P9-CQB-036

Wintering

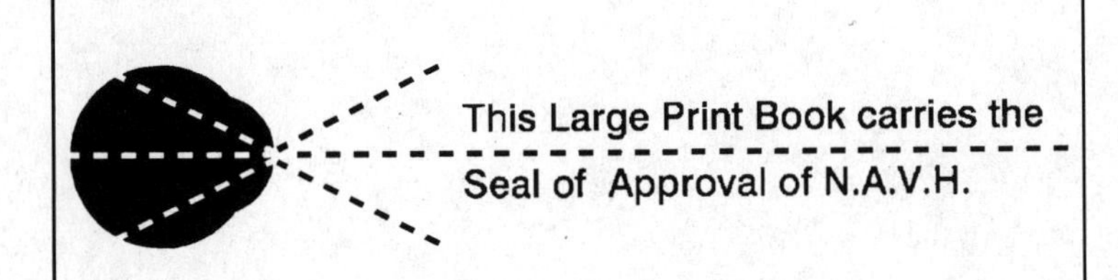
This Large Print Book carries the
Seal of Approval of N.A.V.H.

Wintering

Peter Geye

THORNDIKE PRESS
A part of Gale, Cengage Learning

Farmington Hills, Mich • San Francisco • New York • Waterville, Maine
Meriden, Conn • Mason, Ohio • Chicago

Thorndike Press, a part of Gale, Cengage Learning.

Thorndike Press® Large Print Bill's Bookshelf.
The text of this Large Print edition is unabridged.
Other aspects of the book may vary from the original edition.
Set in 16 pt. Plantin.

LIBRARY OF CONGRESS CATALOGING-IN-PUBLICATION DATA

Names: Geye, Peter, author.
Title: Wintering / by Peter Geye.
Description: Large print edition. | Waterville, Maine : Thorndike Press, 2016. | Series: Thorndike Press large print Bill's bookshelf
Identifiers: LCCN 2016027741| ISBN 9781410493712 (hardcover) | ISBN 1410493717 (hardcover)
Subjects: LCSH: Large type books. | Domestic fiction.
Classification: LCC PS3607.E925 W56 2016b | DDC 813/.6—dc23
LC record available at https://lccn.loc.gov/2016027741

Published in 2016 by arrangement with Alfred A. Knopf, a division of Penguin Random House LLCM

Printed in Mexico
1 2 3 4 5 6 7 20 19 18 17 16

For my boys, Finn and Cormac

And for Dana

The country between Lake Superior and the Lake of the Woods is, like the whole watershed between Hudson's Bay and the Valley of the St. Lawrence, a rugged assemblage of hills, with lakes, rivers, and morasses, of all sizes and shapes, in their intervals. It is, in fact, a drowned land, whose waters have assumed their permanent features by a balance of receipt and discharge.

They all communicate practically with each other, either by water or by portages, so that the traveller may reach the Lake of the Woods by many routes, differing only in danger, labour, and directness.

— JOHN JEREMIAH BIGSBY

Our winters are faithful and unfailing and we take what they bring, but this season has tested even the most devout among us. The thermometer hanging outside my window reads thirty-two degrees below zero. Five degrees warmer than yesterday, which itself was warmer than the day before. I can hear the pines exploding, heartwood turned to splinter and pulp all up and down the Burnt Wood River.

As if the cold weren't enough, yesterday brought another unkindness. Gustav Eide came bearing it: his father's red woolen hat — the one he wore almost every day, the type children wear tobogganing — found by those Bargaard twins as they ice-skated out past the breakwater.

It wasn't the first time Gus came knocking this winter. Back in November he held his own hat in his hands. Gus, with his father's lonesome, lazy eyes, standing bare-headed but buttoned up outside my door.

"I hate to drop in unannounced, Berit," he had said then.

"Since when do we stand on ceremony around here? Come in."

He stepped inside but stood with his back against the door, his eyes studying his bootlaces. I've seen much of this town's woe, its suffering and tragedy, and have marked it all. While I stood there waiting for Gus to speak, I knew my own everlasting sadness was suddenly upon me.

"He disappeared last night, Berit." He spoke without looking up. "He's gone."

I turned and stepped carefully to the bench under the window and sat.

"We found tracks heading up the river," he said.

I looked up at him, now looking down at me. I thought of sitting at his father's bedside the evening before, holding his hand, singing to him. I thought of how Harry had looked at me, his gaze seeming to go through me and into some past only he could see. I was disappearing from his view. This I knew.

Gus came and sat next to me on the bench. "That new sheriff — Ruutu's his name — is leading the search. We went all the way up past the lower falls. The dogs lost his scent around the Devil's Maw. Ruutu's down in Gunflint right now, calling for more help."

He reached over and held my hand, a gesture he surely learned from his father and one that calmed me down, at once familiar and uncanny. There are depths to those Eides no sounding line will ever reach. I knew this about Harry and I have come to know it about Gus, though on that November morning he knew me much better than I did him.

"They're not going to find him, Berit."

He let my hand go and sat back and rubbed the cold from his cheeks.

"Why would you say that? He can't have gone far," I said, thinking again of that faraway look in Harry's eyes.

"We've heard this story before, haven't we?"

"Speak plainly, would you? For the benefit of an old lady?"

Then Gus looked through me just as his father had only hours before. "People searched for don't get found here. Not in these woods." He closed his eyes and shook his head as though to banish some thought. "Put on some coffee? I'll tell you how all this happened."

So I did. I went to the kitchen and filled

the kettle at the sink. As the water poured from the faucet I glanced upriver, where I have kept my eyes more or less since. Two stories began that day in November. One of them was new and the other as old as this land itself. Both of them were borne by the river.

Ruutu and his deputies and Gus and his sister, Signe, and the good people of Gunflint spent a week searching for Harry, every dawn following some new dead end into the wilderness, every dusk emerging from wherever they'd been, tired and cold and no closer to finding him. Gus stopped by each evening to tell me where they'd looked, assuring me every single time they'd never find him. Even still, the next morning he went out with the others. Sometimes three or four parties, following three or four leads. When, finally, they conceded Harry to the wilderness, it was thanks to Gus's insistence. Signe went back home to Minneapolis. Gus back to his job teaching English and history at Arrowhead High School. Ruutu back to our local misdemeanors and traffic violations.

Me? I was still searching in my own fashion. That first morning, I visited Harry's empty bed. There was the iron headboard and the flannel linens and the quilt crumpled at the foot of the bed. Harry was always too warm. The pillow still held the imprint of his head. His medication sat on the bedside table, next to the radio and a half-drunk glass of water. The bureau opposite the bedside table was as old and timeworn as whatever part of Harry stored his memories. I crossed the room and opened the top drawer and noticed straightaway his knit hat was missing. Strangely, the pompom had been snipped off.

I'd passed the previous evening as I had so many others before it, sitting at his bedside, reminding him of who we used to be, feeling at times that I was not only disappearing into the darkness of his mind but from the world altogether. It was no less strange that evening than it had been at the start of his confinement to see a man still so bodily strong becoming a child again. No less strange and no less unbearable.

Of that last night we spent together, I cannot say he exhibited any signs he was about to undertake a disappearance, no word spoken or gesture made that gave me pause. He did nothing that might've forewarned me. That evening I only hoped, as I did every night, that when he finally fell to sleep he would do so with the knowledge of my love, and that when he dreamt it would be of peaceful things.

It was Doctor Ingebrigsten — who grew up in Misquah, went to medical school in Minneapolis, and returned to Arrowhead County because, she said, this place needed one of its own to care for its sickly — who described to Gus and me what it would become like for Harry. "You and I," she said, "we see our past as though it were a bright summer day. The trees green, flowers blossoming, the water shining blue. Harry's going to start seeing less and less of his past until — sadly — everything will seem as though it's taking place in a nighttime blizzard in the dead of winter." She said this on a September morning, with the trees in full autumn blaze — our loveliest time of year — and I wept to think that the man I loved would never register that beauty again, even if he lived another ten years.

That same morning Doctor Ingebrigsten told me the best thing I could do for Harry was to be with him. Sit at his bedside and talk to him and tell him I still loved him. To hold him among us for as long as I could. So I did. Of course I did.

And now it's been half of a winter since Harry vanished, and I can finally rest my thoughts. I ought to feel relief. Of this I'm sure. But do you know what it's like to hold proof of the last heartache you'll ever know in your own raw hands? I hadn't known, either, not until Gus delivered Harry's red hat yesterday morning, a cork bobber sewed on where the pompom should've been. Gus's stories and that damn hat — handed to me like a verdict and never spoken of again — these things have made of my heart what this season has of the splintering pines along the river.

Only after I poured the coffee did Gus remove his gloves and unbutton his coat. His eyes were fixed on the kitchen window, warning of nothing, though their sadness was plain. Outside, the first snow of the season, which had fallen all night, was finally relenting.

I thought of the townsfolk zipping up and brushing it from their cars. They'd make it to the nine o'clock service at Immanuel Lutheran come what may, choosing the cold and snow over the fires of hell any day. Families marching into church, sitting straight-backed in the pews. The wives and children enthralled by Pastor Nils's holy words. The men sitting there beside them, heads bowed or turned heavenward. You'd as likely hear his silent prayers as you would his singing voice at hymn time. For some sixty years I've lived among these people — all my adult life and the end of my childhood. I know how they make you wait.

So I waited for Gus, my hands warmed by my own mug of coffee. After a time, he shifted his eyes from the ceiling and pulled off his coat.

He spoke slowly, almost as if what he said had been rehearsed, though of course it hadn't. "You made him very happy, Berit. You made his life worth living." He paused and looked at me. "Being as he was, though, well, what worth was there in that? I might've gone off myself, knowing what was to come. Hell, I'd have strung myself up from the fish-house ceiling." He put the coffee to his lips but did not drink. "I'm sorry," he said over the lip of the cup. After a sip he went on. "I must've inherited his habit of saying any damn-fool thing that comes to mind." He tried to smile but just couldn't do it. "Lately, I've wondered quite a lot about what memories were still left. Did anything come to him at all?" Again he paused, and did manage a sort of smile. "If he remembered anything, it was good times with you."

"You don't need to butter me up, Gus. I know how it was with him."

As if I'd not spoken at all, he continued. "When Tom and Greta were babies, I used to walk them to sleep. You know, wander around the house at night, whispering to them, singing them lullabies, telling them everything would be all right. I liked to think they could understand me, that my voice soothed them until they eventually calmed down and fell asleep." He actually smiled now. "Of course, they didn't know a damn thing. Only that they were tired and unhappy." He took a deep breath and shook his head. "I wish to Christ he would've said one simple thing before he left. One damn thing."

"I'm sitting here looking at you, Gus, and thinking you're his spitting image. But you certainly didn't get his plainspokenness, did you?"

"You'll have to pardon me, Berit. I don't make a lick of sense in the best of times."

"You said they're not going to find him."

"Of course they aren't."

"Well, I can sit here all winter with you," I said.

He looked up at me and smiled and by some legerdemain placed on the table a small moose-hide portfolio. "You just might have to," he said. "Ruutu found this up on the river." He slid it across the table.

"What is it?"

"Proof that he never found what he was looking for."

I picked it up, opened it to the first page, and saw a hand-drawn map of the shore of Lake Superior.

"I don't know how to talk about this. I don't know if it makes perfect sense or if my mind is starting to go, too. But maybe you can help me understand, Berit."

"Understand what, Gus?"

"Why he walked off. What he left behind." He shook his head. "What happened that winter when I was a kid."

"I know what happened that winter."

"No, you don't. Not all of it."

I got up to refill our coffee, and when I sat back down I said, "Folks are skipping church this morning to search for your father, Pastor Nils is praying for an old man lost in the snow, and here you sit telling stories to his sweetheart."

"I told you, they're not going to find him. They just won't. Pastor Nils is a good man. One of the best. But his prayers won't help my father." His eyes were glassy. "And you? You were more than his sweetheart. You know that as well as I do. You were the only reason he didn't wander off thirty years ago. Hear me out, Berit. And don't think for another minute my father's anything but gone and resting now." He closed his eyes and looked up. "If rest's what he found down there."

I didn't have to wait all winter for Gus to start talking. I didn't even have to wait past that morning. At my kitchen table he started right at the beginning, if that's what it really was. In any case, he began with a late-autumn morning in 1963, thirty-three years before.

Harry stood over the moose-hide book of maps, the light falling from the lamp above the kitchen table between them. The transistor radio buzzed on the counter. "I'm a damned fool for thinking so much of these," he said.

"No, you're not," Gus said, though they troubled him, those maps. Even then.

"I knew from the day I first copied one of these that I'd use them. Don't ask me how." He closed the book and pushed it aside. The Fisher Maps were spread across the table under his elbows, every lake and stream and portage charted with exactitude.

The radio came to life with Monday's news. National then local then sports, talk of the Yankees and Dodgers' World Series beginning the next day. Before the weather forecast came on, Harry reached to shut the radio off and then walked across the great room. There, above the mantel, was the picture Lisbet had painted many years earlier. The one she said reminded her of her husband while he was gone. His head bowed under a rain cap, galluses holding his oilskin pants. His boat — which was his father's boat before him, and as much a part of this town as the Eides themselves — floats on smooth waters. There's a net roller aft, full of nets. Fishboxes up to the gunwales. The painting, *The Nets,* was by his mother's own standards her best.

"Hey, Gus," Harry said, "come over here."

Gus pushed his uneaten eggs away and crossed the room.

Harry kept his eyes on the painting as he spoke. "A few months ago, Charlie Aas gets his art collector friend Ruben Mazecki up here. We'd never met the guy before, some shyster lawyer from Duluth. One of Charlie's cronies. So Ruben's standing right here, wearing a three-piece suit, and some queer hat he won't take off's hanging limp over one eye. He smells like furniture oil.

And he says to your mother, 'I'll give you five thousand dollars for this painting.' "
Harry cocked his head as if to inspect more thoughtfully this painting that had for a decade hung above their fireplace. "Five thousand bucks, right?" His voice trailed off and he peered again at the painting.

"Mom told me about that."

"Of course she did." He looked at him. "It wasn't Mazecki's money. Wasn't his idea, neither. Did you know that?" He closed his eyes. "Goddamn Charlie. Anyway, Mazecki's offer, that's how this whole mess started." He made a gesture to encompass the whole room. The whole house. He stepped closer to the painting and pointed at the sky in the background. "At least she got the horizon right. Lord knows she's been watching it long enough." He put his arm around Gus. "Whatever happens, do not become that man." He nodded at the man in the painting. "That man will fail you sure as he lives."

He let go of Gus's shoulder and stood beneath the painting for several minutes more, still nodding slowly, until he heard the water come on in the bathroom around the corner.

He turned his attention to his son's wondering eyes and smiled. "You should eat your breakfast and shower up. Make it a hot one. It'll be your last for some time." He checked his watch. "We'll leave in an hour."

Later that morning Gus watched his father loading the canoes. Mist rose off the river. His mother came onto the deck, set her coffee on the deck railing, and lit a cigarette.

A moment passed before she said, "You don't have to go."

"Why wouldn't I go?"

"I guess there are about a hundred reasons. You know most of them." She took a sip of her coffee. "For God's sake, how's he going to survive up there? He walks like an old man now."

"He walks like a man who's been bent over the side of a boat all his life."

"Bent over a barrel, you mean." She looked over to the river for a long time. "He walks as if he's given up."

"Or been beaten."

"You always were his great defender."

Gus looked out across the clearing and blinked slowly three times. "I thought you'd be happy we're leaving."

She said nothing, just stood there staring at her husband, first through the ribbons of cigarette smoke, then through the cloud of fog over the clearing between their house and the river. She stubbed her cigarette and dropped the butt in her empty coffee cup. "Whatever happened to your father was a long time ago. Before you were born. Even before he met me."

Gus wanted to slap her. Instead, he said, "I know what happened to him. Everyone does."

"You might think you do." Again she stared across the clearing. When she looked back at Gus she had tears in her eyes.

"Oh, please," he said.

"You need to go to college, Gus. The world's not about to wait on your father's shenanigans. You read the newspaper. The world's going to hell in a handbasket. Don't be a fool."

"I'm not afraid of what's going on."

She wiped her tears, which looked even more fake now that they were gone. "And you think playing around in the woods with him will be good practice? That he can teach you everything you need from his own vast experience?"

Gus just shook his head.

"My God, you are his son, aren't you? The two of you won't see the ice come in up there." She kissed him on the forehead. "You'll be back in a week, that's what I think." She turned and walked into the house.

Gus heard the radio come on inside and his mother tuning the dial, looking for the music station. It took a clear morning for that, though, and after a minute or so she turned the radio off.

On that morning, Gus was eighteen years old and a summer removed from high school graduation. As broad-shouldered as his father.

Harry watched him walk across the clearing and said, once he got to the canoes, "Where'd the kid you used to be go?"

Gus still felt his mother's stinging words. "We all set?"

Harry squatted, grabbed a handful of pebbles from the shore, and let them sift through his big hand. "I should give you one more chance to balk. There are plenty of excuses to stay here."

"I'm not balking."

Harry pointed up at the house. "Head back up there and call one of those colleges that accepted you. Quit this place for good. Farther than you can paddle and walk, leastways."

"I'm not balking. Besides, who would sing

you those songs? Who'd catch you your fish?"

"All right, then. You got your compass? Matches?"

Gus patted the hip pocket of his army pants.

"Said goodbye to your mother?"

"Something like that."

"Is your sister awake?"

"I told her goodbye last night."

"Me, too."

Gus looked into the canoes. "Everything loaded?"

Harry stepped beside him and they stared into them. Each held two number-four Duluth packs. In Gus's the extra paddle and Remington were tied under the thwarts, as were the fishing rods and the ax and pick handles and saws in his father's canoe. In both, cross-country skis and poles were strapped to the tumble-home. Snowshoes hung from two of the packs.

"I think so," Harry said, then looked at the house, upriver, and at his wristwatch in quick, quiet succession. "Gus, buddy, where we're going, well, better men than you or I have gotten lost there."

The waters alongshore were still, the trees coming to light with the morning. Gus was full of fear, because he knew not only what sort of wilderness lay beyond the oxbow in the river, but also that they were risking something else, and that they were leaving something unspoken behind. Despite this fear, he looked back at his father's waiting face and felt almost nothing but a boy's excitement. "If we get lost," he said, "then we'll be doing it together, right?"

Harry's smile was wide. He took a pinch from his tobacco pouch and pushed his canoe into the river.

It wasn't more than a half hour before they reached the lower falls. During the hot summer months, Gus had spent countless hours in these pools, dropping dry flies in the lee waters, swimming with his friends. But when he and Harry stepped out into the shallows now, the water felt as though it had fallen from the moon. That's how cold it was.

They portaged the falls. First the packs, then the canoes yoked over their shoulders. When they put back in above, Harry said, "We might've packed a little lighter."

Gus could see his father's chest heaving under his flannel shirt. Harry worked the snuff loose from his lip and spit it out.

"We could dump your shaving kit," Gus said.

"And live like animals? How about we ditch your little guitar?"

"It's a mandolin."

"That's what I said."

"Or you could just bear up," Gus said.

Harry smiled broadly again and nudged Gus's canoe with the tip of his paddle. "That I could."

Not another half hour passed before they reached the Devil's Maw, where the Burnt Wood split atop the falls. One chute rushed through a jagged stone trough forty feet long before it churned back on itself with a force equal to its own falling. The other ran water into the maw itself. For generations it had been a place of lore and legend that was regarded as being as holy as Immanuel Lutheran. They were still downstream, holding their canoes into the current.

"It's been a while since I've been up this far," Harry said, looking left and right at the gorge walls rising sheer above them.

"She's running light," Gus said. "We were fishing up here this spring and couldn't get close to the falls."

"Fish make it past the lower falls?"

"The big ones do."

"The big ones? Hope your braggadocio don't come back to bite us on the ass. We'll need some big fish, come the months ahead."

Harry rubbed his eyes with the heels of his hands and then stared back up at the falls, maybe wondering if something about them would change. He shook his head. "Who could ever imagine this water might be tamed? Look at it." Even with the slow, autumn flow it was deafening. "Does that look like water that wants to be dammed? Like there's enough dynamite in the world to widen those stone walls? And for what purpose?" He shook his head again. "Men like Charlie are never satisfied until they have more. And then they're still not satisfied." Now he looked at Gus. "Don't matter. He'll have bigger problems than how to dam this river when he wakes up tomorrow."

Gus had of course heard about this nonsense. We all had. Damming not just the Burnt Wood, but half a dozen others leading up into the borderlands. The plans had been whispered about for years. The promise of more iron ore and lumber and copper, lately of hydroelectricity. Harry had long been among the townsfolk who went to meetings to shout about it. Charlie Aas was always shouting back.

"This'll be more work than the lower

falls," Harry said.

"I've been up these falls a hundred times."

"With eighty pounds on your back?" Harry surveyed the options. "You want to take the long way around or split the chutes?"

"It'll take half an hour to go around."

"In the scheme of things, that won't amount to much." Harry looked up at the falls again. "One misstep and our adventure's over."

"I know it," Gus said.

"And our lives." Harry studied the clearing in the woods and the bottom of the trail that led up and around the falls. That would have been the prudent route, and they both knew it. "But we're fresh, eh?"

Harry dug his paddle into the current and steered for the slick talus between the pool at the bottom of the chute and the maw. Gus fell in line, and by the time they'd nosed their canoes onto the shelf they were both damp with brume. Harry stepped out, pulled his boat out of the water, and heaved a Duluth pack over his shoulders, then turned back to Gus. "Stay to the right, bud."

"Like I need to be told that?"

Harry scrabbled up the steep rock steps, using his hands and arms as much as his legs. Gus followed behind, his face at his father's bootheels. Midway up at the Devil's Maw, Gus paused and gaped into the precipice, feeling its cold, sharp exhalation, a breeze with a metallic tang. Suddenly dizzied, he gripped the rocks and pulled himself up and away. The footing was of course chancy and the water hauling over the falls thunderous, so loud that he couldn't hear his own heavy breathing. But as they neared the top, the water quieted beneath them and he heard his father singing.

At first he mistook it for some alien sound coming off the water or out of the earth, some whistling from the treetops up on the ridges. But the longer they climbed the more certain Harry's voice became. Deep and loud, as if he'd just found it along their route. Words of a song Gus had never heard, sung in a language he'd spent four years of high school learning and only one short summer forgetting: *"À la claire fontaine m'en allant promener, / J'ai trouvé l'eau si belle que je m'y suis baigné. / Il y a longtemps que je t'aime, / Jamais je ne t'oublierai. . . ."*

They made camp on the shore of Borealis Lake that evening. They'd been ten hours paddling up the Burnt Wood with only those few short portages and a half hour for lunch ashore. When Harry unfolded himself from his canoe he was stiff as a jackknife. He cracked his back slowly and turned to Gus. "Not a bad first day's paddle, eh?"

"If they're all that easy, I'll be disappointed," Gus said. He meant it, too.

Harry gave him a sly smile. "Oh, you won't be disappointed." He cracked his back again. "How was your boat?"

Gus stroked the smooth cedar gunwale. "Stalwart," he said, because that had been Harry's mantra and prediction for all the months they'd spent building them.

"Stalwart. Indeed, sonny boy."

He hadn't seen his father so at peace for some time and hadn't expected to now, given how many years it had been since he'd last been in a camp anywhere. Gus knew something was off, because that kind of easiness had so rarely been part of Harry's constitution. It made Gus nervous. "We'd better tend to our camp," he said.

"Righto."

As would become their custom, Gus got a line in the water while Harry gathered firewood and started a pot of rice. Two pike fillets were boiled and salted before the rice was done, and they ate off tin plates, the sun setting over the trees behind them. They were silent, as they'd been most of the day, and when they finished eating, Gus scrubbed the pots and plates and stoked the fire before he took his mandolin from its case.

While he fingered a few chords into that beautiful gloaming, his father pulled a length of birchwood from the pile beside the fire and cut it to a length of a foot and a half. The hatchet — like the canoes and sleeping sacks and paddles and damn near half their outfit — was something Harry had made. In a furnace he'd built, he melted the old Buda motor from his own father's retired fishing boat. He cast the hatchets and knives in clay molds, hammered the edges on an anvil, honed them with files, then his belt sander, and finally with emery paper and the sharpening stone. He'd stacked leather for the grips and cut moose hide for the sheaths, and now here he was, on the shore of Borealis Lake, trimming a birch stick by the fire.

He worked, as he always did, as though he were completely free of thought, his hands obeying instinct rather than the instructions of his own mind. Before Gus finished the first song, he'd already cut all the bark from the birch.

Gus stopped playing. "What are you making there?"

Harry sighted the birch up and down,

looked across the fire, and said, "Play me another ditty, would you?"

Gus strummed the mandolin only once before repeating the question.

"I guess," Harry said, "it's going to be a calendar. We can notch all our days on it." He nodded, satisfied, and said, "Now play me that song again, eh?"

So Gus did. He played until the stars jumped out.

For two days they paddled against the Burnt Wood's weakening current, portaging the saults, making lunches over fires on the river's edge, pitching their canvas each night in clearings. Already each was growing used to the silence of the other's company. And to the strange beckonings from the wilderness.

Here the river was narrowing even as the trees on shore grew more distant. On either side they could touch the tall and browning cattails with the blades of their paddles, the boggy water beyond seeping toward the jack pines ashore. Every thirty strokes or so they came upon matted shoreline where moose had come to forage.

As they paddled Harry sang full-voiced: *"Le fils du roi s'en va chassant, / En roulant ma boule. / Avec son grand fusil d'argent, rouli,-roulant, ma boule roulant . . ."*

"What's with the love songs?" Gus said.

"They're chansons. Voyageur songs."

"Why holler about it?"

"You want to surprise some bull along this tight stretch of river? With nowhere to turn? They're hornier than you are right now. We come on one unannounced and you'll have an antler up your ass faster than you could squeal about it." Harry smiled and started singing again. They paddled on.

An hour later, the river and muskeg funneled into a narrow watercourse no more than two feet deep and six feet wide. Their paddles struck the rocky riverbed, sending sharp reverberations into their hands. After a few minutes, Harry stepped from his canoe and unpacked a length of rope. Gus did as Harry did. They knotted their lines to the bows, shouldered and tied off the line, and started dragging their boats single-file up what was left of the river. When the trees closed above them, they had to bend and then crawl through the canopy of boughs and branches.

"I hope this means we're near Burnt Wood Lake," Harry said. "We ought to be."

The river was frigid and already Gus's hands were numb. "Were you expecting this?"

"I wasn't expecting anything. I will not." Harry looked over his shoulder, down the starboard side of his canoe, and fixed Gus with his stare. He remembered that stare, Gus did. All these years later, he recognized it as a warning. For Harry knew, sure as Gus did himself, that asking if he'd been anticipating a tangle of trees and shallow water was his son's first complaint. And them only three days into a trip that would last months.

Gus had not questioned their planning much, but he had wondered — on the night before they departed — why they didn't just drive up to the public access on Burnt Wood Lake and put in there. It would have taken less than an hour from their front door, saved them a lot of unnecessary effort, and spared them this cloying mess of trees.

The reason, Harry had told him, was that since the "voyageurs of yore" didn't have the benefit of being towed up to the public access, neither should he and Gus. This notion sounded noble to Gus, and of course it was in the spirit of their adventure. But clambering on hands and knees to tow his canoe like some blind and stubborn horse, he was unable to check himself. Gus said, "This water is freezing."

"I suppose we'll run into our share of cold

water between now and then," Harry said, still staring down the length of his canoe.

"I thought this was a river," Gus said, rolling now.

Harry got up on one knee, cupped his hand into the water, and brought it up to his mouth. "Gus, bud, there's gonna be stretches that're tougher than others. We're gonna get wet and we're gonna get cold. I'll save you the trouble of discovery on those accounts. Let's not piss in our soup, eh?"

Gus didn't say anything, only pulled his canoe past his father and tunneled farther up the river.

"You have to wonder why we were there," Gus said that November morning he got to talking. "Not just on that stretch of river, but heading into the wilderness beyond. It was so incredibly reckless. To leave at that time of year, for starters. With our provisions? With his miscarriage of a plan? My God." He paused. "And of course I should've been in college. Should have been running to college. But I didn't even think of it. Can you imagine that? What mess of bent and secret lives was leading us into this? How much anger and grief?"

"Folks always chase their sadness around. Into the woods. Up to the attic. Out onto the ice."

Gus closed his eyes. "I guess they do."

"You're chasing yours."

"Maybe," he said. "Or maybe it's chasing me."

"Could be."

"But why was I being petulant three days in? Had he overestimated me? Was I still just a kid? A little boy?" He moved his head like he was nodding yes and shaking no at the same time. "Or were we just in over our heads? Who can say? I only know that when the trees above me lifted and I got off my knees and shook like a wet dog, Burnt Wood Lake opened up right before me. I looked back at my father, still a hundred yards behind, and do you know what I felt?"

I looked at him, waiting.

"Ready to keep going. If I'd felt otherwise, we might've stopped then and there. We might have avoided everything. But I didn't want to. I took a couple steps forward into the river's earliest, feeble currents and mistook their weakness for my strength. When my father hauled up next to me he said nothing, only pointed up the lakeshore. There, standing among the duckweeds and watermeal, in water up to its belly, its dewlap dripping, its huge antlers lit up, was a moose. He was beautiful. And furious, I could tell.

"I said, 'Why isn't he running away? He ought to fear us. I could shoot him right now. He should know that.'

"My father, he only said, 'Yes, I suppose he should.' " He mimicked Harry's voice — a perfect imitation — and then fell silent for a moment. "Good Christ, Berit. The things I didn't know."

I know what some of the folks around here used to think, that for years the worst of them labeled me a boondagger because I could lift a fifty-pound sack of U.S. mail and had no husband. The fact is, there's only been one man in all my years and I simply chose to wait for him. Through the end of my first winter here, then through what seemed an eternity.

Harry was the first person in Gunflint to show me a special gentleness. This was one warm summer morning after I'd strolled the shoreline, plucking flowers from the cracks in the bedrock. He'd been out at his nets, just a sixteen-year-old boy already making a living for himself. He was tying his boat to a cleat on the Lighthouse Road. "You got a fistful of carnivorous flowers there, Miss Lovig," he said.

"Beg your pardon?" I said, surprised to hear his voice at all. More surprised to hear him saying my name.

He finished his knot and stood and offered his hand. "I'm Harry Eide," he said. We shook hands and he continued, "Butterworts." He nodded at the flowers in my hand. "That's what you've got there. You'd have to walk a long way to find them anywhere else."

I looked down at the purple flowers, then up at his fresh and boyish face. He ought to have been smiling. Later he would tell me he hadn't spoken in months. Since February. Which seemed hard to believe then and still does, though I never — not once — had reason to doubt anything he ever said.

"What do you mean by carnivorous?" I asked him.

"They eat bugs. Honest to God."

"How do you know that?"

"My old man taught me."

"How do you know my name?"

"I guess everyone knows that by now."

"My given name's Berit," I said.

He smiled, or, rather, half-smiled, the right side of his mouth curling up, his right eye squinting. "Berit Lovig. Right. It's nice to meet you. Get those flowers in a vase." He took a step to leave, then paused and said, "Butterworts. They only grow here. This kind of butterwort, leastways. Here along the water." He paused a second more, looked as though he was about to say something, but then went up the Lighthouse Road toward the Traveler's Hotel, where he took his lunch each day. Years later he would tell me how hard it had been to leave without saying more. Without saying thanks. Without asking me to join him for lunch. But he didn't do any of those things, and those few minutes on the Lighthouse Road would be our only proper conversation for more than twenty years. I knew from that moment, though, that he was my man. I knew I'd wait for him however long I had to. And I did.

Which is not to say that others didn't come calling. Some did. Charlie Aas, for example. But he was rotten from the word go, and rottener still with each day of his life.

By the time he was elected mayor in 1960 he presided over this town like a drunken lord. Through his strong-arming and sleight of hand he'd hidden his past, one that included charges of poaching and animal cruelty, both beaten, and a short stint in the juvenile correction facility in Duluth for terrorizing that autistic Bargaard child. No doubt there were other transgressions, large and small. I can say that because I experienced Charlie's thuggery myself, and no one but Rebekah Grimm and I ever knew about it.

By 1960 he was known for his mink coat and penny loafers in a town where every other man — even Mr. Nelson, the music teacher at Arrowhead High — wore work boots. Charlie was educated, his degree from the University of Minnesota one of only three or four in Gunflint back then. He was council president at Immanuel Lutheran. A real-estate baron. A bush pilot. A father of four, a daughter and three sons. He was respected because he was feared. Corrupter. Corrupted. Embezzler. Womanizer. Most folks knew all this. Or at least some of it.

But more than anything — and this is why he got away with so much — Charlie was third-generation. His grandfather put a fish house on the harbor shore in 1891. His father, Marcus, used to tussle with Harry's own father for whiskey dollars during Prohibition. All of which is to say that he had pedigree in these parts, crazy as that sounds, and despite his failings. Nothing has ever meant more to people up here than bloodlines.

Charlie parlayed his into public office. Being mayor around here never meant much before Charlie, but he was determined to change that. Partnering with the mining and lumber companies, he made a fortune just for saying we ought to open the borderlands, not protect them. As Harry put it, Charlie's goal was to pillage the wilderness and get rich from the wreckage. Harry's hundred acres along the Burnt Wood River were in the wrong spot. That was part of their problem. But the larger impediment was Harry's integrity and his own clout with the townsfolk.

For a year after he was elected, Charlie fought fair. Or at least out in the open. He and Harry shouted at each other across the church basement, where the town meetings were held in those days, and I was there for many of them. Charlie and his accomplices wore hundred-dollar suits and silk ties, while Harry and a few others sat there in flannel shirts with contrary views. Charlie loved trotting out phrases like "eminent domain" and "the good of the people" and was always talking about jobs. But Harry — whose name had always meant more than Charlie's, despite his office and money — wouldn't budge. And he found allies.

So Charlie reared back. For years he tried to gain the upper hand, buying friends as fast as he made enemies. He was as deft at one as he was at the other, and at times it looked like he and his Republican cronies would have their way with the wilderness. But they never did. Not then. Not ever.

The summer of '63, when Gus and his father weren't out hoisting mostly empty gill nets, they were in the fish house, building their canoes. Harry told Gus he wanted to teach him one true thing before he got out of this place, and the canoes were it. Most nights, after fishing all day and dinner at the Traveler's Hotel, the two of them would put a Bill Monroe record on the turntable and settle into their gentle and quiet labor. It was during those hours that Gus learned about Harry's own father's genius with boats, for every lesson — every word — had its root in something Odd had once said. Odd being Harry's father.

Gus recalled those hours as some of the best of his life. But he also recalled being anxious for their nights in the fish house to end, so he could steal away to meet Cindy Aas at Eddie Riverfish's house.

She was Charlie's only daughter, Gus's age and in the same high school class, and her shine for him was as unexpected and unlikely as snow in August. He'd known her his whole life, of course, and all that time they'd been strict opposites if not outright enemies. A cheerleader and homecoming queen and mediocre student, she liked to drink and smoke. The sort of girl mothers warned their sons about. Gus was quiet, a straight-A student, a letterman on the cross-country ski team, a member of the Chess Club. Those differences would have been enough to lock them in opposite circles, even without the rift between their fathers, and their grandfathers, too.

What they had in common was music. Cindy played the piano at church when her mother wasn't able to, and in the high school band she was first flute. Gus played the guitar in band and could strum any instrument with strings. Those old crones in the church basement used to whisper about the sounds the two of them could make together, but in all their lives Cindy and Gus had hardly spoken to each other.

After graduation that summer, Gus found himself sitting next to her on the deck out back of Eddie's house. It was late enough that the party, stoked all night by beer and marijuana, was finally petering out. Cindy didn't say much. Maybe she didn't say anything, but he remembered her looking up at him and kissing him, as though they'd been going steady for years. And he remembered the great whorling in his gut. And not being able to push her away even though he knew he should.

There in my kitchen, he wasn't comfortable talking about this, even so many years after the offense.

They spent the whole summer sneaking around. Swimming in the cove on the hottest nights, fooling with each other in her friend's basement, driving up to Long Finger Lake with a fifth of vodka and a pack of Pall Malls. She was showing Gus things he'd never seen before, and he loved it. He could still hear the songs on the radio, still remember how her hair gleamed with the moonlight behind it.

It would be months before Gus learned she was ordered into his life. He admitted that that fact complicated the story. But he still felt with absolute certainty that, on those nights up at Long Finger Lake, she was there because she wanted to be, never mind that unexpected wrinkle.

It was on such a night at Long Finger Lake that she told Gus about his mother and her father. They passed a bottle back and forth, toyed with the radio dial between long kisses, talked about friends and music. After a lull in the conversation, Cindy said, "My dad's screwing your mom." Then she laughed, her eyes wide and wild. "Isn't it *scandalous*?"

Before he could answer she reached across the car seat and unzipped his jeans.

He wasn't sure he believed her. Not at first. For all the fun they were having, she was moody and prone to lying. But because of their intimacy — and because intimacy can make the blind see, if not the reverse — he did choose to believe, for the rest of the evening, that what was happening between them was at least as important as whatever his mother and Charlie Aas might be up to. Which is not to say that he wasn't curious. So he started investigating.

He had no idea, though, what he was looking for. His parents had never seemed happy, much less in love. He couldn't recall a single kiss, or a tender word, ever passing between them. As for his own experiences in affairs of the heart, that summer with Cindy was his initiation.

Still, he saw changes at home. Lisbet became glib with Harry, almost mocking. She bought new dresses. Started smoking again. Listened to loud music and spent countless hours on the telephone in hushed conversations with a friend in Chicago. And she started painting again. Feverishly, and sometimes all night long.

And his father? He became more obsessed than ever with his maps. He'd hunker down at the kitchen table with a pot of coffee and his books and pore over them as if the world itself could not impart the truths hidden within those pages. For him this was, Gus thought, a strange posture, to sit anywhere with such focus for so long, especially at their kitchen table, and Harry now reminded him of a wounded animal. Which it turns out he was.

They didn't talk much that season, father and son, but when they did — out tending the nets, or bent over their canoes in the fish house — Harry started telling Gus his war stories. The Hürtgen Forest. The Ardennes. Surprisingly, they had little to do with the men he fought beside or against, or the carnage he saw, though he told of these things, too. What he remembered most was how cold those nights were. Even worse, he said, than he'd grown up with in Gunflint. Gus was of course entranced. He listened with unwavering attention, though he was convinced even then that he didn't truly understand what he was being told, much less why. Any hours he spent alone were given over to questions of what it meant to be a man, and if he was one. Wondering if he had to go to war himself in order to cross that threshold. No doubt he'd have the chance if he wanted it. Maybe even if he didn't, given what JFK was calling the communist threat in Vietnam. He'd heard it was hotter than Hades in the jungles over there.

Things with Cindy came to a head near the end of summer, after Gus overheard his mother on the phone one night. He'd been out with Cindy, half drunk and full of lust. Lisbet was sitting by the fire, drinking a glass of wine, unaware that he'd just come in.

"I guess all the Aases are slumming it this summer," she said, then listened for a moment to what her friend was saying. She took another pull of wine, nodded emphatically, and said, "Yes, of course. But that little trollop will flat wreck Gus. He's no match for her." It was only then she noticed Gus, staring at her from across the room. She only smiled and turned back to her conversation.

Cindy didn't wreck him, even if she was supposed to.

They spent their last night together waiting out a thunderstorm in the fish house. It would be the first and only time they made love, a detail that sent Gus to blushing as he told me. When they finished she lay beneath him, her mouth on his shoulder. He remembered her hand in his hair, the sweat pooled in her belly, how she'd bitten him after he said he loved her, hard, right on the shoulder blade, enough to draw blood.

Then she laughed. "My dad told me I'm done seeing you, but I still wanted to do that with you."

Gus didn't say anything.

"Did I hurt you?" She pushed herself up and looked into his eyes. "Your shoulder, did I hurt it?"

He glanced at the small arc of blood. "No," he said. "Well, maybe a little."

"Good. Whenever it stings, think of me." She got up and dressed while the rain lightened outside. "I was your first time."

Again he said nothing.

"I knew it." She pulled her shirt on. "I hope you liked it. I sure did." Then she knelt down and ran her hand through his hair. "I bet I even love you, too, Gus. I never thought I would." She stood and looked away. "My father told me not to."

She left without saying anything more, and he was still in the fish house later that night, when Harry arrived. If Harry was surprised to see him there, at that hour, he didn't let on. Gus *was* surprised, of course, and stood up guiltily and pretended to be putting some tools away.

"You don't need to do that," Harry said.

"Do what?"

Harry came over and stood beside his canoe on the strongback. "I saw the Aas girl leaving. I was right outside."

Gus turned away, though there was no place to hide.

"Tell me it's just a fling, eh, bud? Tell me you two aren't mixed up in something serious."

"She broke up with me tonight."

He shook his head knowingly.

"It was Mr. Aas told her she couldn't see me anymore."

Gus could remember the look his father gave him then. Tired, fierce, angry. He came over and sat beside him.

"Well, Charlie's a guy wants to be the lead dog. Trouble is, he's only good on the cut trail. Know what I'm saying? He sees you're one who can cut 'em yourself. He doesn't want his daughter jumping on your sled. Anyway, you don't need to worry about Cindy Aas. Likely she'd run away with you right now if you'd have her."

Harry stepped back from his canoe and stood quietly for a long time. Then he said,

"I've built dozens of these, but this is the prettiest one yet." He paused to admire her curves, then looked back at Gus. "My old man, there was a man who could build a boat. I guess you've heard that story, eh?"

"I guess so."

Harry went from the canoe to the door, opened the window set in the top half, and stuck his head out for a minute, then turned back around. "The winds are coming," he said, "bringing that Canadian air on down. The bears are fattening up. My favorite time of year, this." He turned back to Gus. "What about you?"

"What about me?"

"What's your favorite time of year?"

Only then did Gus realize his father had been drinking. He almost never drank. Certainly never got twisted. "What's going on, Dad?"

Harry smiled and glanced out the window again. "Yep, the winds are coming around." He closed the window and stepped back to the canoe. "I've been thinking, bud. How about we take a little adventure? Who's to say we'll ever have this chance again? Who's to say how quickly this world's going straight to hell? You and me, we'll get into our canoes and paddle them up into the borderlands and live like voyageurs this winter. We won't have to worry about a thing. We'll be winterers. What do you say?"

"What would Mom think about that?"

"That's another thing not to worry about."

It was the first time Gus ever heard him defy his mother's iron grip on their family, and it seemed to enliven Harry. "We'll use my maps. Go up the Burnt Wood and through the Minnesota lakes until we cross the Laurentian Divide. From there we'll get on the old voyageurs' highway." He clapped his hands. "Thompson had to winter unexpectedly up on Holy Lake. Rumors are the fort's still there. Hidden in the woods. We'll find it. Make a go of it. Just the two of us. We'll have a hell of a time."

Gus must have looked doubtful, because Harry said, "What?"

"Isn't this the sort of trip that needs planning?"

"I've been planning this for as long as you've been alive. Longer. We'll leave in two weeks."

" 'I'll go,' that's what I said, instinctively. I was certain — who knows how — that my father was at the crossroads of his great dream and his worst nightmare. I knew he would need me."

Gus looked at the fire for a moment and

said, “I’ve recalled that scene in the fish house a thousand times. I can still see the turn of expression on my father’s face, like a photograph in a gilded frame. And even if that picture now has a cautionary caption, there was no such warning then. Or else I didn’t notice it. Or refused to.” He looked over at me. “What did not escape me was the awful mood around our house those days before we left. My father had an unreal focus. He likened our adventure to going to battle, and said we should prepare as though that’s what we were doing. So we did. He bought me a Ruger handgun. He bought powerful binoculars. He dug from the attic the field pants he’d worn in the Ardennes. He never said a word to my mother that I heard.

“And though I had misgivings — obvious ones, too — one overwhelming thing drove me on: on the borderlands, my father would need me as much as I’d need him. That’s what made me so blindly ready to go off with him. What boy doesn’t wait his whole childhood to walk alongside his father on equal terms?”

Gus sat there in my house, staring into the fireplace, the expression on his face — well, he wore it like an old coat he’d inherited from Harry. I could see his memories traveling back as he called them up one by one, willing to speak of them only after he was sure that no errors would accompany them in the retelling. It was all I could do not to fall in love with Harry all over again, sitting there looking at his son in my home.

"What if I'd seen right then the folly of it? I'd already been accepted by four colleges, which was the best built-in excuse I've ever had for not doing something else. What if I'd said no, that I didn't want to go?" Again he looked up from the fire. "You can't imagine how many times I've asked myself that question."

We sat silently for a minute or two before I offered him another cup of coffee.

"No, thank you. I'd best get moving." He got up and walked to the door and put on his coat.

"It's no secret Charlie's been a lout his whole life," I said. "No secret about him and your mother. So why mention him at all?"

"To understand why we went in the first place, you need to start with Charlie. In order to understand any of this, you need to know everything about that crooked bastard."

"He's the reason you and Harry went north that winter?"

"One of them, yes. Maybe the main reason."

"What about your mother?"

Gus nodded his head slowly. Was he agreeing with me? He kept nodding and then closed his eyes, as he would do so often in these sessions. Once he opened them, he said, "Why didn't he just go to you then, Berit? It would've been so easy. None of this would ever have happened. Not to him. Not to me." He nodded yet again, as if the idea was just now taking shape in his mind. "My father and his friends, by then they'd done enough to stop the developers, timber and mining both. I don't believe that was a danger anymore. My father would've known that better than anybody." He looked at me. "So was Charlie the reason my father took me north? The answer is yes. Absolutely."

Before Charlie was elected mayor, before he went after Harry's wife, before he sent his daughter to cow Gus, he was just a young bully. I should know, and I can offer an example from the spring of 1942.

For six months, every young man from Duluth to the Canadian border had been ready to fight. Harry had been at basic training in Fort Dix for three weeks. Charlie's brother, George, was anxious to enlist himself. But Charlie? He came home from the University of Minnesota with his diploma and a medical exemption his father had paid for, already grooming Charlie to run the family's business.

Not that they had a legitimate enterprise. The Aas clan — even back then — was focused on back-door deals. I already mentioned that Charlie's grandfather had his hand in whiskey smuggling during Prohibition. Marcus was a rival to Odd Eide, who was Hosea Grimm's right hand. But as Hosea's empire went the way of his sanity, fueled by Odd's striking out on his own, and as Charlie's father, Marcus, Jr., came of age, the Aas family became the kingpins of Arrowhead County. By the time Hosea passed away, they controlled the real-estate market and ran a couple saloons and, for a few years, even a family restaurant and the confectionery on the Lighthouse Road. What these businesses had in common was that they were all duplicitous, each fronting some other endeavor or working in concert with something crooked. Politics. Tourism. The church. They had a hand in it all, like minor and pathetic gangsters. And Charlie was the natural heir to every bit of it. Home from college, he was anxious to prove his grit, and any target would do.

During those years I was running the post office myself, Rebekah having gone properly and finally as mad as a March hare. Though, in fairness, there was no shortage of craziness back then, what with all the mothers and wives stopping by daily in hopes of letters from their sons and husbands. Failing that, they'd settle for news of any sort. So it was a busy time to be sorting mail. And to be offering kind and hopeful words.

I was sorting a bag of those letters when

Charlie came in. I was alone in the apothecary except for Rebekah's dog, a yappy little schnauzer that patrolled the sales floor like a sentinel. She growled as Charlie leaned against the counter smoking a cigarette, her black lips quivering. I could smell the whiskey on Charlie's breath even from behind the counter. He was paunchy and red-faced but it wasn't hard to see the handsome in him. I'll admit that, much as it pains me to say it. Everyone thought so.

"Now, Miss Lovig, I know you've been patient. Biding your time. And I appreciate it," Charlie said. "But your lucky day is upon us." He made a show of crushing out his cigarette, then set his hat on the counter. "What say you and I take a stroll up the Lighthouse Road? We'll wait for the moon to rise and then, well, I'll give you a chance to see what all the fuss is about."

"I beg your pardon, Mr. Aas?"

That leer, it was as ugly a thing as I've ever seen. "Come on, now, Berit. This is your chance. Get out from under this roof and that hobgoblin upstairs. I'll show you a time!"

"Please leave," I said. It took some courage to say it, and I could feel the weight of his black eyes on me. It wouldn't have been unheard of for him to smack me right across the counter. Or worse. When he said nothing, I turned away from his stare and whispered, "There's no mail for you today."

"You goddamn cooze." He stepped back slowly and spread his arms wide, stabbing at me with his hateful eyes. "You ain't seen the last of Charlie Aas. I'll be back for you."

The next day he was there before lunch. This time he walked in the front door with a gargantuan dog he kept on a shot-peened length of chain. This beast was rumored to have descended from the legendary Ovcharkas that had guarded the logging camp up on the Burnt Wood River, back in the days of Gus's great-grandmother.

Of course, excepting Rebekah's little yapper, dogs weren't allowed in the apothecary, and straightaway I told Charlie to take his mongrel outside. In answer, he jerked the chain sharply. The dog looked up at him, then sat back on its haunches. Charlie squatted and rubbed its belly for a long minute. The schnauzer was growling all the while, quickstepping in circles, its little ears pinned back, its teeth clenched and bared.

"You'd better rein that little bitch in," Charlie said as he stood up. "Czar here's got a pecker like a stick of dynamite and he ain't afraid to use it." He kicked his brute's hind leg out to show what he said was true.

"You see what I'm saying, Berit Lovig?" He nodded down at the dog's genitals. "All I have to do is cluck my tongue and Czar here will rip that little shit in half. I couldn't stop him if I wanted to. That's just how it is."

"Take that hellhound out of here, Mr. Aas. Right this minute."

"You call old Czar here a hellhound?" Charlie said, feigning indignation. "You might stop to consider what that makes me." He made another great show of taking a cigarette from his shirt pocket. He struck a wooden match and lit the tip of the cigarette. Rather than blowing out the match, he let it burn down to his fingers and didn't flinch when the flame touched his skin. Nor did he drop the match. He merely smiled and exhaled smoke from his cigarette. "You've been warned. Consider that little rat warned, too." He stomped his foot at the schnauzer and howled like a dog himself.

His message was sent. Of course it was. And I was properly terrified. It's easy to look a fiend in the eye and know that much. But it wasn't enough for him to leave me scared. For that man, nothing was ever enough.

Two days later I went onto the porch to shake out the rugs. It was early morning and no one was about. I opened the door, hung the rugs over the railing, and then noticed the schnauzer in the empty flower box. Or, rather, I noticed half of her, the hind legs and tail and rump all torn or eaten away. I screamed. I screamed and ran inside, wanting to tell Rebekah. It was her dog, after all. I thought, too, of calling the sheriff. But, like everyone else in town, the sheriff was just another lackey on the Aas payroll. So I fetched a paper sack and my gardening gloves and carried the remains to the rubbish bin out back, dumped them in, and spent the rest of that week and most of the next frightened of what he might do.

It was six weeks later when his final revenge came. In any case, that's what I always considered it. I read that warm morning that a new post office would be built, near the library on the highway running through town, the apothecary, according to the *Ax & Beacon,* having become unsuitable as a federal building. The article cited fire hazards and vermin infestation, neither of which was factual. There had never been an inspection. Never a letter. Never a word of any sort that might have questioned the building's integrity. Charlie was finally learning how to wield his influence.

Nowadays the book of maps sits on the mantel, between deer-antler bookends, in Gus's great room. Above the mantel, a scaled-down replica of David Thompson's epic map of the Northwest Territory hangs where the painting of Harry in his fishing boat once did. It is, Gus admits, a peculiar choice. It could even be mistaken as an affront to his father and his own maps, given their history, to say nothing of their proximity to Thompson's replica. But he likes to think it's to the contrary, that the juxtaposition is in fact a fitting homage.

The only sound beyond the chafing fire was the ticking of the grandfather clock in the corner. It was the first morning he'd invited me in, and I cannot say how strange it felt to be there without Harry down the hall. Even the coffee steaming from mugs on the table sent me back to those nights I spent watching Harry's mind begin fading away. And Gus sitting at the head of the table in much the same posture that Harry always assumed — chin both jutting and hanging, eyes watery, hands folded before him. All of it so eerie and wonderful that it would have been easy to get swamped by sad memories.

But Gus was quick to speak. "This is chart eight," he said, pointing at the volume open in his lap. "The map of Burnt Wood Lake."

I leaned in for a look.

The map was puckered by water from dozens of lakes and rivers and streams, from snow and rain and rising mist. The pencil lines, too, are fading, but they, at least, are not gone yet. "Someday," Gus said, "maybe when my grandsons are old men themselves, no lines at all will be left. These beautiful wind roses. The sketches. They'll fade right into oblivion, the paper thinning and thinning and turning to dust in somebody's hands. Why I can take any comfort in such thoughts, I couldn't say."

Chart 8, excerpted from one of Thompson's maps, shows the source of the river as a small bay on the southeastern shore of the lake. In truth, the bay was rounder and much larger than this chart suggests. "My father knew it was off-scale. One glance at a Fisher Map proved that. But he also knew that to reach our first portage we only needed to paddle to the northernmost point of the lake. From there we would continue to bear north and cross the Laurentian Divide between Lake Tramontane and Ostro Lake." He took a sip of his coffee and peered at it closely. "That's what he told me. As though it were simple as walking up the Lighthouse Road."

All morning, he held that book of maps while he talked.

They bobbed in their canoes where the bay met the broader waters of Burnt Wood Lake, which opened up in all directions. On Thompson's map there are only three islands, but Gus could see no fewer than a dozen as Harry pointed to one and said, "Let's have lunch over there. We'll plan the rest of our day after some vittles."

So they paddled the half mile of open water to that island, trolling rubber leaches behind them. They each reeled in a few small pikes before landing on the southern shore, skirted by bedrock that rose into a tuft of scrub spruce and dormant blueberry bushes. They went ashore, and Gus gathered wood and built the cook fire while Harry readied a pot of coffee and got some rice on. They boiled the fish and when the rice was done settled into their lunch, forking bites straight from the pots.

"I suppose we'll tire of this fish," Harry said, "but, sweet Christ, it tastes good now."

Gus was already sick of boiled fish and rice, but didn't have the heart to say so.

"This time the day after tomorrow we'll cross the divide, then on to Lake Biwanago and the old voyageurs' highway. It's all downhill from there." He spoke with his mouth full of food, chewing around his words.

"How far from Biwanago?"

Harry sat on his bootheels and sipped his coffee. "No more than sixty miles as the crow flies, most of that on water. But things get a little dicey past Biwanago. The maps are truer up there, sure. But that country'll all be strange. Country we've never seen, leastways. And getting colder and darker, eh? There's that."

He stood slowly, cracked his back, walked over to his canoe, and pulled out the birchwood calendar. He checked the notches in it — only four, though to Gus it felt like two weeks — and put it back in the pack, then turned to the maps. "Even if we get turned around up here, we'll beat the snow."

This had been his aim: to reach the fort before the first snow. Gus could tell it pleased him to be on schedule, even though that proved to be fallacious and meaningless. Harry was punctual to a fault. As exact as the sun- or moonrise, both of which he daily knew by heart.

I remember him winding his old Schaffhausen wristwatch at our lunch table, sandwich crumbs still on his plate. Almost nothing pleased me as much as his easy pleasure after a meal. He wound the watch then, on that island, before stepping to shore and washing their lunch dishes while Gus lay back against a rock and let the sun warm his face. In that moment he was utterly content, all misgivings arrested by both time and place.

Harry came back to their dwindling fire, poured himself the last of the coffee, and said, "How are you holding up, bud?"

Gus held his hand up to block the sun. "I'm good."

Harry sat down and slapped him on the knee. "I should say you are. If the measure of a man's his ability to carry a load, you're as fine as they come."

"Is that the measure?"

"It's one of them."

"But there are others?"

Harry smiled. "I sure as hell hope so." He took a sip of coffee and lay back himself.

"So, we'll get to Biwanago in a day or two," Gus said. He was thinking of their route, but also found himself curious about their destination. They hadn't talked about it since that night in the fish house. Gus had trusted that what his father'd said was true, that the plan was reasonable and sound. Why wouldn't he? Harry had never done anything unreasonable in his life. Though it was now dawning on Gus, having reached what could have been called their first milestone, that he had no idea where in fact they were headed.

"Then up the Balsam River, along the border. A day's paddle. Maybe less. Lots of portages and white water, but then the water gets smooth and big." He sat up on his elbow and took another sip. "That river's the last place we'll know for certain where we are."

"What does that mean?"

Harry lay back down. "Like I said, that's new country up there. Big country. I've never been north of the divide. Can you believe that?"

The truth was, Gus didn't know what the divide was, or where it was, or even what it was supposed to look like. Still, it was hard to believe that his father had never crossed it — a man who'd been to war in Europe, who could walk through any forest with the same sovereignty he had going down his hallway to the bathroom, who knew practically everything. Nothing seemed beyond him. Yet that's exactly what he was describing: a world beyond him. Now that seemed hard to believe.

"Does it matter you've never crossed the divide?"

"La Vérendrye, Thompson, a hundred others like them, a thousand others, all of them passed through this neck of the woods. They all went across Biwanago. Hell, before La Vérendrye or Thompson made it, somebody else did. Some Frenchman or Scotsman three hundred years ago. When that man came through he didn't have any map or the slightest damn notion of where he was. That's a historical fact. That man — whoever he was — thought he was headed to the Orient, with China just up the river." He waved at the water. "At least I know we ain't on our way to China, eh?" He slapped Gus's knee again and wrestled himself up off the ground. "Not only that, but he had to worry about the natives in the woods. He didn't know what fine folks they were. And he was paddling along in a birchbark canoe. They sewed those goddamn things together with the split roots of black spruce. Roots.

He didn't have one of these stalwart vessels." He winked and took a step toward his boat and nudged it with his toe. "*And* he didn't know when winter was coming. Hadn't a clue what winter means around here. So does it matter that I haven't crossed the divide? I reckon it does not. Not in comparison, leastways."

This answer did nothing to allay Gus's rising doubt. More to hasten it. Because Harry was dodging the question, Gus could see that even then. Perhaps he was right to.

Now he refilled our coffee mugs and stood at the kitchen counter. "To tell you the truth, I'd be hard-pressed to articulate what it was I wanted to know. Maybe just: 'You know where we're going, right?' Or: 'I'm safe with you, right?' In any case, all I could muster was a boyish and anxious reiteration of the question that came up only moments before: 'What do you mean, the river's the last place we'll know for certain where we are?' "

He gestured at the book of maps sitting on the table between our coffee cups. "Where my father was going — where we were going —"

I picked up the book and listened as he continued his story.

"You've come a long way," Harry said,

"without asking to see the maps. Here, have a look." He handed the book of maps to him. "Turn to chart sixteen."

This showed the Balsam River fanning into a glut of thirty or forty unnamed islands. They, in turn, spread to a vast lake called Kaseiganagah. He studied the map for a moment and then glanced at his father, who was staring down on him.

"You see?" Harry said.

Gus said nothing, just turned the page to chart seventeen, which was devoted to the western half of Kaseiganagah. Along the south shore another fifty islands were marked, each shoreline more jagged than the one before. Sketched in the corner of the chart a snarling bear reared up, its paw swatting the air. The words *Îles des Chasseurs* crawled along the northern edge of the lake in beautiful looping calligraphy.

"What's Chasseurs?" Gus asked.

"Turn the page. Keep looking."

Again Gus did as he was told, pausing for a minute or two to study each of the maps. They grew increasingly more vague until he got to chart twenty-four. Holy Lake. It had almost no detail but for a house on the shore of a northern bay marked *Fort le Croix*. In the corner, instead of a bear, a single man in a canoe was paddling through the rain.

Gus turned the final page. Chart twenty-five was drawn to an entirely different scale and covered what must have been fifty miles of broadening lakes and rivers, none of them named. No compass rose, no arrow pointing north. No sketches, only the words L'EXTRÉMITÉ — TROP LOIN, written not in a script like *Îles des Chasseurs* or *Fort le Croix* but in bold block letters. Ominous letters.

"Find the fort before twenty-five, eh?" Harry said.

"Fort le Croix?" Gus said.

"Home sweet home," Harry said.

Gus flipped through the maps again. "I still don't understand. Every place is certainly somewhere."

"Now you sound like a philosopher. Or Pastor Nils."

Harry stood and went to the coffeepot still sitting on a rock near the fire. He removed his handkerchief from his trouser pocket and dumped the grounds into it, wrapped them up, and cinched the cloth with a piece of twine. He stowed the coffee in the food pack and rinsed the pot on the shore, then filled it again and brought it over to douse the last glowing embers of the fire.

"You're wondering the right things, bud," he said. "I'm wondering them myself." He packed the coffeepot and stood at his canoe. "Fort le Croix? The miles between here and there? The season ahead? It's all out there, there's no doubt of that." He looked out at the lake and then he turned his gaze on the sky in the south. He seemed ready to say more for a long time before finally adding, "And maybe there's more than that. Likely there is. If not now, then en route." He used a hand to block the sunlight. "En route, indeed."

He stepped into his canoe and back-stroked twice and waited for Gus ten feet offshore. When he, too, was on the water, Harry pinched a wad of snoose into his cheek and tossed him the sack, so Gus took a dip himself. Harry spit on the water and said, "Our concern now is crossing those miles. It's finding the fort. It's getting settled in before winter does." He worked the tobacco in his cheek and spit again. "All those boys before us did it. We can, too."

When Gus didn't answer, Harry said, "You bet we will."

"Even now I recall that afternoon clearly," Gus said. "We paddled around the islands on Burnt Wood Lake and into her northeastern bays, my father singing all the while. It was warm enough that I took my shirt off for an hour after lunch." He looked across the great room at the map above the mantel. "It was, of all our days up there, among the finest. All of which ought to have made my father's lying less forgivable." Now he turned to me. "But instead of looking back in anger, I've decided I owe my father a kind of thanks that isn't often required nowadays." He pointed over at the map. "On this scaled-down version of Thompson's Northwest Territory, our time on the border traveled only inches in a world six feet wide. All those unseen lakes and rivers? A thousand miles north? A thousand west? They weren't meant for us. But those miles we did travel, my father's apocryphal fort? They taught me more — about myself, about him, about loyalty and love — than I've ever learned since. No doubt about it.

"My father did lie to me. There's no denying that. But there was also — in his lie — a kind of truth that honesty could never have conveyed."

"What does that mean?" I was now the one to ask. They were the first words I'd spoken in what seemed an hour.

Gus sat back down across the table from me. "I told my wife the same story last night. When she asked what my father taught me, I told her I couldn't put it into words. But then I lay awake watching the snow fall outside and came up with this: how brave a thing it was for him to try to rediscover something, even if it was only himself, not a continent."

That sounded just right, and I smiled, if not actually, then to myself. But when I looked up Gus's gaze was fierce.

"There's this, too, though I didn't say it to Sarah: I thought how wise he was to lure his rival out into the woods, where every fight's fair."

My eyes must have widened, because Gus looked at me even more fiercely and said, "I told you you didn't know the whole story."

But Gus didn't know the whole story, either. Who ever does?

After our second morning together I could already see that the story he was telling — to explain a man we both dearly loved — was lacking a few things Gus didn't know. Things that I *did* know but couldn't speak of. I'm talking about what happened many years ago to his grandfather, Odd Einar Eide, which I saw firsthand and understood better than anyone. It still stuns me, almost sixty years later, to think of it. But even more than Odd's story, I was thinking about Rebekah Grimm and the shadow she cast over Harry's life. And so over Gus's, too. Secreting my knowledge felt like a betrayal, like I was sending Gus out into the woods to hunt bear with a slingshot when behind my back I held his father's trusty Remington, oiled and loaded and sighted true. But about Rebekah I simply didn't know where to begin. I knew that anything I said, any expression of sympathy or fondness, would be met with doubt. In fact, it would be met with a religious certainty to the contrary. This sort of thinking was as ingrained in Gus as it had been in his father, and nothing I might say would discourage it. Just as nothing I ever told Harry changed his thinking. Not about Rebekah. Not one inch.

Harry came by his grievances against Rebekah honestly, I'll give him that. He rarely spoke of his father, whom he adored and admired and knew as well as a person can know someone else. Harry would never share that man with anyone. But of his mother — whom he scorned and knew not at all — he spoke often.

I heard, as everyone had, that Rebekah abandoned Odd in Duluth when Harry was little more than a newborn. Just up and left one summer morning. She ferried herself back to Gunflint and took her place next to Hosea Grimm like he was a prophet and she a hapless disciple of his foolishness. Meanwhile, Odd settled his own affairs in Duluth, packed a box of baby formula, swaddled his boy, and carried him aboard a boat named after his mother. Once the two of them motored home, he set up shop in the fish house, and carved out a living tossing nets and building boats.

This was the popular version of their story, the one whispered over drinks at the Traveler's Hotel saloon, coffee in the church basement, and fishing bobbers up on Long Finger Lake. The one I overheard in pieces over the apothecary's counter. But you never would have heard it from Rebekah or Odd or Harry. For them, the story of their blood was sacrosanct. People avoided the subject with them as though it were poisonous. Children were born into old families up here knowing to give it a wide berth.

So it came as a surprise to me when, some months after Harry and I took up, he mentioned his mother.

"It's a pity and a sad thing to see that woman — *Miss Grimm* — tucked away up there in that rest home. No one to bring her flowers."

"I bring her flowers," I told him. "I did just yesterday."

He seemed insulted. "You don't work for her anymore."

"You think I don't know that?"

"So you don't have to go see her anymore," he said.

"Are you saying you don't want me to?"

"I'm saying you've done your service. Her friends can keep her company now."

I remember wondering if we were arguing. What I said was "I'm her friend. Her only friend."

"You're not her friend."

"Of course I am."

"Well, far be it from me to say who your friends are," he said. "Just know she won't be a regular topic of conversation, eh?"

But as I said, he brought her up often. Never "How's my mother?" or "Will you say hello for me?" or "Do you think I ought to pay her a visit?" What he did say was cutting or worse. "I suppose Miss Grimm's ranting hardly registers with the rest of the seniles up there at the home," or "I bet there's no one left to empty Miss Grimm's bedpan up there, eh?" or "I bet they've replaced the goose down in her pillow with porcupine quills by now."

His barbs were so entirely out of character that at moments I felt that I was talking with another man altogether. That the kind and gentle and lonely man I already loved was someone I'd invented to salve my own loneliness, which in fact had been increased by his mother's absence from my everyday life.

At night, in the new house Harry had built for me, pacing around, trying to get used to the quiet thrill of it all, I began thinking of how I might tell him about her. Things I'd come to know during the many years I lived with her. My first nights in the apothecary were terrifying. I was only seventeen years old and living with a phantom. I knew that about Rebekah before I knew anything else. Each night at seven-thirty she closed the door to her room. She expected complete silence until five-thirty the next morning, when she wanted her breakfast to be served. Tea, oatmeal with butter and brown sugar, a piece of dry white toast, a glass of orange juice. At seven the store was to be opened, such store as it was. She sold hats, or anyway had hats for sale. Thousands of them, each one a particular clue to her eccentricity. In all those years, I wonder if we sold a dozen of them. That was half of her enterprise. The viable half was the post office. By some vagary of small-town life, she was allowed to operate it. Rather, I operated it.

My job was to service the counter and sort the mail and receive packages and letters. Every morning I shook the rugs and swept the floor. At noon, I locked the door and ascended the two flights of stairs to our apartment, where I prepared her lunch. Crackers and cheese and peeled carrots (every day, year after year after year, I ate the same thing myself). Then back to the counter until three-thirty, when I locked the door again. It was in the two hours before dinner that I had my only freedom. Most often I'd walk to the end of the Lighthouse Road and stroll the shoreline. How clearly I remember that view of the apothecary. I swear, every time I looked I could see Rebekah looming in the big window on the third floor. How much time did I spend watching the town's figurehead beating against the waves of her own grief?

At night, because I couldn't fall asleep and had been banished to silence, I'd go and stand at the window myself, trying to see what she saw. Or didn't see. I now realize it was a practice inspired more by curiosity than by empathy. Though the one led eventually to the other.

In springtime, I watched the evenings growing longer as the ice came apart and ashore. I watched the townsfolk coming out after the long winter, children running in the streets, lovers sitting on benches along the Lighthouse Road. In summer, I watched high-schoolers diving from the breakwater into the harbor, their lives so very different than mine. I watched kids throwing sandwich crusts to gulls hovering above their picnics. I watched the scant harbor traffic.

More than a few times I saw Harry sidle his beautiful boat up to the harbormaster's dock to refuel. In the cool months of autumn, I watched the smoke from Harry's fish-house chimney filter up across the isthmus. Seeing these things didn't help me understand Rebekah any better. I think the opposite might have been true.

During the winter nights that followed, when darkness fell before suppertime, the window only reflected the view inside. The lamp that lent light to the likenesses in the glass. The rocking chair and davenport and braided rug. My own face. It came as a surprise every time to see myself there. It was as though I'd forgotten I was actually part of the odd domesticity that Rebekah and I were playing out against all our silence and stiltedness. In fact, it was easy to forget myself up there, plain as I was. Or what was then thought of as handsome, a word no woman ever aspired to. I had always known this about myself and accepted it as I would have a limp. But Rebekah, she was a graceful woman, as strikingly tragic as an aged movie star, with the sort of beauty that made it easy for me to forget my own plainness. So I took pleasure in her loveliness and wondered what it would be like to see such elegance in one's own reflection. Or did she see this at all? Maybe she saw only loneliness. Certainly that's what I saw when I looked past her prettiness, whether across the kitchen table or down on the Lighthouse Road.

I wondered other things, too. In fact, I spent much of my early life here obsessing about her. But she was then, as she remained always, as mysterious and furtive and unpredictable as the northern lights. And as distant. No amount of curiosity could bring her any closer. Asking around didn't help, either. Once I became friendly with the townswomen, I'd sneak questions about Rebekah into our conversations at the mail counter: Was she ever married? What about her father, Hosea? Did she ever smile? Was my work at the apothecary satisfactory?

It took a long time to work up the courage to ask about Harry. One day Claire Veilleux came in to send her daughter a care package. About Rebekah's age, Claire had lived here from the day of her birth and was considered by most to be a kind and generous woman. We chatted pleasantly for a few minutes. I took her package and weighed it and was getting ready to take her payment when Freddy Riverfish walked in. He doffed his cap and I turned for his mail and handed it to him.

"Harry Eide's today, too," he said.

He often fetched Harry's mail as well. So I handed it to him without question. He doffed his cap again and left.

I remember looking at Claire Veilleux and saying, "Why does Harry Eide never come for his own mail?"

Bless her, she blushed deeply and stammered, then managed, "Miss Lovig, the answer to that question is buried out there." She pointed out the window toward the lake. "You could ask Rebekah or Harry, but neither would have an answer. That's the sad truth." She put her mail in her purse and looked back at me. "But let me tell you something. There are truths that run deep and truths that run shallow. And there are truths that do neither. Do you understand?"

I must have looked doubtful.

"When you're older, perhaps after you've had to lie to people you care about, or let go of that which you didn't think you could, well, maybe then you'll understand."

Claire Veilleux left that day with a sympathetic smile. For some twenty-five years I lived with Rebekah and wondered often what Claire meant about all these different truths. When I cared for her in times of sickness, which were frequent, I wondered. As I did when I helped her bathe and dress as she grew feebler. In her last years in the apothecary, I wondered as I helped her to the toilet. When, eventually, her eyes were so bad that I read to her for an hour, sometimes longer, I wondered. And I wondered then, as I read to her and as she fell asleep in her rocking chair, harboring all the feelings she must've had, how she could ever sleep. But despite everything we shared, she never once betrayed herself or the past I was so eager to know. To this day — now more than twenty-two years after her death — I do not know what it is to lie to someone I love. And until Harry himself vanished up the river last month, I never knew what it was to let go of something I didn't think I ever could. And because I'm an honest woman, I can say his disappearance hasn't brought me one iota closer to understanding Rebekah Grimm. If anything, his vanishing and the stories it has provoked in his son have made her even more of an enigma.

I can't say standing up in that same window these days has lent any clarity, either. And there have been a few such days lately, now that we're set to begin work on the historical society, a project made possible because Gus's sister donated the apothecary to the municipality of Gunflint, population 1,201.

It's been a strange string of ownership for this place. Strange and tangled, as so many things are. The apothecary was sold to Lisbet when Rebekah moved to the Lutheran Home back in the spring of 1963. By any definition it was a slap in Harry's face that a place he so deplored was suddenly his property. Even if it was only his property until he and Lisbet divorced less than two years later.

Not long after the divorce, Lisbet moved back to Chicago. By then I had moved into a rented house up on Eighth Avenue and on my walks through town I would often pause and stare up at the old apothecary. For years afterward it loomed over the town like some stately and remnant white pine. Paint peeled from the siding. Weeds overtook the lawn. The porch swing fell from its chains. Every five years the plywood over the windows was replaced by Harry or Gus. They must have felt they owed it to the townsfolk to keep what was in there hidden away. And then Signe, putting her estate in order, wiped her hands free of the place, with not a single condition to her donation. She only wanted out from under it. So now it has another chance to become a part of the fabric of life in Gunflint.

Bonnie Hanrahan and Lenora Lemay talked me into helping to curate the historical society, and certainly we'll do our best. Though to be honest I took their coaxing as a compliment and agreed without needing to think it over for even a second. Perhaps I should have. I've been back a few times by now and always feel a kind of presence in here. Please don't think me a quack. I'm no Gnostic and don't believe in sixth senses. Still and all, my memories have been especially piqued when I've stood up there in the apartment looking out that old pane of glass.

On the last occasion I got thinking that perhaps Rebekah was long past waiting. Maybe she'd spent her time in that high window wanting to jump through it. This thought put a chill right down my spine and left me feeling heartbroken for days. Because, for all of her coldness and eccentricity, I was actually very fond of her. I might even say I loved her.

There were moments when her guard went down, when she entered a room or a conversation as if she'd been delivered into another life that wasn't smothered by personal history. It's true those moments were infrequent, but suddenly she could be witty or blithe, even warm. Sometimes they'd come at the breakfast table. She'd recall a scene from the story I read her the night before and she'd laugh. Or maybe it was a story she heard on WTIP that led her to questions. *Does this new desegregation law mean the Norwegians and Swedes up here will be forced to walk the same road to school? Eight cents to send a letter? I'd better capture a hawk when they fly through this fall.* On the rare instance when she sold a hat, she was moved to something like giddiness. The tone of her voice would change. The tension around her eyes and lips would release and she could smile like a woman thirty years younger. Those moods might last a minute or an hour, but she was lovely then.

I've not thought often enough about those happy times, though I found myself reminiscing when last I was up on the third floor. It felt good — quite good — to recall the sound of her laughter. It lingered in my mind and got me thinking about how that window was something like a crystal ball for me. How it looked onto a future that might have been very grim if not for those glimpses of Harry and his fishing boat.

But as soon as the thought of him crossed my mind, I was struck by the notion that

Rebekah and I might have been waiting and wishing for the same man.

The first day beyond Burnt Wood Lake was the last of their easy days. The weather was fair, their lungs and legs were fresh, their outfit was complete. The fish were biting, and that night they ate walleye breaded in crackers and fried in oleo, so their guts were well pleased. They were equal on the water, which surprised Gus as much as it did Harry, but he was commended for it. He saw, with every paddle stroke, a stoutheartedness he'd always known in his father but was thrilled to discover in himself. The looming voyage made sense for the entire day. They found the first portage and crossed two more lakes before making camp and finding a long night's sleep.

Already the next morning the maps proved unfaithful to the country, accounting for fewer and fewer of the lakes and portages, and by the third afternoon on this stretch they were relying more on compass and feel than on charts. The fact that they were lost — paddling shorelines for hours, looking for access into the woods, cutting trail through cedar swamps or pine stands when they couldn't find any — didn't seem to alarm Harry. And because he was nonchalant, even confident, Gus put his own worries aside. Until the night the wind came.

They were four or five days beyond Burnt Wood Lake when a squalling, screaming rain ambushed them on what they guessed was Malcolm Lake. They took shelter in the lee of its craggy shore, which didn't provide much. Whitecaps swamped their canoes. Lightning split thunderheads. Late in the afternoon they found a place to camp along a narrow arm of the lake and pitched their canvas between two trees on the granite shore. With everything too wet for them to start a fire, they ate jerky and crackers for dinner and then hoisted the food packs into a swaying pine before settling in.

All night the wind hollered. The flapping canvas and dropping temperatures made sleep fitful. Twice Gus was shaken wide awake by the sound of a snapping tree. At one point Harry crept from the tent to check on the canoes. When he came back in and burrowed into his sleeping sack he said, "It's unnatural, that wind."

The rain relented before dawn and Gus had an hour of peaceable sleep. When he woke, he crawled from the tent and saw his father staring across the lake. Atop the ridge that they'd canoed under the evening before, all the pines had been blown over. Hundreds of trees. Thousands. A mile of trees, felled in a single night. They could have built a lodge from them.

Harry turned and smiled. He held his compass in his hands, the wind blowing the pompom on his red hat like a rooster's tail on a weathervane. "A perfect day for scouting, eh?" He had to shout to make his voice heard above the relentless gale.

He pointed up the narrows. "North!" he said. "Look at that rise." He moved next to Gus and leaned into his shoulder. "A hill like that could damn well be the divide." He turned and looked again up the lake. "What do you think?"

Gus scanned the ridge once more. "I think we're lucky we didn't get crushed by timber last night."

"I guess any night you don't die under a falling tree is a lucky one," Harry said. He had a dopey look on his face.

Gus looked up the narrows. "You really think that could be the divide?"

"I'll make coffee, then we'll go have a

look."

They launched only one canoe, Harry taking the helm. Even though it was no great distance up the narrows, they were paddling into the northerly wind funneling down the gorge, and it took them nearly half an hour. Near the end of the lake Gus saw a sort of line, a change in the light. The wind was visible above it, and below it the air was clear and hard. As they passed under it, the atmosphere suddenly felt almost weightless. The wind — noisy as a passing train when upon them — now quieted, nothing more than a faint whistling.

Harry turned to look back at Gus in the stern. "Creepy, eh?"

It was ominous, all that shifting light and sound. When Gus turned back himself to study the lake behind them, he thought, *We're gone. There's no turning back. Not now.*

They gently beached the canoe on talus black with rainwater. They heard the unmistakable hammering of a waterfall and followed the sound west by climbing a steep escarpment. The roar was soon imminent and everywhere and Gus expected to see falls at any minute, but they ventured as far north as they did west before they found it twenty minutes later. A pool of water the size of a baseball infield, rimmed with fallen trees and knifelike rocks, caught the water falling from thirty feet above. It was beautiful. The mist rising. The cedar trees lining the falls and drooping under all that wetness. The wind forgotten in this seam of the earth.

Harry sat down on a rotted-out cedar half submerged in the pool. "Goddamnit," he said, his voice hoarse. He coughed and spit and said "Goddamnit" again, as if maybe Gus hadn't heard him the first time.

"What's wrong?"

"This water's flowing the wrong way." He snapped a branch off the fallen tree and threw it into the shallow creek running from the pool, as though he expected it to flow up the falls instead of down. He watched it bounce between rocks for a moment and said, "Obviously." He shook his head and added, "What kind of a fool would think a rise like this would go farther down the other side?"

"What's the big deal?"

He shook his head. "I'm not thinking straight. We can't have that." He turned and looked up at the falls.

"We should still go look," Gus said. He was rightly confused by his father's mood swing.

Harry said nothing, just started wading around the edge of the water. It was hazardous alongside those falls, the rocks slick and sharp and given to shifting underfoot. The temperature must have fallen thirty degrees overnight, which made the water feel warmer but the air biting and cruel. When they reached the top, the ground flattened and spread out in a tangle of warped cedars. They stumbled through the grove in water up to their thighs, the wind back in their faces. When they came through the trees a lake opened wide and white with churning water. All along the southern shore the cliffs dwarfed the ones in the gorge below.

A look like panic came over Harry's face — almost as if he'd been slapped — and he surveyed their surroundings like a simpleton for a few long minutes. But then his face lit up. He took the book of maps from his daypack and flipped between two pages, then studied these cliffs again. "This could damn well be Rouge Lake. That means we're on track after all." Now he looked behind them, from where they'd just come, and conjured with the maps and his memory for a long time. He nodded emphatically. "Yes, sir, I think this might very well be Rouge."

Gus pulled himself up into the crotch of a

cedar and sat with his back to the open water. The wind blew through his wet pants and burned cold. "It won't be easy through here," he said. "It's like a ball of yarn, all these trees. Won't be easy up those falls with the boats, either." He pointed behind him. "It'll take us all day."

Harry squinted up at Gus. "We've been at this long enough for a day off, eh? What say we tackle this portage tomorrow? Maybe give this wind a chance to blow itself out?"

"I'm for that," Gus said.

They started back down; in spots it was so steep that it seemed impossible they'd climbed it without aid of a ladder or ropes. Before returning to the canoe, they foraged in the undergrowth of the cedar swamp for deadfall. They found four good logs and loaded them into the canoe and paddled back to their campsite, the gunwales not more than six inches above the waterline.

After all those days of going strong it was strange to idle around the campsite, but that's just what they did. Harry roused a huge fire and Gus went to work on the deadfall, quartering all the logs before splitting them with the hatchet. They hung a rope between two trees and washed their clothes and hung them near the heat of the fire to dry. Gus made a pot of coffee, and by noon they'd done all the chores.

Harry sat with his feet toward the fire and took the Remington apart, carefully wiping out the barrel after all the rain the day before. Gus watched him, feeling drowsy and hungry and in some back room of himself, like he wished he'd never joined this expedition. His father must have read his mood, because he said, "You look like you came out on the wrong end of a bad night's sleep."

"I've had better. That's for sure."

Harry was oiling the pins, squinting down his nose at his work.

"I was going to fish," Gus said, "but I think I'll take a nap."

Harry kept working on the gun. "A nap would do you well. I'll wake you for dinner."

So Gus climbed under their canvas and wrapped himself in the sleeping sack. He slept hard that afternoon. When he woke it was to a sound like a baaing sheep somewhere near. His right arm and shoulder tingled from sleeping on them wrong. He lay there listening to the strange sound while the wind ruffled the canvas. After a while his blood washed the prickling out of his arm and he sat up. Through the tent flap he could see Harry up the shore, standing in plain sight beside a boulder the size of a bear and aiming the Remington across the lake.

Gus had seen that look on his face before — a great many times — and he knew there was game in his sights. He crawled up to the flap and peered out. On the opposite shore, a fawn stood with its hind end to them, its bleats carrying across the water on the strong wind coming down the cliff. He could still see vestiges of the fawn's spots.

Gus swept his glance between the deer and Harry for what seemed ten minutes. Twice his father lowered the gun and closed his eyes with the countenance of a man at prayer. When he opened his eyes again he retrained his sights on the fawn. Then he noticed Gus crouching in the tent, aimed a third time, and fired.

Gus was surprised to see the fawn merely flinch and buck. It seemed impossible that Harry would have missed so easy a shot, but Gus felt relieved when the fawn only bawled louder.

Harry slung the Remington over his shoulder and walked briskly toward him. Once within earshot, he shouted, "Grab the hunting knife and come on."

Gus rummaged through the pack and found the knife, put on his sweater and boots, and stepped out of the tent. The fawn still hadn't moved.

"What's going on?" he said.

"You're not going to believe this."

They jumped into a canoe and crossed the narrows. Harry splashed into the knee-deep water and took a few cautious steps forward. The fawn looked at him and baaed frantically before burying its nose in the rocks. Or what Gus thought were rocks. In fact it was the fawn's mother. The doe was headshot, her legs splayed like a marionette cut from its strings.

Gus was having trouble sorting it all out. Between the fawn and the doe and his having just woken up, he thought that perhaps he was only dreaming. He tried to wake himself again, better this time, but found himself still standing at the canoe, watching his father step cautiously toward the fawn, his hand outstretched as though the little deer were a dog.

When he was within twenty feet he turned and glanced at Gus, looking confused himself. He shrugged and widened his eyes as though to ask, *What should I do?*

Gus shrugged back.

Ten feet from the fawn Harry stopped, stood tall, and put his hands at his sides. The fawn sniffed its mother, licked her ear, then turned and ran up the craggy shoreline. Gus and Harry watched it go.

He might still have thought he was dreaming if, a minute later, he hadn't crossed the beach, looked down, and seen the dead doe. He stood beside his father, who had his hat in his hand as if he were paying respects.

"What the hell?" Gus said.

Harry still had the Remington slung over his shoulder. He removed it and checked the safety and laid it on a rock. "I'm sitting there drinking a cup of coffee while you were napping. The wind was back up. Fierce again." He whirled his hands above his head as though this needed to be acted out. "I'd already put the gun away. So I get up to take a piss and have a look around. I'm walking up the shore" — he pointed across the lake at the huge boulder — "and looking up at the ridge, where the trees are down, and, no kidding, I see this doe and her fawn coming along the edge. I mean the *very* edge. A gust comes down and, I shit you not, the doe's blown right off the cliff. Or she slips. Anyway, she lands here." He gestured at her.

"Bullshit," Gus said.

"I'm not making this up. Look at her legs. Look at her goddamned neck."

"Then why'd you shoot her?"

"Because she wasn't dead!"

Gus stared up at the cliff. "She fell from there and didn't die?"

Harry scratched his head and put his hat back on. "That's thirty or forty feet if it's ten, eh? Just fell off. Two minutes later, that fawn comes walking up the rocks, bawling its fool head off. You heard it."

"I think it woke me."

Harry waved a hand above his head. "She just fell off. She landed here. She was still alive."

"How?"

"I have no idea. None in the world. When I saw her twitching I went for the gun. Got it out of the case and walked over to that rock. That's when I saw the fawn." He reached under his hat and scratched again. "How in the *hell*?"

They both stood over the deer for a spell until Harry said, "I had to shoot her." He knelt and grabbed one of its hind legs. "It must be broken in a hundred spots." He took the other hind leg in his hand. "They're all broken in a hundred spots." He stood back up and looked at Gus. "I guess we gut her."

"I can do it," Gus said.

"No. It was my shot."

Gus took the knife from his belt and

handed it to his father, who unsheathed it and knelt and rolled the doe onto her back. Before he cut into her he glanced up. "I guess the snow's gonna beat us now, eh, bud?"

They spent two or three days at their camp on the narrows, waiting for the wind to blow through and jerking the venison. By the time they portaged up those falls, their larder was heavier than when they'd left home.

Gus had suggested when they broke camp earlier that morning that they wait for the fog to lift, but Harry insisted the sun would burn it off. It hadn't. Half a day later they were paddling slowly, still staring into the whiteness. Every twenty strokes the trees hanging over the water came into view through the fog and Gus felt relieved. It was short in lasting, though, for the fog would swallow them back up almost immediately.

Harry sang the whole time. One of those chansons that had become anthem. *"Petit rocher de la haute montagne, / Je viens ici finir cette champagne. / Ah! doux échos, entendez mes soupirs, / En languissant je vais bientôt mourir. . . .*" Gus hummed along even as he wondered what the hell the words meant.

They paddled for another hour before Harry stopped singing, rested his paddle, and stretched his back. "Half a goddamn day," he said. "We've been four hours on this lake and it just won't quit."

"Could be Biwanago," Gus said, though he had no hope that it was.

Harry studied the fog in each direction. "And this weather. Christ almighty."

Gus took his compass from the hip pocket of his pants. Before he even took a reading, his father said, "Dead west."

Gus held the compass up anyway.

"Dead fucking west," Harry told him.

"Biwanago goes east and west," Gus said.

"It's not Biwanago, Gus." Then Harry gripped his paddle and dug in for a hard pull.

But it was Biwanago. Most likely, anyway. They cut through that misty morning for another half hour before the fog was gone all at once. Not like smoke rising, which was what Gus was used to, but as if it had been shattered and shot across the water like blowing snow. Green pines suddenly came into view against a soft blue sky, the trees here dense and unbroken.

They paddled until they came to a point of gnarly granite. Gus moved ahead of his father without a word and passed into a long, narrow bay. Before he was halfway across he heard rushing water. He turned to look at his father, who had his ear canted toward the sound as though God himself were whispering across the water.

"Hear that?" Harry said as his canoe slid beside Gus's.

"Yup."

"Sounds heavy."

Now Harry pulled out his compass, took his measure, and looked up at the sky. Their canoes came together and Gus made them trice by hooking his paddle over his father's gunwale. The air was as still as the inside of a church. They sat in that stillness for a moment before Gus noticed that their canoes were being pulled slowly toward the sound of the rushing water.

They put ashore well above the falls. Gus could see the mist rising downstream. Harry was hunched over the strap of his Duluth pack, and when he stood he had the book of maps in a grip so tight Gus thought the veins in his hands might burst.

They walked the rocky shoreline to the sault. The first chute dropped five feet into a roiling white pool before spitting out into a hundred yards of churning water, its narrow path pocked with boulders and laced with fallen trees. At the end of the view, where the water veered west, it also appeared to slow down and smooth out.

Harry looked back toward the big lake behind them, tapping the moose hide onto his freshly shaven chin. "How in the hell did we miss it?"

"Miss what?" Gus said.

"The divide, Gus. The height of land." He thumbed through the pages and mumbled something Gus couldn't understand. Then Harry shook his head fiercely, glanced heavenward, squatted, and cupped a handful of water up to his mouth. When he stood back up, he said, "Maybe it's time we turned around, eh, bud?"

Gus spun to face him. "You mean go home?"

Harry arched his eyebrows.

"Are you kidding me?"

"We're in a spot here. A hell of a spot. This" — he pointed down at the water, spread his arms toward the forest and sky above, and shook the book of maps like a pastor wielding the Bible — "is not where we are."

"Of course this is where we are," Gus said.

"It's where we're supposed to be, too." Though they were back on course, where they wanted to be, Gus recognized it as the most dangerous place he'd ever been. He felt charged, electric, like some current as strong as the river's was coursing through him. "The mouth of the Balsam River. Right on course."

Harry pocketed the maps and turned to face the rapids. "I do reckon this is the Balsam, Gus. But think about how we got here. It's blind goddamn luck. Right now, from here, we can feel our way home. Before we get into real trouble."

Gus laughed. "Haven't you been talking all this time about the authentic experience? About La Vérendrye and Thompson and the voyageurs? You and me. Right here. Unsure of our maps? Winter nipping at our heels? 'We're winterers!' you said. You must have said it fifty times." He said all this at once and didn't wait for his father's response. Instead, he pushed past him and marched back up the shoreline. When he reached his canoe he hefted the first Duluth pack from it, shouldered it, pulled the tumpline over his forehead, walked toward the edge of the sault, and dropped it. Harry hadn't moved except to cross his arms over his ragg-wool sweater. When Gus passed again, Harry whispered his name but did nothing to stop him.

Gus passed him twice more. Once with the second pack and then with his canoe. Under the first chute, with a longer view of the rapids, he studied them for a route that obviously wasn't there. The course was too narrow, with too many downed trees.

Harry had come to his side, holding the book of maps again. "There used to be a portage here," he said.

"I guess some trees must've grown in the last hundred years," Gus said.

"Might've been more than a portage. Could even have been an old logging road."

"There was never a logging road here."

"Gus, bud."

"What?"

"We need to slow down. Take stock."

"Why?"

"We're right where we're supposed to be. You're right. But we're also lost."

"We're not lost. We're fucking vanished."

Harry didn't say anything. Instead, he turned and walked the edge of the river back up past the sault.

Gus studied the rapids again. *I can float it,* he thought. *Fix a line, scrabble along the shoreline.* As soon as he thought it, this much was settled.

He was fixing a bowline when he saw his father come tentatively around the sault. He set his pack on the shore, winded, bent over.

"You want some help?" Gus said.

"No." Harry went back for the rest of his gear.

Gus had never seen his father over-matched before, and the sight of it spooked him even more than his own outburst had. Before he could make sense of any of it, he looped the rope over his shoulder and cinched it tight.

He pushed his canoe into the water and hadn't taken ten steps before he realized he was at the mercy of the stream. Between the current and the heavy canoe before him, he had no recourse. His legs couldn't keep up with the flow, and in seconds he was pulled under. The rope twisted and he was on his back on the streambed, looking up through the coursing water. He felt relief rather than panic, even found a moment to think how beautiful the blur above was before he rolled over and got to his feet. He felt electric again, as if he could have lifted from the surface of that stream like a hatching mayfly.

Now the water was waist-deep. As cold and swift as snowmelt under the Devil's Maw. Gus searched for better footing, grabbed hold of a deadfall branch jutting from the shore, and heeled the canoe. He untangled the rope from his waist and pulled himself into shallower water. He was only halfway down the rapids but already they were losing their vigor. The water slowed and widened into a river.

When he reached the bend, the canoe settled on the river bottom and he looked back at his father, still standing under the falls. It was the greatest distance between them since they'd left home, and Gus relished it. He relished, too, that his hour's hard work was done while Harry still had hell to pay. This, he knew, was a dangerous thought.

He turned to look west, where the river was wide and flat. The terrain climbed again on the northern shore, and white pines towered on the ridge. On the southern shore, the water seeped through duckweeds and water lilies to a muskeg thick with cedar trees. Gus opted for the northern shore, where he beached his canoe and unpacked dry clothes. When he reached into the cargo pocket of his wet pants, it was empty. No compass.

It was almost Christmas, and Gus had helped me up to the third floor of the apothecary. We stood at the window, looking down on the Lighthouse Road, its streetlights strung with garlands and white bulbs. The morning was shadowy, brooding, the lake still holding the darkness of the night before. We stood at the window for some time before he turned and examined the empty room.

"What's it like being back here?" he said.

I was still looking out the window. "I've been back a few times already, and each time seems like it was long ago."

"Everything seems to have happened long ago."

"You're not old enough to talk like that," I told him.

He had his satchel over his shoulder. He wore a tweed coat. By every report he was a fine teacher. Every student's favorite. He put his hands deep in his coat pockets.

"Why did you love him, Berit? What was it about him?"

"He was gentle. And funny. He was plain to see, even if most of him was hidden." I glanced out the window again. "He loved me back. His love made me feel alive. That was very important. He was strong. I adored his strength."

"You had that in common, eh?"

"Don't ever mistake age for strength."

Gus smiled his father's smile again. They were the same, those two. Every time Gus smiled I could have taken his face in my hands and kissed him and been a younger woman again.

"I hate this place," Gus said after a while. "I hate it because he did. Everything I love or hate. Everything I know. Everything I don't know. It's all because of him."

"That can't be true."

"It's true of the things that matter most."

We looked out at the lake for a few more long minutes.

"You're really going to make it into a museum?" he said.

"A historical society."

He shook his head. "Sure, because this place needs its history on display."

"Isn't that what all these talks are, Gus?

Your own history on display? For me, at least?"

"History and memory aren't the same thing."

"How are they different?"

He faced me. "History doesn't abide acts of the imagination but memories depend on it. And memories are as much what we've forgotten as what we recall. History cannot be forgotten."

"You don't seem to have forgotten much."

"I spend more time remembering than most, I guess."

"And all this remembering, it's taking a toll on you, isn't it?"

He turned away. "Even though it feels good to talk about it. Isn't that how it goes?"

"So often, yes."

"Is it the same for you, being here? The memories?"

I looked around the room. I could picture Rebekah sitting in her rocking chair, the kitchen across the hall, could smell the herring frying in the skillet. I could see the basket of yarn and the amber light of the floor lamp. I thought of how much harder it was to stand beside him and listen to his stories, to be reminded in so many ways of his father, than it was to stand here looking at an empty room. "I don't have any strong feelings about this place. But why would I? It was just where I waited for my life to happen. And when it finally did happen, that was somewhere else."

"How in God's name did you pass all that time here?"

"I worked. I looked after Rebekah. I read books. Lots of them. You should see the boxes still down in the basement." I paused. Should I say more? What I spent most of my time waiting for? "I spent more time than was right wondering if I was becoming Rebekah. Middle-aged. Alone. *Lonely.* Waiting for something to change — for someone to come. I thought about your father. I thought about what a life with him would be like. I pined away for him because I got a feeling around him. I was right about it, too, but I spent nearly half of my life quite sure I might have to let that feeling drift away. I didn't want to do that. There was too much to it. Too much happiness waiting to be had. I knew that for certain, so I waited. Lord, did I wait."

"For a long time."

"It was worth it."

Again he smiled. A minute passed before he said, "The last time I saw you, I was talking about the Balsam River?"

"You were. About the sault and losing

your compass."

He nodded. "I wanted to tell you something else. Something that happened soon after that. It was important.

"I'd quit counting days by then. Even though my father notched them into his calendar each night, I'd quit. However many days had passed since we washed out of the Balsam and onto those islands of Kaseiganagah, we were by this day properly and irrefutably lost. And because it had been raining more or less since we cleared the last of those islands — and because I had neither compass nor any inclination to wonder — I couldn't have said if we were lost north or west.

"My father was no longer singing his chansons. He'd hardly spoken in days. He'd stashed the red hat in favor of his poncho's hood, and he paddled through those days like the angel of death."

Gus put the heels of his hands over his eyes and held them there. "The day I'm talking about, I paddled on his starboard flank. Watched the eddies trail his canoe. Watched them as they caught the rain and funneled down into the depths." He lowered his hands. "The lake was black with rain. Like the lake out there." He nodded out the window. "And just as cold.

"My father, he seemed to have a new and manic resolve to move ahead. Even if it meant floating into oblivion." He paused yet again, staring through the window at the lake. "From here, I can see that's just what was happening. My father was discovering the wilderness in himself. It must have seemed as large and unaccommodating as the lands we were traveling through."

"Oh, Gustav," I said.

"What I didn't know, and what makes it all so much more unfathomable — what ought to make it *unforgivable* — is that he knew not only where he was headed but also what would come after us. *Who* would come after us. And why."

I wished that there was a place to sit, that the old davenport was there in front of the window. It was one thing to listen to him talk about his father, to watch the memories working on him. It was another thing altogether to revisit my own lovesickness. Every word about Harry from his lips found a deeper and darker place in me. A feeling I didn't like. It exhausted me. But there was nowhere to sit up in the apothecary's attic. "Is there something you're not telling me, Gus?"

There might have been tears in his eyes. "I've spent so many nights between then and now wondering why he dragged me along with him. I've been angry. Appalled. Sad. But I've spent just as many days giddy with excitement. Like a little boy. So I've always said to myself: *Let the sleeping dog lie.* And I have. At least some of the time. Christ, I have Sarah and the kids as proof that I've been able to put it behind me. But now, telling you all of this — I don't know, Berit. I'm scared."

"To tell me?"

"No. To look back anymore."

"Maybe that's because you're a father yourself. Or because you're afraid you're becoming your father."

"That's what Sarah said."

"Can we both be wrong?"

At this I could tell he wanted to smile. He didn't, though. "There are so many similarities between him and me, I can see that," he said. "But what I think really scares me are the countless ways I'm not like him. And because the past is getting farther and farther behind me, and the end coming closer and closer, I'm afraid I'll never meet the man in myself that I saw in him."

"Everyone's past disappears. That's only natural."

"Parts of it do. You're right. But other parts don't. You know that as well as I do.

There are things that can never be forgotten, no matter how hard we try to."

I caught his eyes in the reflection of the window. "You have your children, Gus. And Sarah. You don't need to become your father."

He closed his eyes and turned his head toward the ceiling.

"You'd better help me down the stairs," I said.

And he did. I put my free hand through his arm and he walked slowly beside me, step by step. When we got outside, the morning was warmer than it looked. The sun was coming out from behind the low clouds. We stood there on the porch.

"Here's what I wanted to tell you. A few days beyond the Balsam River, a cold, rainy day, we turned into the heavy waters of some swamp. My father paused to take his pointless reckoning, and the rain turned to snow by degrees so deliberate and measurable it seemed to be happening out of time altogether. He pulled his hood back and looked up into the snow. And my father — the same man you knew, Berit — he wept. I was stunned. Too stunned to say a word. I just watched him. And after a moment he turned to me and said, 'We'll never find our way back.'

"I felt no fear or anxiety. None at all, even though I was certain we'd die in that wilderness. That I'd die without so much as a compass in my pocket. That we would never be found. What a thing for a boy my age to know. Or for a man to carry around his whole life."

I took his hands in mine.

"How can I convey any of this, Berit? How can I tell Sarah and our kids that our whole life, all of our happiness, it's all been make-believe, because my father and I died up on the borderlands?"

I squeezed his hands tightly.

"We died over and over and over again."

I'd be lying if I said my talks with Gus didn't fill me with a kind of purpose. Maybe even hope. I loved to be so daily reminded of Harry, both bodily and in Gus's manner of speech — how carefully he chose his words, the pauses between them, his conscience plain to see. Harry had been the same in every respect.

But our talks troubled me, too, and the hours after we'd part — when I was left alone with the stories he'd told me, sorting them out, remembering my own version of Harry, writing things down — troubled me even more.

That morning in December, after he guided me down the stairs at the old apothecary and helped me into my truck, after I'd driven through town and turned up the Burnt Wood Trail toward home, I got to thinking about what he'd said about our being able to forget some things. It was easy to see he was right, even though I'd never thought of it exactly like that before. All I had to do was conjure the image of Harry's face. The sweet lines around his eyes. The mess of hair that framed it. The soft lips that ought to have been anything but. My God, how I missed him. How I remembered him. But what had I already forgotten? And where had it gone?

When I got home I went to my bureau and opened the top drawer and took from it the only picture that was ever taken of Harry and me together. His shirt collar askew. His eyes cast off to the side as if there were some imminent danger he'd just noticed. He looked nervous. Caught. I know because he told me that the expression mimicked his feelings on that day. In the photograph we're standing outside the Normandy Hotel in downtown Minneapolis. It was one of only a handful of trips we ever took.

That expression is the one he always wore in public when I was around, which is why most of our time was spent in private, mostly nights here, at my house by the river. We'd have dinner together. Play cribbage by the fire, sipping Harry's aquavit. All our time together felt stolen, clandestine. It did then, and does even more so now. That would be troubling enough, but now there's this: All of those nights together — some thirty years of them — have dissolved into one. Or what I remember as one. Time is already doing its job.

Thank goodness for the photograph. It seems to be almost like evidence that we were together. I studied it closely that morning and realized that our love was in its final act. I'd spent nearly as much time waiting for him as I had with him, and now he was gone. But how would the rest of it go, without Harry here to be a part of it? Or part of it only in my memory — what there was of it — and in the stories his son was telling me?

I stood at the bureau for a long time, looking at us. When I could bear it no longer, I turned my gaze out the window, at the river curling into the trees and rocks. I stared at the river for many minutes. As I did, my reflection came into relief on the glass, and I saw my face suspended over the river. Crying. I hadn't even noticed I was. And I thought of Harry crying into the snow.

Had it been necessary for him to go into the borderlands, for the two of them to have gotten lost up there, so that we might be together? Did the moment when he finally came to me depend on all that had happened up there? And if so, what did that say about our love?

After that morning in the swamp — under the falling snow, with Harry's weeping — came a week of days and nights surrendered completely to the wilderness.

Each morning broke in fog, and Harry and Gus decamped in silence. Always in silence. Harry was no longer checking the maps. They hardly ever spoke. The sound of their paddles scooping through the water was symphonic.

The first of those mornings they canoed across a shallow lake and found a stand of spruce. The trees were draped with old-man's beard that hung white, covered with the morning's frost. Gus passed beneath them thinking that ghosts guarded the world, and he felt all the safer for it.

They paddled streams that turned to swamps and back again to streams without giving up their currents, without a tree in sight above the brown reeds. On the smaller lakes, even the water lilies had gone brown alongshore. When they found the woods again, the only green thing left among them was the lichen and moss. The pines had gone to black against the wan light.

Another morning they woke on a beach, and when Gus walked around the curve of the shore for a piss, he found a riot of paw prints in the sand. He followed them to where they ended in bloodstains and the wolves whose tracks they were had caught their prey. A deer's four hooves was all that remained.

They portaged through woods and on trails and over granite ridges that had been fractured. Crossing one of them, Harry said, "Wasn't that last cold snap these rocks could no longer stand. No, sir, the cold that busted them came a thousand years ago."

It was the first thing he'd said that day.

Each morning came later, each evening sooner. The moon rose after dark, low and bulbous through the trees, as golden as if it had been dipped in bourbon. The sun rose in turn the next morning and provided as little light or warmth as the moon it replaced.

They slept under their tent with a fire burning at the open end of the canvas. Some nights they'd spoon together for the body heat. It snowed twice overnight. On starry nights, Gus could see his father's sleeping face as though it were in broad daylight. Harry slept untroubled, which troubled his son greatly.

There were log-jammed creeks where the water had stopped altogether, only to rise again as if from the soil itself a quarter mile down the streambed.

The stands of aspen and birch were white as bones.

And one day's walk was through burnt-over timber. Miles of black, and only the white clouds above to break it. Their boots were coal-black when they took them off that night. "I guess it's the devil's stand of timber we crossed today, eh, bud?"

Gus couldn't shake the blackness from his mind. "I guess it's all the devil's timber up here."

Harry laughed out loud and said, "Good thing we don't go in for that hocus-pocus!"

It was the last thing he said until days later. The birds were all gone. There were no chirping insects. No rustling leaves left on the trees. Gus found conversation with their snapping campfires at night instead.

The last of those nights he woke with a start. Their fire had died and his teeth were chattering, and when he stepped out of the tent to restoke the flames, he saw the pines on the opposite shore backlit by their own celestial fires: the aurora borealis, shimmering orange and red across the starlit heavens.

Surely, he thought, there was a way to burn with them.

They paddled through the morning and past lunchtime and still there was no end to the lake. Now the wind was stiff in their faces, the sun falling over their port shoulders. Gus looked toward the shore. He felt like they were being watched.

The cliffs and skerries they'd left behind that morning had given over to drab rolling hills. Between their aimlessness and the difficult paddling and their general and persistent silence, they had not yet spoken that day.

Gus, trying to change the subject in his mind, finally said, "Think we're in Minnesota or Canada?"

"It doesn't matter."

"I'm hungry." Gus nearly had to shout to get his voice above the wind.

"Eat some jerky."

"I want a steak."

"A steak?"

"And some spuds."

"You'll need a beer, then. And a crock of corn. While we're at it, how about a slice of rhubarb pie for dessert?"

"And a gallon of strong black coffee."

Harry looked ahead. "The coffee I could give you," he said.

Their canoes drifted together and they both idly surveyed the lake.

"Dad, what are we going to do?"

"We'll paddle until we find a campsite." Harry dipped the tin cup he'd tied to the canoe's thwart into the lake and brought it up for a drink.

"The sun's gonna set in an hour."

"Then we ought to quit lollygagging." He dipped his cup for another drink and took up his paddle again.

"We're in real trouble, aren't we?" Gus said, and though he'd felt the certainty of this for some time, saying it aloud made it entirely more bothersome.

"We don't know trouble yet." Harry nudged his son's canoe away. "Hell, we haven't even met trouble's third cousin."

It was no relief for Gus to hear his father's voice after so many days of its absence.

An hour later the shore to their right opened into a bay bulwarked by a beaver lodge.

They paddled ahead as the sun settled behind them. The calm water was an improvement over going hard against the relentless wind.

Harry said, "There'll be someplace to pitch our tent on this bay."

"I thought the same thing."

Gus scanned the shoreline. The forest stood in ranks. Cedar trees on the far shore, letting into a shadowy muskeg. Birch trees behind them. Maples ahead. Tall, rugged white pines where they steered their canoes.

"That could be rice over there." Harry pointed the tip of his paddle toward the cedars. "I used to do some ricing with my old man and Mr. Riverfish. I bet I could dust the cobwebs off the old brainbox and harvest us some. It's about the right season, if I recall."

"We aren't short on rice," Gus said. And they weren't. Rice and oats and buckwheat they'd packed in. Dried fruit. A sack of onions and another sack of potatoes. Sugar. Ten pounds each of oleo, salt, and coffee. Four jars of peanut butter. Six tins of crackers. Chocolate bars. More than a hundred pounds of food split into two packs. They'd hunt and fish for the rest of their provisions.

"There's a spot," Harry said, pointing now to a moon-shaped beach of granite in the shadow of the white pines.

When they went ashore, Gus said, "I didn't think we'd ever see this much open ground again." A dozen towering pines were scattered across what was otherwise a clearing the size of a highway intersection. In contrast to recent campsites, this was a royal find. They wandered from tree to tree, looking up at the canopy of heavy boughs as though at a cathedral ceiling.

"We'll have no trouble finding a place to raise our tent here, eh, bud?"

"I guess not."

Harry looked out over the lake for a clear view of the sky. "We have half an hour of light left. You collect firewood, I'll get the tent up?"

"Sure."

Gus took the hatchet from the pack and walked along the perimeter, gathering fallen branches, the wood in such abundance that he felt like a thief. He brought the first armful to a spot between two trees eight feet apart, giving them both a place to rest their backs while they sat fireside. He kicked the duff clear, exposing a natural bowl in the granite, and piled the firewood beside it. He collected another several armloads and built a fire.

Harry joined him beside the flames after

the tent was up. "It's my turn to make dinner, isn't it?"

"I can eat jerky."

"Instead of steak and potatoes."

Gus smiled.

"Naw, go catch us a fish to fry up," Harry said. "I'll get a pot of rice going."

Gus went straightaway to the canoe, untied his rod from the thwarts, grabbed his tackle box, and stepped down to the shoreline. He tied a spinner onto his line and studied the falling darkness. Already there were stars flickering into view. He could hear the fire crack behind him.

But for the expanse of the water before him, casting into those stars shining off the surface seemed not so different than fishing the lakes he frequented around Gunflint. He wished he had a bucket of minnows and the right jig, for there surely were walleyes out on the ledge he'd noticed as they peeled their canoes ashore. But he'd have to make do and hope the spinner worked.

After five minutes his father came down to the shore and waded into the water to fill their pot. "Thought you'd have three lunkers by now," he said, squinting up and down the shore. "What are you using?"

"A spinner," Gus said, and cast again.

"Throw a Rapala right off the end of that

log." He pointed to their left and turned back to camp. "A silver one."

Gus waited for him to reach the fire, then bit the spinner from his line and took a Rapala from the tackle box, tied it on his line, and cast it up the shore. The lure landed only feet from the log. He kept the tip of the rod extended as far offshore as he could. Before he'd reeled it halfway home there was a strike. He set the hook and stepped waist-deep into water to fight the fish, holding his rod high above his head. After a couple runs he landed the fish by its gills, a pike as long as his forearm even as its tail curled up into a beautiful *J*.

They ate fish and rice, scrubbed the pots and plates when they were finished, and sat in the fire's warmth, drinking coffee, an hour later.

"I lost my compass," Gus said.

Harry took a sip of his coffee. "You did?"

"Way back on that river. When I went under."

"What good have our compasses been anyway?"

Gus reached for the coffeepot and refilled his cup, then stood and walked around the fire to refill his father's. "I don't understand, Dad."

"You don't understand what?"

"Whatever the hell's happened."

"Well, we've gotten in up to our necks. That's what's happened."

"Obviously. I'm wondering what we're going to do about it." He went back to his side of the fire and sat down against the tree. "We should've turned around when you said to."

"Nope. Not true at all. I was a coward for saying that." Harry sat up. "When the sun comes up, I'll make a good, long study of the maps. This lake here is enormous. The biggest we've been on since Kaseiganagah. It shouldn't be impossible to figure out which one it is and work from there."

"We'll never find that fort. No chance."

Harry looked at him for a long time with what Gus thought was maybe regret or apology. He'd felt that same expression settle over his own face hundreds of times over the years, trying to convey to Sarah or their children the depth of his feelings without having the words to express them. But that night, he mistook what was on his father's face for irritation. "What?" he said.

"You've been tremendous up here, bud. You kept us going when I wanted to quit. I had no idea you were so strong. That you could work so hard. If we keep it together, we'll be fine. If we don't find the fort, we'll find another place to winter. Hell, we'll build a wigwam if it comes to that."

"A wigwam?"

"Sure, as a last resort. I only mean to say we'll be okay."

"A wigwam," Gus said. *"Wigwam."* Having nothing more to say, he moved toward the tent.

Harry, speaking to himself, said, "I'll be to bed soon myself."

He woke in the middle of the night. He searched the darkness for his father but realized he was alone. He watched the fire's shadow dancing on the canvas, then fell back to sleep and woke again, hours later, to Harry's snoring, so he unzipped his sleeping sack, pulled on his trousers and boots and sweater, and brushed the tent flap aside.

The world outside was perfectly still. A heavy frost had settled overnight, bleaching everything a brilliant white. The lake was still as glass except for a beaver's wake along the far shore. It couldn't have been more than twenty degrees.

Gus walked the shore with the little garden spade and a roll of toilet paper in a coffee can. Thirty paces beyond the canoes, he stopped and set the can on a tree stump, lowered his britches, and squatted, resting his elbow on the stump and watching the beaver across the bay. The thought occurred to him that he was still asleep and dreaming, but an echelon of late-migrating geese came gaggling overhead, and for the first time in days he realized which way was south.

It was then that he saw it: a shack sitting on a knoll among blueberry bushes and deadfall. He cocked his head and rubbed his eyes and looked again. The shack was still there. Cracked windows hung on either side of a door falling from its rusted hinges. A roof of wooden shingles was cloaked in moss, two steps smothered in ferns. The river-rock foundation was held together by ancient mortar, the chimney fashioned of the same materials.

Gus again tried to wipe the sight of it from his eyes. Still it remained. He took a cautious step forward. "Hello?" he called, as if some voyageur might emerge from the collapsing doorway. But no man had crossed that threshold in years. Without taking his eyes from the empty doorway, Gus shouted for his father.

Harry pulled the door free. The shanty filled

with sunlight and they stepped inside. A mound of husked pinecones sat on the middle of the puncheon floor, but otherwise there was no sign of life. Gus and Harry looked at each other, then slowly poked around the shack.

It was fifteen feet square. Along the southern wall a single bunk not much wider than one of their canoes sat on four birchwood legs. There were two wooden boxes beneath it. On the opposite wall, a small woodstove occupied the hearth and a tin flue rose up the chimney. In lieu of a mantel, three empty shelves hung on the pine-board walls. On the ceiling joists timber planks were stacked neatly. They appeared to be old floorboards. There was no furniture save for the bunk and shelves. The whole place canted toward the water.

"My, oh, my," Harry whispered. He clapped Gus on the shoulder and then pulled the boxes from beneath the bunk.

The first one held two wooden buckets and a length of coiled rope. In the second was a jar of eight-penny nails, a carton of shotgun shells, a useless pack of wooden matches, two dozen paraffin candles, a stack of composition notebooks wrapped in cellophane, and a small sleeve that held the yellowing pages of a Bible.

Harry removed and replaced each item and pushed the boxes back under the bunk. He sat there on his heels and began chuckling and then erupted into such a fit that he fell on his rump, which only made him laugh more. When he collected himself he said, "This'll do better than a wigwam, eh?" He stood still, laughing, and wiped a tear from his eye.

Unlike his father, Gus could not see the humor in their finding the shack. He felt more lost than ever. "This isn't Fort le Croix, is it?" he said.

"No, it sure isn't."

"What is it, then?"

Harry took another look around the shack. "I don't know, bud." He wiped his eyes again and went to stand beside him. "I don't know how this place got here or how we did, either. But it's a good thing we found each other. I'm ready to admit that now."

"Now that what?" Gus said.

Harry put his arm around his son. "Now that we're here." He gave him a shake. "Now that we've discovered this place."

"We didn't discover anything."

"Have you ever been here before?"

"Of course not."

"Then call it a discovery."

■ ■ ■ ■

After they moved their gear into the shack, after they swept it out and took a more complete inventory, after they inspected the roof and floor and surveyed the area around it — finding the remnants of a garden now overgrown with creeper — they stood outside, looking at the shack. From the thigh pocket of his army pants, Harry removed a flask and unscrewed the cap and offered it to Gus without a word.

Without a word in return he took a short drink. All that fire and flavor after a month of fish and jerky was heavenly, even as the whiskey made him gag. He handed the flask back.

His father raised the flask toward the house. "To wintering," he said, then took a long swallow. Then another. "God*damn.*" He took a third pull for good measure. "A hell of a reward, eh, bud? Those voyageurs used to haul rum by the barrel to their winter forts. I figured a couple sips wouldn't hurt us."

"Let's not talk about voyageurs anymore."

"Fair enough." Harry held out the flask again, but Gus shook his head, and he screwed the cap back on. "We can finish this with dinner."

Now it was Gus's turn to cry. As he stood there, the whiskey still hot in his gut, his relief came at him furiously. There would be no more paddling. No more cutting through woods and swamps and rivers barely as wide as their canoes. They were home, even if they'd never known where they were headed.

Harry pulled his son into his arms and held him while he got rid of his tears. They'd be his last in the borderlands, Gus would see to that.

Gus recalled how the nights so often ended, pacing around the kitchen cradling his babies, finally drowsing after their fitful, colicky sleep. Sometimes he would nearly nod off with them while standing there looking out the window, watching the first reach into the darkness, twice seeing a fox cross the deck, stop to lift his nose toward the bird feeders, then jumping down onto the snow-covered yard. Usually it was his daughter, Greta, in his arms, Tom being quick to sleep. Gus could still see her eyes fluttering shut, and feel the heaviness of his eyelids and the lightness of her against his chest.

But above all, he could remember the quiet of those nights and mornings. So quiet he could hear Greta breathing. So quiet he could hear the flakes falling when it snowed, the drips of icicles in springtime, or Sarah rolling over in bed on the other side of the house.

When he woke that first morning at the shack it was to a similar silence. After a month of sleeping under a canvas tent, the quiet indoors was unsettling. It took him a long minute to realize where he was. He listened for any sound at all, but then gave up. Not even the wind moving the pine trees outside. He peeled himself from the sleeping sack on the floor and walked to the window. The world was white with frost again.

Harry was in a canoe fifty feet offshore, hunched over the gunwale and holding the end of a length of rope that disappeared into the steaming water. Gus watched as he marked the rope, then pulled it hand over hand. He wrote something in the book of maps, made five paddle strokes up the shore, and dropped the rope back in again. For ten minutes Gus stood at the window before he finally went outside and hailed his father.

As Harry paddled back toward shore, Gus said, "What are you doing out there?"

"Getting the lay of the lake bottom," Harry said as he stepped out of the canoe. "So we know where to fish when the ice comes."

"It's cold enough I'm surprised the water isn't frozen already."

"That'll happen soon enough," Harry said. "Water's not more than knee-deep for thirty feet off the point here, then it drops off. Twenty, twenty-five feet sheer. A good place to jig once the ice sets. We won't have to travel far." He nodded, satisfied with his soundings. "How'd you sleep last night?"

"It felt good to wake up warm and dry, that's for sure."

"You won't get any argument from me on that account."

"Whose place do you suppose it is?"

"I was wondering the same thing. I reckon it's a trapper's shack. Some fella who got tired of trudging all these miles through cold and snow for a hundred dollars' worth of beaver pelts."

"But there's no trapping gear."

"True. So maybe it's a hunting camp." He looked up at the shack for a moment. "It's a lonely son of a gun who comes out here to hunt by himself, though, ain't it? Hardly fit for a big party, is it?"

"No," Gus said. "It hasn't been used in a while."

"Likely we don't have to worry about the proud owner jumping us for trespassing."

"Or anyone else, either," Gus said.

Harry forced a smile then. "There are some things I need to tell you, bud."

"All right."

"You'll want to punch me in the gut when you hear them."

"I doubt that, but go ahead."

Harry looked at the lake, then at the book of maps in his hand. "Fort le Croix —"

"What about it?"

"There never was such a place."

"What does that mean?"

"What I just said. There never was a Fort le Croix up here. Or any other fort."

"I don't get it. Where were we going, then?"

"Here, I reckon."

"What if we didn't find here?"

"Hell, here or someplace like it. I told you before, we were going to be fine regardless. Set up a wigwam. I used to spend a week at a time with Freddy Riverfish up on his trap-lines. In the deepest part of winter. We were fine then, so we'd have been all right, you and me, without any shack."

"What about the maps?"

Harry looked at the book in his hand again. "Yeah, the maps."

"We followed them. They got us to Kasei-ganagah, didn't they?"

"They sure did."

Gus was out of questions. He sat there, waiting for the truth.

On those mornings with his own children, once Gus had finally soothed them to sleep, sometimes while it was still dark outside but just as often after sunrise, when the house was warming with the morning, he would sit back in the big chair beside his fireplace and put his feet on the ottoman and pull the afghan from behind his shoulder. Greta or Tom would nestle into him, their fine and unruly hair tickling his chin. He would spread the afghan over them and close his eyes and fall asleep while their little hands lay between them.

Gus told me that, of all the things he'd done in his life, none ever seemed as wonderful as getting his children to sleep. Keeping them warm. Giving his exhausted wife a few hours' rest herself before it was time to nurse the baby again.

Sitting with his father at the shack after he'd admitted that Fort le Croix was a hoax? That morning, and being with his father, was just as important as those mornings with his own children so many years later. He knew that now.

And he did not — as his father had said — want to hit him. He wanted to hug him.

That morning at the shack, the soundings recorded, Harry explained how the maps came to be. They began as true facsimiles, Harry said. He told Gus how he'd always wanted to follow the old voyageur maps into the wilderness, so he started copying them on long winter nights. But as Signe and Gus got older and as his marriage and livelihood took their dives — fewer fish biting, fewer folks buying his handsome canoes, Lisbet becoming as anxious and aloof and distant as the city she came from — these maps became a means of seeing the world differently. Especially his own place in it. Harry began to imagine everything north of the divide. He so desperately needed to find that world, and to find himself in the bargain.

"I remember watching you at the kitchen table," Gus said. "Drawing those things. I thought they were so cool. I wanted to be like you."

"You don't want to be like me, that's a fact. Surely you know that now." Harry looked at him. "And I don't want you to be, either. That's why I brought you up here. One of the reasons, leastways."

"I still don't understand," Gus said, meaning that he didn't understand *anything.* About the maps, about why they were there, about what was to come, about what his family was anymore.

"Maybe you never will understand. Could be you'll understand only if you get married and have kids yourself someday."

Gus gave him a blank look. "You can't honestly have thought we could survive the winter in a wigwam."

"Wasn't long ago that every living soul in this part of the world did exactly that. Winter and summer both. Ten generations of Freddy's people made out just fine in wigwams before our people showed up."

Gus walked to the water's edge, his head hung down.

"Get married and have kids, bud, you'll think surviving the winter in a wigwam's not only possible but a dream come true."

Gus didn't turn around.

"Anything that came before your wife and kids? That doesn't mean a damn thing."

He turned around then and stared at his father.

"I know you've been watching your mother and me. You're old enough to see what's going on. It must all seem damn crazy. Parts of it are. But just wait a little, and know while you're waiting that I'd never let anything happen to you. Not ever."

Now Harry walked over and wrapped his

arms around him. "I should've brought proper maps, I can see that now. I overestimated myself. I've got a long history of doing that. But we're here now. We're safe. We've got a whole new season to figure the rest of it out."

Gus shook himself free. "We're up here so you can decide what to do about Mom?"

"Christ almighty, bud, I don't know. I can tell you that all the horseshit that's going on between us is as much my fault as hers. That's usually the case when things get this far gone." He nodded his head yes, then shook it no. "We'll have plenty of nights to chew the fat off that bone, I'd guess. What we don't have is much time to get ready for winter."

He opened the book of maps and tore a sheet from it. "I made a list of things to do this morning," he said, handing it to Gus.

Who read: WOOD. CACHE. MEAT. LOOKOUT?

Then Harry ripped out the sheet he'd written his soundings on, folded it up, and slipped it in the pocket of his flannel shirt. "Ready to get to work?"

Too baffled to say anything, Gus just stood there looking at his father.

"One more thing," Harry said. He smiled, kissed the moose-hide binding of the book, then winked at Gus and threw the maps into the lake.

I remember once, many years ago, when Claire Veilleux came into the apothecary with her granddaughter. They collected their letters and were ready to leave but met Eleanor Rusk and her newborn daughter at the doorway. Eleanor was then only twenty or twenty-one and this was her first baby. I wasn't part of their conversation, simply overhead it from my perch behind the counter.

After pleasantries and a word or two about the baby, Claire said, "Yes, well, they do teach us to love in ways we never knew we could, don't they?" She ought to have known something about loving children, having five sons and five daughters herself.

That comment has stayed with me ever since, and I've often wondered what I've missed out on by not having any children of my own. I used to watch Gus and Signe gallivant through town and wish they were mine. But that wish, too, was decades ago.

They might have been mine were it not for Lisbet, whose grand entrance into the life of this town quashed my prospects with Harry. Like so many before her, she arrived by water, though not on some ferry or fishing boat. Her father — a law professor at the University of Chicago, president of the Chicago Yacht Club, political confidant of Adlai Stevenson — steered his thirty-six-foot sloop into Gunflint's harbor like an Annapolis bluejacket. Lisbet and her mother stood topside, looking like breezy models on the cover of *McCall's.* Stylish and scrubbed, with a highborn air of invincibility. It wouldn't be too much to say that at first glance they seemed regal.

That air was shortly dispatched. Once her father docked the sloop in one of the slips along the Lighthouse Road, he went straight to the Traveler's Hotel and took two rooms. Though the tavern wasn't open, he offered the hotel manager fifteen dollars to stand behind the bar and pour apple wine. After the first glass, he offered him another ten bucks to leave the bottle on the bar and retrieve his wife and daughter from the harbor. After six hours on that barstool, he hadn't yet figured out why the string of bartenders weren't converting the change from American currency into Canadian. He thought he'd docked in Port Arthur.

Lisbet's mother was perhaps even more striking than her daughter. She left her hotel room only for meals in the Traveler's Hotel dining room, wore ridiculous gowns, and seemed always on the verge of fainting. Whereas Lisbet — given her parents' aloofness and her own fierce independence — spent the week freely roaming Gunflint.

I'd noticed her several times. She was uninhibited and loose-lipped and seemed proud that her family's adventure was dreamed up as a solution to her spell at Passavant Hospital in Chicago, where the plants were plastic and the windows covered with bars. She'd landed there after an episode in which she drank a bottle of her mother's champagne and stole her father's Cadillac. She admitted these things to me, standing before the counter while I was sorting the mail.

On the third or fourth day, I saw her sitting on the breakwater with her ubiquitous sketchbook open in her lap. That's the spot where she first saw Harry Eide, and I watched her watching him. For a long time. Later, standing in front of the counter at the post office again, she told me, "It was the most perfect moment of my entire *life,* seeing that man. He's like something out of Homer."

He'd cruised past her, tipping his cap as he went. He wore oilskin pants and red galluses. He motored around Fisherman's Point and into Eide Cove, and suddenly it was her solemn vow to have him.

"I doubt he owns a suit jacket," she said, and then looked out the window, though his boat was gone. "Does he have a girl?"

Well, I might have stepped in. Steered her away. Run to Harry's fish house to tell him how he made me feel, how I saw us together, how I wanted him and nothing else. I could have. But I didn't think I needed to, because I had no idea she'd be so true to her word. If I'd come to know anything of Lisbet during our short conversations, it was that she liked to talk — and talk big — and that had never counted for much in my life before then.

That evening, she saw Harry sitting in the Traveler's Hotel dining room, and he looked even more exceptional than he had on his boat. That was the word she used the next morning. He ordered a pork chop and a baked potato and a crock of creamed corn. She was surprised to see a glass of milk before him, but even that glitch in the picture she was building in her mind didn't deter her. She found it charming. The whiskey he ordered with his coffee and pie made him irresistible. Her father, she added, ate like a woman, only steamed green vegetables, white fish, salad, and sweet German wine.

By now, Harry had traded his oilskin pants for a pair of worn-hard dungarees but still wore his canvas work shirt, one side of his collar turned in, the other turned up. His face had a week-old beard scratched across it, and his hair probably hadn't seen a comb in his whole adult life. She described all this as if I hadn't registered every last detail every time I'd closed my eyes and begged for my real life to begin.

Lisbet saw him again the next night, and the night after. Each time, she allowed herself more generous fantasies. The firmness of his body. A sagacious streak borne by hours of contemplation out on his fishing boat each day. Finally, how he would be in bed. She was graphic about this last supposition. He would be silent, unlike her father, whom she'd heard bleating like a sheep on those rare occasions he'd made love with her mother. She imagined that when they finished he'd say something to make her see the heavenly night in a new light. That she spoke so uninhibitedly about such things proved at once that I could never be a friend to this strange city girl, even as she was trying to make one of me.

She came the next morning, too. She lingered by the window, looking out at the harbor and telling me how she'd brazenly flirted with Harry from across the dining room the night before. When they passed each other in the lobby after dinner, she told him to meet her at the harbor for a walk in the morning. She was waiting for him now, both uncertain he'd come and positive he wouldn't miss it. She had her sketchbook along and she kept flipping it open and closed.

How could he have stayed away? And why would he? As sure as the clock struck nine, he was standing there by the water, in his dungarees again, but with his shirt tucked in, his collar right. She passed me a devilish smile — as though I were a part of her ploy — and went out to meet him.

She accepted his offered cigarette. He asked her about the sketchbook, which she had shown me more than once, standing at the counter. There were several pictures of him in his boat. Of the lake and the sky and woods. Even I, never having seen a true work of art, could tell she was gifted. Perhaps even more. She wanted to show him her work, but couldn't bear it — turning to one drawing, then another, always closing the book before he could see them. I thought she was faking that coyness. I watched them smile and laugh and smoke before they walked away. I saw her father's sloop sail out of the harbor three days later, but I didn't see Lisbet again until she came back, a month later.

For years I was haunted by what came to pass between them on that day they turned up the alley by the Traveler's Hotel, no doubt heading to Harry's fish house. I was aware even then that something decisive was happening, and as much to me as to either of them.

It would be nearly half my life before I finally found out. Being proper, I never asked Harry. And Harry, being a gentleman, wouldn't have answered if I had. But Lisbet, well, in the late winter of 1965 she gave evidence that she'd been waiting all that time to bring the story to me. It was my first season living in the house that Harry built for me on the Burnt Wood River. He and Signe and Gus had been my only guests until that morning she came to my door.

Our lives were by then so bound together that only deaths could untangle some of the knots, but at that moment she and Harry were in the middle of their messy divorce. I'd made friends with Gus and Signe not because I had any ulterior motives, simply because it was only natural, given the amount of time Harry and I were now spending together. Standing at my door, Lisbet looked very much as she had as a young woman in the apothecary all those years before. She was still nearly as beautiful, even if she wore her lifetime of disappointment in the lines around her eyes. She held me in those eyes, standing there in my kitchen. I offered her coffee, which she rejected with a wave of her hand.

"Harry has built you a lovely home, eh, Miss Lovig? He once did the same for me."

"I paid Harry as I would any other carpenter, Lisbet."

"I suppose you have paid him, if that's what you'd prefer to call it."

I bristled, of course, but didn't know what to say. If I'd been in her shoes, I might have confronted me, too.

"Harry and I are divorcing. I'm sure he's told you. I'm sure you know why. I'm sure you see the reason why every time you catch your reflection."

"Oh, Lisbet, let's be honest about all of this."

"You want honesty? Certainly, let's be

honest. Harry has a habit of the grand gesture. Standing here under this vaulted ceiling, no doubt you're daily reminded of that. But he was the same with me."

She walked across the kitchen and stood close to me. "We made love the first day we met. Right on the floor of the fish house. It was the first real thing I'd ever done." Her eyes narrowed and wandered to the carpet. "On a blanket on the floor. Wood shavings in my hair. It felt terrible and wonderful. And I had been exactly right about him." Now she looked back up at me and her eyes widened again. "I actually thought of you while I lay there, watching my life come to me. I thought of you because I didn't want to become you. A spinster before you had a single gray hair." She looked up and down her nose at me. "I wanted to be the woman I was in just that moment. When we finished he got up and walked across the room and brought me a glass of water. He lit a cigarette and handed it to me. Then he said, 'You'll stay here. You'll be my gal. We'll get married.'

"You know as well as I do that he never says anything he doesn't mean sincerely, I'll give him that. It's one of his great faults."

She took a long look around my house, then shook her head.

"He asked me to marry him even with you sitting down there at the apothecary, taking care of that meshuga in the attic. He ought to have built you a castle for all you did for him." She opened her hands as though everything were plain to see.

"The grand gesture, Berit. Marrying the first girl who'd have him. Forsaking a mother he had no right to. Endangering his son that season up in the woods. Now your quaint little house right up the road. How convenient for you both."

"You're a cruel and selfish woman," I told her.

"You're not?"

"Harry's my friend, and if he's divorcing you, it's because you've failed him and made him miserable."

Her eyes widened — so wide the lines around them smoothed — and her lips pursed. "I'm not blind, Berit. I'm not a fool. Do you think I didn't know he was in love with you before I ever met him? Do you think I came here because he was some great catch? I married him because I wanted to be the girl on the floor of his fish house, not a girl like you."

"And you were that girl. You should've been happy. Anyone else on earth would've been."

She lit a cigarette. "You're simpler than I thought."

"What about your children? Signe's still so young."

"That takes some nerve, mentioning my children." An ugly, awful snarl crossed her face. "But I suppose you wouldn't understand about that — barren as your life truly is." She stepped closer to me. "But that brings us to why I'm here in the first place. You can have Harry. For God's sake, please, take him. But leave my children out of your pathetic tryst." She walked to the door. "They're mine," she turned to say before leaving, "not yours."

I've thought of that day often, of the hatred in her voice, and the hurt. I've thought of it every time Gus and I have sat down to talk about what happened up on the borderlands. And each time it comes to mind, whenever I look at his sad eyes and listen to his sad voice, I'm sure that I never could've been a mother, much as I've begun to feel like I am to him.

And maybe I should have been. Maybe that's how it was supposed to go. Maybe everyone involved would have been happier for it. The last time Gus and I talked, he spoke of her and said a few things that buoy this very notion. He'd just finished telling me about Harry throwing the book of maps into the lake. He paused then and stared into his hands for a moment before saying, as if we were having a different conversation altogether, "I never knew my mother very well. I was only seven or eight years old when she told me she'd never wanted to have children. She told me she wasn't suited for it." He looked up at me and smiled. "She wasn't. But she tried. I'll give her credit for that. She took us to the park and for walks up the river. She made us eat our vegetables and drink our milk and do our homework. She taught us to say 'please' and 'thank you.' She read to us at bedtime when we were tykes. But, my God, her unhappiness was overwhelming. Even before I knew what unhappiness was. Signe always chalked our mother's moods up to the fact that she was not from here. That she felt imprisoned. Impoverished. She wasn't from here, true. But she did come here of her own volition. Came running, in fact, to be with my dad. No one's ever disputed that part of the story."

I thought he might cry — his eyes were glossing up. "But I loved her. Very much. I loved her the way only a scorned child could. I still do."

■ ■ ■ ■

What's uncanny is that Rebekah foretold all of this. It wasn't her first act of clairvoyance, but it was her most chilling.

On the day Harry and Lisbet sneaked off to the fish house, I watched them go from the porch. Under the pretense of needing to shake out the rug, I stood in a haze of dust and counted their steps. When the air finally cleared, I turned to go back inside. There Rebekah stood, sharp and straight as a kitchen knife. As though she were privy to the thoughts in my head, she said, "You might take comfort in knowing that the Eide men have never chosen their women well." She kept her eyes on the alleyway. "He's a fool for falling for that one." Now she edged her chin up and pointed it in their direction. "She's a vixen and a vamp. I saw it the minute she stepped off that boat. She'll never make a mother. You can see it in how she always expects to be looked at, how she carries that sketchbook around like she knows us better than we know ourselves." She lowered her sharp chin. "All that girl really wants is a life she doesn't have."

"How do you know all that?"

"How could I not? I've spent most of my

life being just like her."

She went back into the apothecary and I followed with the rug. Inside, I laid it in front of the counter and went to my stool. Rebekah rearranged a couple of the hats on the display table in the middle of the floor, then stepped back, satisfied, and said, "It's no coincidence she's from Chicago. I was, too."

"I didn't know that."

"Not born there, but I spent time in Chicago as a girl. I grew up in an orphanage in Wisconsin."

"Oh?"

"I never knew my mother or father. For all I know they never were."

"Never were what?"

She looked at me with her breathtaking condescension. "Never were anything. When I was twelve I stole some money and left the orphanage and went to Chicago. I worked in a brothel."

"Dear Lord."

"I wasn't one of the girls. I took the coats. Lit cigarettes for the johns. I was all promise. All fantasy."

"I thought Hosea was your father."

"He took me in." She looked hard across the room. "But he wasn't my father. Any more than that girl will one day be a mother to Harry's children."

She started to go upstairs but stopped and stared at me again from across the room. "He might have come for you. I know that. And I'm sorry he hasn't. It's my fault he never did. He thinks you're forbidden. Because of me. Because you work here. He can't abide me."

I said nothing. I couldn't. It was the only time she ever brought him up in conversation, and I was frankly struck mute.

She took the first step and then turned with her final thought on the matter. "But someday he'll realize that you have nothing to do with me. Someday he'll realize that he's made a terrible mistake, taking the walk he did just now. Someday, his children will need the likes of you. No one should go through life without a mother." She took another step. "Or, anyway, without someone to mother them."

"Likely we'll freeze to death before we starve." This was Harry speaking, later that first morning at what by now they were calling "the trapper's shack." "We ought to start with four cords of firewood. Four cords and a good idea where to find more."

Four cords without a chain saw? Gus could hardly imagine the labor.

"You start with the gathering, eh?" Harry said. "I'll get to work around here."

"Sure," Gus said.

"Start with that birch." Harry pointed across the bay. "Pull out as much deadfall as you can. Paddle it back. Birch'll burn cleaner than these others." He waved his hands to suggest the cedar and pine and maple.

So Gus grabbed a saw and hatchet and paddled across the bay. The sun rose behind the trees, and the whiteness of their bark and the frost still heavy on the ground magnified the glare tenfold. He put ashore and started into the woods. For every tree that stood another had fallen, and he pulled a few logs from the ferns. They were pulpy and moss-covered, and where there was no moss their bark had been weathered black. He walked farther into the trees, and the ground began to rise as if with the sun.

At the top was a knoll of smooth granite, the downside of which opened into a stand of bur oaks. Two dozen of them, the ground beneath covered with fallen leaves and acorns. Beyond the oaks, the forest deepened again. Gus wandered around under the shelter of those alien oaks. Woolgathering, his father would have called it, though he himself considered it simply taking stock of their situation, which was more confounding now than it had ever been.

He walked to the far side of the oaks, acorns cracking beneath the vulcanized rubber of his boot soles. Stubborn leaves still hung in clumps in the branches above. The oaks were always the last to give up. But bur oaks this far north? He thought about that.

And he wondered, Why had his father thrown the maps in the water? Why had he made them in the first place? Most pressingly, why had he relied on them while knowing full well their fallibility? Gus looked up again at the bur oaks. There would be days ahead when the sun would barely stretch above their stately limbs, days when the temperature at noon would be forty degrees below zero. Who in their right mind would venture *toward* days like that? With only those maps now on the bottom of the lake? In answer to his questions, he sat down against one of the oaks and fought some strange and sad happiness running roughshod through his thoughts.

He sat there for a long time. When he looked up again he noticed that several of the younger oaks were dead. No leaves clung to their branches. The bark on their trunks was duller than the living trees'. He crawled over to one and began swinging the hatchet. Slowly and empty-minded at first but then faster, madly. The sun rose above the tree he was chopping, shining down through the skeletal limbs without warming the morning at all. He chopped through a quarter of the tree with the hatchet, then took up the saw and started on the opposite side.

With only the hatchet and saw it took an hour to fell that tree. Why he did it Gus never could fathom, not then, not years later. Not ever. But it was down, and he stood over it, his hands blistered, his sweater soaked through with sweat. It would take another two hours to shear the branches from it and a full day to get the trunk back to the lake without a horse and sled. Splitting the hardwood would be brutish work, much harder than splitting birch. But he resolved that somehow he'd get that wood back to the shack, that they would live off the warmth it provided.

He walked up one side of the fallen tree, started back down the other, and noticed there on the ground a pile of bear scat bigger than his boot.

He canoed only one load of birchwood back to the shack that day, six trunks as fat as his leg. He unloaded them and checked inside for his father. Harry was gone, but there was a pot of warm coffee on the stove. He'd repaired the door and built a table barely large enough for two plates and two cups. He'd unpacked their foodstuffs and the kitchen implements. For all their enormous weight over the portages and through the scrub, the supplies looked pathetic on the shelves. Gus poured himself a cup of coffee and stepped outside. He stacked the logs against the shack's lee wall.

It had been his intention to fetch more

birch, but when he gave his canoe a pull across the shallows he saw, fluttering underwater not far from shore, the book of maps. He fished it out with the tip of his fishing rod, brought it back to the shack, and laid the maps page by page across the boards overhead on the joists, where his father wouldn't see them.

They ate hunks of jerky and after dinner sat on either side of the little table, their legs crossed, sipping coffee. The cribbage board sat between them but they didn't play.

"Have we got enough gun for a bear?" Gus asked.

"What do you want with a bear?"

"I saw a pile of scat big as your head in a stand of trees over there."

Harry smiled. "How you gonna bait a bear?"

He couldn't say why, but he didn't tell his father about the bur oaks and acorns. He didn't tell him about chopping down one of the dead oaks. Didn't tell him about finding the maps, either. He wanted secrets of his own, Gus did. He wanted his own discoveries. He wanted there to be things his father simply didn't know.

"Have we got enough gun?"

"Sure we do. But the bears'll be going to

bed soon, and we've got a few things to do before we start hunting. That pile of wood you brought home today might not get us through the night."

"We'll have wood." Gus went for more coffee and poured them each a cup. "The bears won't go into hibernation for a few weeks yet. It's been warm. Almost no snow."

Harry nodded. "I admit, a few pounds of bear fat might be good for the larder. I found a bushel of mushrooms today. Fry those things up in bear fat and we'd be the happiest shitheads this country ever saw." He nodded again. "Get some wood, then get yourself a bear if you can. Even a small boar's, what, seventy-five pounds of meat? We could use that."

"We'll have the neighbors over for a barbecue," Gus said, leaning back on his stool and putting his hands behind his head. "But I guess we're not expecting company."

The dopey smile Harry had been wearing since they'd found the shack vanished all at once. "Well," he said, picking a piece of jerky from his teeth, "that's the thing."

Gus sat up. Put his hands flat on the table. Even all these years later, he could still feel his pulse quicken to think of it. "What's the thing?"

Harry took a long sip of coffee and looked

over Gus's head, his eyes lighting on the windows on either side of the door. "We might have company yet," he said. He reached over his shoulder for the coffeepot and filled his cup with the dregs. "I should've saved a bit of the hooch for this." He set the coffeepot on the floor and feigned a smile. "This all happened years ago. Before you and your sister were born. Before your mother even came to town. Before I knew a damn thing." He got up with his cup and took a step in each direction but then stood by the stove. "Me and Charlie and Charlie's big brother, George, and Freddy Riverfish, all night we're at a card game in the fish house. Finished a jar apiece of old man Hakonsson's home-burnt. We're all potted and quarrelsome and I'd lost my ass in the stud game, so I offer the boys a wager: ten bucks a man I'll go down into the Devil's Maw."

"The Devil's Maw?"

"Why, hell yes, they'll take that wager." Harry sat back down and wedged his boots off. He set them under the stove and pulled his socks off, too. "We come falling out of the fish house at sunup. Stumble down to the boat slide. Freddy's looking up at the sky. It's already eighty degrees and promising nothing if not more heat. He says he'll buy me breakfast if I'll quit this nonsense. But I'm primed. Ready to go. And so's Charlie. He tells Freddy to pull his skirt up.

"So here we go. Out the cove and around the point and up the Burnt Wood. But before we even make it to the highway bridge, the water craps out and we have to beach the boat. The hoppers go scattering like buckshot, and by now Freddy and George have pooled six bucks and the promise of steaks at the Traveler's if we quit.

"But Charlie, he's not ready to call it a day. He's got to get his brother up to the falls. He says, 'You goddamn welshes. Get your pants wet.' So we start walking. Ropes and a lantern and a fresh jar of home-burnt for the morning's task. The four of us marching up the shallow river.

"Christ almighty, were we a haggard bunch. George Aas was almost a friend. Hell, he *was* one. Very different than his old man and brother. George's the one who brought his brother along to that card game. George, just back from Iwo Jima minus an arm and jumpy as a June bug, but a good man." He rubbed the knuckles of each of his forefingers into his eyes. "George had joined the marines the minute he could. Went off to Fort Pendleton despite his old man's being against it. He trained as a flamethrower, George did, and he was in the first wave of soldiers to hit the beach on that goddamn island." Again he rubbed his eyes. "Georgie said he thought it was abandoned, just a ghost island. They marched across that beach without so much as a whisper from the Japs. Not until they reached the first line of defense did the bullets start flying. And did they ever. He said it was like waking from a dream. Turns out the Japs were all dug in, had miles and miles of tunnels and bunkers, goddamn gophers. And there's Georgie, blasting his flamethrower into one of the holes in the ground. He turns around and, *rat-a-tat-tat,* some Jap in another hole blows his arm right off. He lays there for half of a day, bleeding out, before he got found and tended to by the medics. A real hero, which is not something to be said lightly. Not ever. Anyway, it wouldn't have taken that. Georgie could always see the forest for the trees, which his brother just couldn't stand.

"Then there's Freddy Riverfish. He's mean as a badger and always was. I'd been on a ship on the Atlantic a month earlier, the sound of Sturmgewehrs still came to me every time I shut my eyes. Of course, Charlie's the exception in our crew. Pretty as a French maid, Charlie was. Wearing a goddamn golf shirt. His hair done up in pomade." Harry looked like he'd just swallowed a glassful of sour milk. "Or maybe with the devil's own spit, for Chrissakes. Anyway, there's your crew, and we're dragging ass up the Burnt Wood. Water's cold and we're passing the jar back and forth and before I pour the last drops down my gullet we're standing under the Devil's Maw. Even as light as the water's running, it's still too much. So Charlie says, 'We'll have to dam it.'

" 'Dam it?' George says. 'Hell, no.' He wades ashore and Freddy goes with him, and before I get one foot up the falls the two of them are passed out on the beach. But Charlie, he's right behind me. Step for step. Why he's so hot to get into the Devil's Maw I couldn't imagine, but he was. And it was making me nervous. He had that look in his eye I came to know well over the years. That look like he was about to put some wild idea to the test. I've never seen much craziness, but I saw it in him. And not for the first time on that day. Not the first by a long shot."

Gus knew the look his father was talking about. He'd seen the same glint in Cindy's eyes up on Long Finger Lake. The moonshine lighting it up. Those nights in his car, kissing fierce, he'd confused that look with desire. But, listening to his father, he thought it over and realized what it was — the Aas wires getting crossed. He shivered to think he'd missed it.

"In the oxbow there, a heap of driftwood's piled up, and I start carrying it across the river. Water's not more than knee-deep, but swift there at the chutes. Charlie and I, we have to work together. Wedge a couple logs into the rocks above the maw. Float a bunch more across the water. Choose our steps carefully. We're busy as goddamn beavers.

"Meanwhile, the boys onshore are drooling on their shirtsleeves. Sun's burning their necks. I kick Freddy in the ass. Charlie fills his hat with water and pours it over his brother's head, and he bolts upright but then falls over just as quick, because the arm he thought would hold him up wasn't there. This sets Charlie howling. He slaps his knee with his hat and says, 'I guess some Jap mixed your left hand into his chow mein, eh, Georgie?'

"Georgie scrambles up and gets in his brother's face. 'You're a lousy son of a bitch, Charlie. A no-account shithead.' Charlie steps back and laughs again and calls him a sourpuss. Georgie takes a half-step back but then spins around and kicks Charlie square in the ass. Sends him stumbling into the water alongshore. Charlie fills his hat again in the same motion and keeps splashing his brother. Freddy, he gets between them, and when Charlie makes another run he pushes him aside and Charlie ends up back on his ass in the shallows. I guess this cooled him down a little, because, the next thing I know, we're all standing on the lip of the maw."

The expression on Harry's face, it was as though he was looking straight down into it now, sitting in the trapper's shack. "You and me, we were right there. Day one of this great adventure." He looked at Gus. "Not two hours from home. Remember?"

"Of course I do."

"I should've told you this story right then and there. I should have had you look into that hole."

"I've looked into the Devil's Maw a hundred times, Dad."

"But you never looked into it knowing what I'm about to tell you."

"Which is what?"

"Charlie ties a lantern onto a rope and lights it and starts lowering it. He plays out maybe thirty feet of rope and — poof! — the light's just gone. I start thinking maybe this isn't the best idea I ever had, but since

I'm not about to renege and lose the bet, I harness myself up. Fix the free end of the rope to that cedar tree that grows out of the bedrock there. I'm all ready and Charlie says, 'I'll hold the rope.' I tell him he can hold his dick." He smiled at this. But frowned a second later.

"Then I'm rappelling into the maw. One minute I hear all the hootin' above, the next it's gone. Water's dripping from above and spraying from the walls and it's cold. Ninety degrees out on the river, and twenty feet down you could've stored your milk and eggs."

Harry paused for a long time, staring again down into his empty coffee cup. "Christ almighty —"

"What was it like?"

Without looking up, Harry said, "First and foremost, it was dark. You can't imagine. And cold, like I said.

"I lit a lantern. The walls were smooth and wet. There was a rock shelf on the other side of the shaft that I tried to swing over to, but I couldn't reach it. So I just hung there for a few minutes, looking down." He stopped talking, brought the cup closer to his eyes, and stared into it. "I've thought about hanging there in the Devil's Maw an awful lot over the years. I sure wish I'd gone deeper. Found the bottom. I'd have been the only person on earth to know what was down there." He finally lifted his gaze.

"But I didn't have enough rope. I clumsily dropped the lantern and watched its light plummet for what seemed a damn long time. Never heard it shatter or splash. It was just gone, gone, gone. But where? What happened to it? All these years later, is it still shining down there? I wondered the same thing about the flames that Georgie threw into those tunnels on Iwo Jima. Where'd that go? Into the fires of hell? Or did it catch some Japanese machine-gunner and burn him up?"

He finally set the coffee cup on the table, pushed it to the center like he was tempted to pick it back up but didn't want to. He did keep his eye on it, though.

" 'Well?' Charlie says when I climb back out.

"My arms were about to fall off and I was breathing hard and steaming like a racehorse. 'Well, what?'

"Freddy and George are standing there. They want to know, too. But I say, 'Pay me, you louts.' And faster than they can pull their money out they're piling it into my hand. Ten bucks apiece, everything I'd lost at the stud game and half again as much.

Then George starts looking very serious. 'Out with it,' he says."

"And?" Gus asked.

Harry looked at him like there was a punch line in the offing. " 'George, you're not going to believe this!' I tell him. 'Those walls are streaked with gold! Gold and diamonds and rubies bigger than your brother's goddamn head.' Then I turned to Charlie. 'And a spring's running fast with hundred-proof home-burnt! And beautiful ladies, ready and waiting for a dandy like you.'

"I untied myself from the rope and made a gesture of handing it to Charlie. 'Of course, we'll need a stronger rope to lower your fat ass down.'

" 'Just tell us what you saw down there. What the hell is it?' Charlie says.

"I told him his potbelly was blocking out the sun and I couldn't see a damn thing through it."

Harry, straight-faced and fierce-eyed, said, "And there's one-armed George, standing with his back against that cedar tree, chuckling at his little brother. He was still learning to live without his arm, always seeming like he was about to tip over. 'It's just a hole in the rock, you rube.'

"Of course, Charlie's madder than a fox

in a trap. He tells George to shut the hell up, that he'll rip his other arm off and beat the snot out of him with it. Then he turns to me and says, 'I ought to give you a beating, too.'

"To which I say, 'Feel like giving it a try?' "

Harry reached for the cup, then stopped and leaned back in his chair. "George wants to know if there's a bottom. 'To the hole?' I say. 'I didn't get there, but it stands to reason there's got to be one.'

"Charlie, he can't stand it and says, 'You wouldn't know reason if it kissed you on the lips.'

" 'Maybe not, but I know more than you do.' He took a step toward me and raised his fist. He might have swung it, too, but Freddy Riverfish steps in, and nobody — I mean nobody — tussled with him. Not back then. Not ever. He was always right beside me. So Charlie pockets his fist and says to me, 'You think you got the market on ancient wisdom, Harry Eide.'

" 'What the hell's ancient wisdom?' I asked him, then I looked from man to man. 'I just went down the Devil's Maw, with you assholes holding the rope. Ain't that the opposite of wisdom?' "

He got up and walked to the window, bent down to look up at the sky, and turned back to Gus for a long minute before he said, "Freddy and I, we hike it back down the falls and camp our asses down there in the cool mist off the river. He tells me about how his granddad and great-granddad used to come up here and make offerings. They'd throw tobacco into the maw, trying to get things right with the spirits. Freddy, he's as fallen away from his religion as I'd ever been from any faith at all, and from our spot on the beach there it seemed like a waste of snoose, is all. Better to save it and just accept there were places in this world you could never reach. Spirits, too. Beliefs. Things that just couldn't be known. Things not meant to be known. Freddy was always going on about the things we couldn't know. It wasn't a philosophy. He would never have called it that. Myself, I thought all those talks were more like blacksmithing — hammering out the impossibly hard and nearly unbendable parts of life.

"Of course, given all that day had had to offer, our fires were stoked and we jabbered on for half an hour while waiting for the Aas boys to finish their squabbling. No doubt we got it all figured out, too, what with the home-burnt and the hot sun."

He went back to the table and sat down across from Gus. "Only one of the Aas boys ever came down those falls."

Gus stuttered something about the story he'd always heard, that George Aas drowned up there, but he could hardly get a word out, let alone string any questions together.

"Charlie's sliding on his ass, hollering about something we can't hear. He's waving his arms and hurrying toward us. We stand up, Freddy and I, and step into the shallows. What's going on, we want to know.

"Charlie bends over to catch his breath, then says, 'George! He jumped into the Devil's Maw! He goddamn killed himself!'

" 'Killed himself?' Freddy says. Untruer words could not have been spoken. George, who'd lived through Iwo Jima, who'd just spent all night with us yucking it up, laughing more than he had in his whole life, he'd jumped into the Devil's Maw? No chance of that. No way, nohow."

Gus's wide eyes asked the question his voice couldn't form.

"Charlie killed him dead."

"Why?"

"How could I know the answer to that?"

"But —"

"There was nothing to be done. No one knew that better than I did. If George was in the Devil's Maw he was gone forever. But we hiked it back up there, Freddy and

I. We got on our bellies and shouted into the maw. Charlie's standing there without an ounce of concern on his fat, sunburned face. He lit a cigarette and says, 'What a sad day. What a sad, sad day.' But he wasn't sad. There was even a hint of goddamn joy in his voice. 'Suppose we better get back to town and let folks know George is gone.'

"Freddy and I were floored, of course. Speechless, and frankly a little bit scared. I was, leastways. But what else *was* there to do? Gone is gone. George was never going to be found."

"Did anyone ever try?"

"Try how?"

"Get ladders? More rope? More lanterns?"

"Didn't you hear the story I just told? About how deep that hole was?" He kept right on. "A few weeks later, the Aas family put up a cenotaph for him."

"What's a cenotaph?"

Harry looked lost and sad. "Gravestones for the unfound. That's what cenotaphs are for. He might as well have been left on that battlefield on Iwo Jima, the poor bastard."

Gus was still rightly bewildered. "So . . . George didn't jump?"

"Of course not. He was pushed. By his brother. Charlie."

"But nothing ever happened to Charlie.

He never got in trouble for this?"

"No one knew. Or, anyway, no one could ever prove it."

Gus sat there staring at his father through the candlelight. For a long time Harry didn't say anything. Somehow Gus knew enough not to prod him. He knew to wait.

When Harry spoke again his voice had hardened. "Remember last winter, when we hit the deer on the highway down around Misquah? The look in her eyes?"

Gus nodded.

"Those whitetails are about the quickest thing in the woods, but that girl couldn't move. We plowed right into her. Goddamn flattened her, right? Well, that was me and Freddy. We didn't know what to do. And we didn't all these years since, either. I don't think we ever even talked about it, Freddy and I. Not until this year."

"Why now?"

Harry looked at him across the table. "Why now? You don't really have to ask, do you?"

"What does all this mean?"

"Last month, that night in the fish house, when we decided to come up here, you remember that night?"

"Of course I do."

"Well, before I came to the fish house,

Freddy and I were in Two Harbors."

"Why?"

"We were talking to a newspaper reporter from the *Tribune.*"

"Why? I don't understand any of this."

"There's a lot to understand."

"So explain it to me." He was scared and confused and he didn't like the look on his father's face. "Tell me what you're talking about."

"Remember when the coffers at Immanuel Lutheran came up empty a few years ago?"

Gus nodded.

"That was Charlie Aas, council president. Now, what did he do with the money? I don't know. Maybe some debts require the good Lord's money."

"What does that have to do with George?"

"It doesn't have anything to do with George. It has to do with Charlie. That's what I'm telling you." Harry could see the confusion on Gus's face. "Listen to me. Just listen. You remember when Bud Nardahl was voted out of the mayor's office?"

"Yeah."

"Was Charlie's work, too. Now he's fighting to dam up the Burnt Wood. He's in the pocket of the lumber and mining companies. You name it, he's up to his double chin in it. That's what I'm telling you." Harry was getting heated. "Do I need to remind you about his girl? You and her and that summer fling?"

Gus shook his head.

Harry took a long, deep breath. "And of course there's the matter of your mother."

Now Gus felt embarrassed. Like a dolt or a little kid. Innocent and naïve. "You have proof? That's why you were talking to the reporter?"

"Charlie's gotten a little big for his britches. He's been heard, down at the Traveler's Saloon, after a few too many. Bragging's the word, I guess. Hinting, maybe. About how he put himself right in line way back when. Made sure the family was his. Word's been getting around, and Freddy and I, we took it to the reporter. About George, and everything else, too." Harry rapped his knuckles on the table. "None of this is simple, bud. Of course it isn't. But the bottom line is, Charlie's been having his say on every damn thing for too long. Now it's time for some comeuppance.

"This summer, Freddy and I were fishing the Hex hatch on Long Finger and we got to talking. Freddy's made it his special project to keep the rivers free. He's as sick about your mother and Charlie as I am. He'd like to put a bullet in Charlie's brain, same as me. But we can't, of course. So out there in our canoe we got to talking about what we *can* do. Which led us to that *Tribune* reporter in Two Harbors. After we talked to that old pencilneck, we've had some chats with the county attorney and the sheriff, too." Harry sat back in his chair, took another deep breath, and looked, for a moment, like he was relieved. "Who knows what Freddy's been dealing with since we left?"

Gus replayed the sequence of their conversation back to the start. "What does any of this have to do with having company?"

"It'll take some time for everything to catch up with Charlie. Lots of folks will need to have lots of conversations about lots of different things. In the meantime, Charlie sure ain't gonna sit on his hands down in Gunflint."

"Charlie's coming after you?" Gus ventured. "After us?"

Harry took hold of Gus with his stare. "Likely he'll pay us a visit, yes. If he can find us, which he'll try pretty hard to do."

Now it was Gus's turn to walk over to the window. "Why would he come here?"

"Whether it's brothers on the Burnt Wood River or generals on a Pacific island, boys will always be looking for a place to tangle."

Gus turned back to his father. "*How* could he find us?"

"There's nowhere to hide from what needs to come, bud. We're here because whatever finds us needs to end after it does. This business between me and Charlie would never have a chance of ending in Gunflint. It needs this place. Needs winter, which is soon to get here."

Gus was then acutely aware of his own anger, both at himself for being so green and at his father for withholding so much. "I can't believe this. Are you out of your mind?"

"Charlie knows only one way. His way. He thinks the world is simple, but it isn't. He thinks people are simple, but they're not. Just he is."

"This is bullshit," Gus said, and he could feel his voice quaver.

"No, it's not, Gus. This is life. Come back over here. Sit down."

"No."

"Bud, there's nothing to be afraid of. The thing isn't what is a man capable of, it's what he's able to do. In town, with all his cronies, Charlie is able to do a whole lot. He's obviously capable of anything. Anywhere. But out here, he's got no advantage. He could bring his ten best hunting buddies and we'd still outnumber them."

They stared at each other for a long time across the candlelit shack, Gus growing furious. He took one step forward and two steps back. He cleared his throat. "How could you drag me into this?"

And Harry smiled. Not a mocking smile, but one that conveyed a kind of pity. Or at least that's how Gus understood it. "You were in this even if you didn't know it. There's no two ways about it. To Charlie, we're the same person. He hates you as much as he hates me. He hates that you're my son." His smile was gone now. "But do you know whose sons aren't in this? Charlie's. Of all the differences between me and him, that's the biggest. That's my advantage."

Gus woke in the morning to the sound of his father's razor on the strop. Harry stood at the window in his underwear and socks, his face lathered up, looking at his reflection in the glass. He must have heard Gus stir, because his gaze shifted from his own face to Gus's. He brought the razor up his chin, rinsed it in a bowl of water, shaved another swath, and paused to look at Gus over his shoulder. He pointed to the stove with his razor. "There's coffee," he said.

"It's still dark out," Gus said.

Harry turned his attention back to shaving. "It's damn near six." He took another stripe of his stubble with the straight blade.

"I'm not getting up yet."

"You won't sleep at all if we're freezing our balls off."

Gus rolled over. "No more telling me what to do. I don't even want to talk to you."

"You'll be a lonely son of a gun up here,

you quit talking to me."

"Right. Because your stories are so good." Gus kicked free of his sleeping sack and stepped from the bunk. He went right past his father and out the door to take a piss and came back in while his father was finishing on his neck.

"Don't be a pantywaist, Gus. We've got work to do. You could wake up tomorrow with a foot of snow on the ground."

Gus poured himself a cup of coffee and watched as his father toweled his face.

"Get back at those birches, eh?" Harry said. He pulled his pants on over his union suit.

Gus took a sip of his coffee and offered his father a gallant and challenging stare. "I've told you there will be wood. I've told you ten times. But I'm not going over there in the dark. It's pointless."

Harry hung the towel from its hook next to the window. "You're afraid of the dark now, too?"

"What else am I afraid of?" Gus shot back.

Harry was deliberate in his response. He put his shirt on before he spoke. He sat down to tie his bootlaces. "Far as I can tell, you're afraid of what's true."

"I'll tell you what I'm afraid of," Gus said. "I'm afraid I'm in the middle of nowhere and my dad — who *tricked* me into coming here — is going nuts. That's what I'm afraid of."

"You're not seeing things right."

Furious, Gus couldn't stand the ridiculous expression on his father's face. "You were just standing at the window there, staring at yourself. What did *you* see?"

"An old fool, that's what I saw. But an old fool who's ready, which is more than you can say. I saw an old fool who understands what's coming." He donned his sweater and his red hat and stood over his pack. He pulled out the Ruger in its holster and ran his belt through the loop. "You had any sense, you'd start looking for what's coming, too. And it might not be the worst idea to train your eyes to see in the dark." Then he walked calmly out the door.

Gus went to the window and watched his father's shadow move around the shack. He wanted to follow him. To assault him. To scream. To do some goddamn thing. But he stood at the window instead, drinking his coffee and waiting for the light.

But he was back under the bur oaks before the sun was up. He'd left the saw and hatchet at the shack and had the Remington over his shoulder. The gun was loaded and he had six cartridges in his jacket pocket. His hunting knife hung from his belt. The book of maps was in the leg pocket of his army pants.

On the edge of the stand, he found a pile of deadfall and made it his blind. A breeze came through the trees onto his face. He scanned the clearing and watched it fill with the morning's light. He kept his ear cocked to the wind, the Remington leaning against the tree trunk.

Then he studied the maps one at a time. There was nothing in them to remind him of the miles and lakes and rivers that had led them to the shack. The memories of traversing the borderlands were already disappearing. It would be years before they would return to him with any sort of fluency, and by then he was certain that in the decades between that morning in the bur oaks and the present day his memory had reshaped some of the facts. He was just as sure that his memories had failed him altogether in other respects. But certain memories were not prey to fallibility. That morning in the bear blind was one of them.

He spent a long time in the blind parsing their situation. He admitted his fear because he could feel it so plainly. And it was worse now, with the threat of Charlie Aas imminent. The pistol on his father's belt was as frightening as any white water they'd had to paddle, as ominous as any wind-torn night. But he felt something else accompanying the fear, something transformative, a certain firmness of spirit. His shoulder muscles danced.

He remembered looking back through the woods, back toward the shack, and thinking that the pistol seemed ludicrous. Like maybe his father thought he was still in Luxembourg and the Huns were about to step out of the forest to besiege their fort. He remembered thinking that his father was a fool.

But if he was a fool, he had no advantage on Gus. At least not on that day.

Who could say how much time had passed in the blind? An hour, maybe two? But when the bear emerged from the darkness of the woods, when she buried her snout in the fallen leaves and acorns and sat on her fat haunches and ate like a glutton, when she moved from one spot to another and another and several more, Gus watched from the blind, and when he got up and stepped over the deadfall and walked toward the sow, the wind blowing in his face so she had no scent of him, the Remington still leaning in the notch against the tree, one step farther behind him with each stride he took, when all this had passed and finally she looked up and fixed him with her soft eyes and stood on all fours, and when he moved toward her like maybe they were grappling partners, him smiling and rubbing his hands together like it was time to get at it, when that bear snorted once and huffed once and turned and hurried back into the darkness she'd come from, after all of this Gus stood there yowling like a madman and felt certain that facing the old sow had its provenance in his own ancestral blood.

A week or more passed with hardly a word between the two of them. Each morning Gus went back to the oaks and waited for the bear to return. Though her sign was everywhere — more scat, trees clawed to hell, tracks trailing into the denser woods beyond — he didn't see her again until the day the first lasting snow came. By then he'd worn a path from the shore into the oaks and made a regular shanty of the deadfall blind. He took his spot that morning, while the snow began, and waited. When the bear didn't show, he figured she'd gone into hibernation, what with the cold, fresh weather. So he left the blind an hour after sunrise, had sawed three inches into his oak, and was already sweating when he heard her grunts. There, not twenty yards behind him, sitting on her flanks, staring at him with her dark eyes, her nose and ears twitching, the bear waited. Gus looked quickly at the Remington resting in its notch in the blind, the barrel camouflaged by the dead branches.

The bear grunted again and ran a paw through the snow like she was drawing a line. She was larger than he remembered. He jimmied the saw blade from the trunk and the bear sat up as though prodded, took a step toward him, shuffled back, then another step forward, her nose low to the ground, her eyes never once leaving his. Gus could hardly draw a breath.

A long moment passed before he found his wits and moved slowly toward the blind. The bear stood watching on her hind paws, but he kept walking slowly, and backward. When he got there he reached for the gun. The bear took another step toward him.

The twenty yards between them might as well have been twenty inches, given how near she felt, so close he could smell her and see the wet of her eyes. And she felt nearer still when he raised the Remington to his shoulder and sighted her, first through the scope and then with both eyes open down the barrel. Her eyes remained fixed in return.

By that time in his life, Gus had killed over a dozen deer. Countless grouse and ducks and wild turkeys. A stringer of hares each winter since the fourth grade. He could hit a soup can from a hundred yards even with a stiff wind on his cheek. When he lowered the gun barrel after pulling the trigger, there was no earthly reason that the bear shouldn't have been lying in a heap. But she wasn't. In fact, by the time he ejected the spent cartridge and levered another into the chamber and raised the rifle again, the sow was already near the dark edge of the pines. Gus blinked and she was gone.

The air reverberated with the shot. His hands thrummed. He checked the magazine to prove he'd actually pulled the trigger. One cartridge was indeed spent. Five remained. He walked slowly to the spot where the bear had stood. Blood had sprayed across the snow and followed the footfalls running toward the dark woods. The drops might as well have been electric lights, so bright were they against the snow.

He patted his hip to check for his knife, loaded another cartridge into the magazine, and followed the tracks into the woods. The pines were so dense so soon that it seemed impossible the bear could have shouldered through them, but her bloody trail kept unfurling before him. The trampled saplings and low-hanging boughs offered more proof of her passage. Gus pressed on.

After some time clearings between trees opened and the bear's gait lengthened. She was still bleeding, but not as much. His shot hit her in the right shoulder or ribs, since the blood trailed on the starboard side of her tracks, a stain for each new stride. The terrain began to arch and fall. Boulders the size of the bear herself cropped up, covered in snow, and more than once Gus startled at the sight of one. He walked for a quarter mile before the land dropped into a sharp valley where a wide creek ran along the bottom. He could see where the bear had paused on the shore. A pool of blood had already cooled in the snow, and Gus could see where her haunches had rested while she drank. He stopped for a moment himself, took a drink from his canteen, and wiped the sweat from his brow.

The snow had stopped and he felt a fleeting relief. It must have been past noon, judging by the light behind the clouds. They promised nothing if not more snow. As if thinking this had made it so, light flakes began blowing through the trees above, bringing with it a different tang to the air and a new kind of dread.

He hiked upstream first, looking for the trail of blood to begin again on the opposite bank. For fifteen minutes he cased the shore, then backtracked for an hour until he spotted her trail heading up a steep embankment, above where the creek's course narrowed into a sault choked with boulders and driftwood. It was by then snowing hard, the bear's blood pinkening under the white of it.

The hillside rose steady and steep for perhaps two hundred feet. Pines and spruce again, thick and dark. He crossed the creek over the sault on a snow-covered log and he prowled the dense woods for hours. The snow had stopped and started three times before the sky lightened. When the sun came out it was already resting over the southwestern treetops. Gus was ravenous and tired and had lost the bear's trail entirely. Obeying one law of the woods, he'd violated another, and now he was lost. As sure as the sun would set, he would have to spend the night in those woods. And with what? No food. An empty canteen. No cover. He had his hat and gloves, but he'd sweated through his shirt and long johns and his boots were soaked from the snow.

Harry would have heard the shot and assumed he was now tracking his prey or field-dressing his kill. He'd have taken it for granted that Gus would leave enough time to get out of the woods in the daylight, would've left the carcass behind when dusk approached. Harry wouldn't start worrying until sunset, and even if on some instinct he'd paddled across the bay and discovered Gus's canoe and then the bur oaks with hours of light left, the snow would've covered the tracks, the bear's and his alike.

He needed shelter. And fire. He was sure of this, if nothing else.

So he wandered through the gloaming. Just down a slope he found a spruce, its boughs dead and rust-colored and covered with snow. He walked around it. The tree had snapped eight or so feet aboveground and the trunk rested against the hillside. Gus crawled under the boughs at the open end. Four feet inside, the ground was dry. He broke dozens of dead limbs to clear enough room to stretch out, which he did. Through the interstices of the boughs above he caught the first moments of darkness as they arrived.

Years later, what he remembered most was

his simple and unadulterated fear, unaccompanied by any other emotion. At times it felt like a physical thing, as real as the dead tree or the snow. For a spell he lay in the grip of it, unable to open his eyes, much less start a fire. But he must have moved. He survived, after all.

He didn't recall building the fire or stockpiling the wood to burn through the night, or melting snow in his canteen, and knew he had only because it was half full in the morning. Nor did he remember stripping down to his skivvies and hanging his wet clothes near the fire to dry, though he did recall waking nearly naked and shivering only inches from the flames. And weeping long enough that his clothes had dried and he put them back on and he felt parched.

He thought a lot about the bear that night. How, if he hadn't been in the woods to shoot her that day, she might have finished her acorns, taken a long study of the falling snow, and come to just such a place as that fallen spruce, where she would have curled into herself and settled down for the winter without need of a fire to keep her warm.

He remembered waking and his fear still looming there in the fire's warm light. He cursed everything that night. His father. His mother. The maps. The canoes. Charlie Aas.

The bear and the woods and the snow. He cursed the stars, too, when they showed on and off from behind the clouds. Their brightness made the night somehow more sinister than the sheer darkness, lighting up the snow and shining back blue and reminding him with every tiny wink how lost he was.

It occurred to him more than once that he would never be rescued. That the woods and the night had swallowed him and that he was already lost forever and just didn't know it yet. He would die curled up under the tree, starved or frozen or both. Years later, it struck him how unlike the bear he was in this respect, how fragile the night made him.

He told me — slowly, very quietly — that he thought often of how many nights had passed between then and now. He allowed that if he'd ever seen any evidence of God it was in his shivering and intermittent sleep that night under the tree. All of it — the fire and snow and stars and moon and darkness all around — hinted at such. But even more than these physical things, it was the feeling that accompanied him as he prayed that tested his doubt. He prayed clumsily, ardently, all through the night. He prayed like a beggar. And he had never felt so alone or so far away or so helpless as when uttering those words. The words themselves he could no longer recall. But the vulnerability alongside them? That feeling stayed with him in the years since, whenever some danger presented itself. And thus he had his religion. And thus his God had always been an orphan to the ones found in the holy books.

Gus woke to the sight of his father walking toward him. Walking and then running and then throwing a sleeping sack over him. He kissed him on the cheeks and forehead until Gus pushed him away. Harry pulled off his coat and wedged it under his head. Then he stoked the fire with all the wood that remained, blowing into the embers until the flames grew as tall as he was. He took a chocolate bar from his hip pocket, ripped it open, and broke a piece off, then knelt and put it in Gus's mouth. His son took the rest of the candy from him and sat up. He guzzled from the canteen and stuffed the rest of the chocolate into his mouth.

"What the hell, bud?" Harry said.

One of the logs toppled from the fire and Gus kicked it back into the flames.

"We're a long way from the shack," Harry continued. "And there's six inches of snow on the ground."

Gus's mouth was full of candy. He couldn't have spoken even if he'd wanted to.

"Your tracks are almost gone. It's a miracle I found you." Harry was pressing back tears as he spoke. "If not for the fire, bud, I might not have." He gazed into the fire and followed the flames as they turned to smoke and rose into the dawn. The sky was purple and clear.

"I shot a bear," Gus said, wiping chocolate from his chin. "I was tracking it."

Harry was still staring at the smoke. "And you didn't notice it getting dark?"

"I —"

"You didn't notice the snow?" Again he pressed back his tears. "You should've known better than to do just about everything you did. I taught you better than that."

Gus turned away. "Yeah, most of what you taught me isn't really holding up out here."

Harry waited for Gus to look back at him. "You're right about that," he said when Gus finally met his eyes. "I guess I thought we were back on track."

"There's no track," Gus said. "Not that I see, anyway."

Harry nodded. He came and sat down next to him.

"I know I shouldn't have shot the bear. That was stupid."

Harry nodded again.

"I know I shouldn't have tracked her till dark. I know all that stuff."

"You warming any?"

Now Gus nodded. They sat there beside the fire for a long time before Harry said, "There's something you should see."

Gus stood and wore the sleeping sack over his shoulders like a cape as he followed his father for a minute or two, until they came to the hilltop. Gus took in the steep drop to a lake that appeared black as coal against the snow-white world around it. Then he noticed tracks along the ridgeline between the bent pines.

He looked at his father, who pointed to where the tracks first appeared and gestured for Gus to move ahead. After twenty paces he was standing beside the dead bear. She was blanketed in snow, her snout resting on her forepaws. They weren't a hundred yards from where he'd slept the night before.

"There's your girl."

Gus could see where his father had brushed the snow away to reveal the bullet wound on the sow's right flank, where blood had frozen in her matted coat. He knelt and swept the snow from her face. Her eyes were closed.

Gus stood and knocked the snow from his trousers, then looked back at the fire through the woods.

"You okay?" Harry said.

"Yeah. Or I'll be okay. Why not?"

"Listen," Harry said. "For everything you did wrong last night — for everything that went wrong last night — there's one thing you got right. You survived. You did everything right after you got lost."

"Maybe," he said.

His father rested a hand on his shoulder and they stood there in silence until Harry took one of the bear's hind legs and told Gus to grab the other. Together they dragged the bear back to the fire.

Harry said, "You want to learn how to do this?"

"I don't think so. My plan is never to hunt bear again."

"You want to keep me company anyway?"

Gus, in answer, sat down by the flames.

His father removed his coat and unbuttoned and rolled up his shirtsleeves, then pulled the knife from his belt. He knelt down and rolled the bear on its back, and sang softly while he went to work. *"Un loup hurlant vint près de ma cabane, / Voir si mon feu n'avait plus de boucane, / Je lui ai dit: Retire-toi d'ici, / Car, par ma foi, je perc'rai ton habit!"*

When the bear was skinned Harry slit open its gut and yanked the offal from its belly. Soon after, he took the bear's heart from its chest and offered it to Gus. "Freddy Riverfish would say to take a bite. You want one?"

"No way," Gus said. "That isn't happening."

Harry's smile was mischievous. He raised the bear's heart up to the morning sun, then brought it down to his open mouth.

"I can't imagine why you'd want to spend another minute in here." This was Gus talking. We stood again in the apothecary, on the main floor. "All this dust. Everything faded and worn." He shook his head. "It's ghostly."

"Ghosts are the stuff of dreams, Gus."

"This place is a dream," he said.

He by then had taken on the countenance of someone wearied by his own story. I thought he might say something more about his father and their winter — there was almost never a preamble, and he started each memory like a man running out of a burning house — but instead he said something that surprised me. "It's always bothered me that my father had to spend his childhood living in the fish house. Poor as a peasant. While she lived here. Feeding filet mignon to those dogs of hers. Starting fires with ten-dollar bills."

"All that money, Gus, what did it buy her?"

"Hey, she was warm at night. She didn't have to spend her time worrying about which way the wind was blowing."

"Fortunes turn, though, don't they? Just look at you and your sister. Consider the legacy of Rebekah and Hosea Grimm and put yours next to theirs. I don't need to point out that the same building you think your father must have pined away for is one that your sister just gave away. Not sold, given. Your family name will be right above the door."

"We've come honestly by what's ours, Berit."

"Oh, I know that. Of course I do. But that sign came at a price and Thea Eide — your great-grandmother — paid it. Odd Eide paid it. Your father, he paid it, too. You're paying some yourself, no doubt."

He looked at me.

"Other people paid other prices, Gus. That's all I want to say. I don't mean to harp. But there's not a soul in this town who doesn't owe something to their neighbor."

He took in the big open room and drew a deep breath. "That's why you're curating this place? There can't be very many other reasons to."

I crossed the room and hung my coat on the hook by the door and turned again. "I told you before, this place isn't as fraught with meaning for me as it is for you."

"Even before my mother made this her trysting place, my father had us understand we were not to come here. We were not to speak with Rebekah. We were not to so much as look in her direction. Like she was some sort of sorceress. A Medusa."

"She was a great many things, but a sorceress? No. Far from it. And she was beautiful, not hideous."

"I don't know, she turned plenty of folks to stone."

"More like she was made of stone herself," I said. "Of all the heartbreaking lives this town has harbored, Rebekah's was the most so. The most."

Gus rolled his eyes.

"It's true. And you owe her much. Harry had it otherwise. I know why, and I understand, and I'm sure I could never convince you to feel differently. But you'd be a fool not to look around. There are things for you to see here."

"Such as what?"

I said nothing, just walked to the staircase and started up, rounding the newel post on the second-floor landing and heading up to the attic, where I went to the kitchen table. A hundred years it had stood there. Now I swept a sheet off it and Gus walked over and looked at the portrait lying on the table.

"Your mother's," I said.

He stared at it intently. "She could only see something through if she was painting it," he said. "Or destroying it."

"She saw you and your sister through to the end."

"Now you're her champion?"

"Certainly not. But as it was with Rebekah, so it was with your mother. They were complicated women. Their lives weren't easy, either one. Rebekah's especially."

"Not easy? She never knew anything except ease."

"She didn't have to hoist gill nets, it's true. But ease? You're mistaken about that."

"What was hard for her? Tell me."

"Try to imagine what it would've been like for a woman to abandon her child back then. Seventy years ago, Gus. Women were treated very differently in those days. Even a woman with her means. She might as well have been a leper."

He looked doubtful.

"She made a decision that cost her any

chance for a normal life."

"You said it — she made a decision."

"Have you ever thought about how much easier it would've been for her to leave from behind this window? To be with your grandfather? To raise your father?"

"Then why didn't she?"

"Because she didn't know how to. She didn't know how to love herself, much less the people she cared about."

"What does her gravestone say?"

"Gus."

"Tell me. You know."

"It says, 'I have loved.' "

"That's right."

"She learned how to love by staring through this godforsaken window. By looking down on a life she could only regret not being a part of."

"Nonsense."

"How could she be a mother? She was no one's child."

"What's that supposed to mean?"

"She was an orphan. She never had anyone."

He stepped away from the painting and shook his head again.

"Think of all you and your father went through. And I don't just mean that winter. I mean all your years together. Think of all the questions you ever asked him. Think of all the questions your children have asked you. All the things you've taught one another. Think of all the love you've known. She never knew any of that."

"She could've come down from this place anytime at all. She could've said she was sorry. Any of the million days she spent up here, she could have quit this for good. None of us were ever very far away."

"And what if she had come down? Your father, he'd have forgiven her? No, he wouldn't have so much as looked at her. In fact, he might have struck her down. And you? You'd have forgiven her?"

He was almost shaking, he was so upset.

"She knew where she stood with those closest to her, or who should've been. She was scared and alone. All she ever knew was loneliness. Loneliness she brought on herself, true. But she had to live with it all the same."

"My father, he had his own share of loneliness."

"Of course he did. But he also had you and Signe. He knew your love."

Gus walked slowly back toward the portrait.

"Signe was here to see her paint it. Part of it, anyway. So many years ago. Still, I remember it very well. Charlie Aas was here, too. And because Rebekah was here, so was I."

The layers of light and subject in that painting are unlike anything I've ever seen. In the center of the canvas, Rebekah Grimm sits in her rocking chair, holding a hat. The background is a view of the lake from the window, and waves are coming across it from the south. The portrait streams from dark-as-night blue on the left edge of the canvas to indigo as soft as the blue of Rebekah's iris. It is as if the waves are bringing the light, or, perhaps, the dark. Maybe both. Her eyes — indeed, all of her — seem to gather the thousand shades of blue between the two edges before casting the color back onto itself. Her face is oversized. Not exactly caricature, though not far from it. But beautiful and youthful. The only thing that isn't a shade of blue is the pink hat in her hands.

"All those years ago, when your mother bought this place, Rebekah made it a condition of the sale that your mother paint her portrait. She never showed it to your father, I'm certain of that.

"I remember Signe. She didn't know enough to be leery of Charlie Aas yet. She was only twelve years old. She didn't know how to be amazed yet, either. By your mother's talent or the particulars of that gathering. All those people in the same room. What it all meant. All the endings it foreshadowed." I got a chill just thinking of it. "Your mother, though? Well, she was right at home. She explained that they'd been working mostly at night or in the afternoon, but on that day they were into the morning light. She wasn't sure the composition would work, so she asked Signe what she thought.

"What in the world was Signe supposed to say?" I asked. "It seemed cruel, putting that question to a child. But Signe, she surprised me. She said, 'It looks sad.' Oh, I can remember it perfectly. *Perfectly.* I was just delighted."

Gus smiled and shook his head as though it was beside the point to explain about Signe, and it was. After a moment he said, "She was a beautiful artist. There's just no getting around that, is there?" He took a deep breath. "If only she'd been as gentle with her family as she was with her brush-strokes."

I sat down on the chair beside the table and told Gus about the rest of that morning.

I wish I could say why it was such a

memorable day. Partly, of course, it was Lisbet and Charlie being there together. So brazen they were, even if they had their excuses. Charlie was her real-estate agent, after all. Partly, though, and maybe more important, it was because I saw in that gathering three generations of Eide women in the same spot, and what Signe had said about the painting could have been said many times over about the incongruity of their being in one another's company.

Signe asked her mother, "How long have you been painting this?"

"We started the day we bought the place. Miss Grimm is a determined subject. She sits for hours on end without so much as batting an eye."

"I've had much practice," Rebekah said, her voice sharp. It would have been the first time Signe had ever heard her speak.

The girl looked at Rebekah sitting in the rocking chair, her eyes cast down on that hat in her lap. By 1963 I'd spent more than twenty-five years with her and I thought I'd seen every expression she was capable of, but there was a new depth to her sadness with Signe in the room. And what did Signe herself see? It was impossible to tell. She was every bit as stoic and straight-faced as her mother.

"Miss Lovig," Lisbet said, "why don't you put water on for tea? Maybe we'll take a break and Signe can spend some time with her grandmother."

And because it was my place, I went to the kitchen and put a pot of water on the stove. From where I stood, I could watch Signe and Rebekah. They said nothing to each other, only sat there by the window. Rebekah with her hollow gaze on the water, Signe with her eyes on the woman she'd spent her whole young life not knowing. Charlie and Lisbet, they stood on the edge of the kitchen and lit cigarettes and watched Signe as though she were a puppy. It wasn't long before they found an excuse to fetch something from Lisbet's car and went downstairs.

It was only then Rebekah said, "Your mother, she's running around with another man? With Charlie Aas, no less. Charlie's a swine."

This was Rebekah's way. She spoke to almost no one. She hardly ever left her seat at the window, entertained almost no visitors. Still, she knew the color of everyone's underclothes.

"An oinking pig." She almost smiled before her expression turned sour. "He's not the first hornswoggler who'd have us believe this backwater's the headwaters of the world. It is certainly not. That's one thing you should know."

Signe looked at her for a long time before her eyes widened. "Miss Grimm, are you blind?"

"I can still see light and dark. But not much more."

Signe didn't say anything.

"Don't pity me, child. I've seen enough in my life."

Signe still didn't speak. She stared at Rebekah, rather too freely, as far as good manners went.

"How old are you, Signe Eide?"

"I'm almost thirteen."

"That means your father is now forty-three. Am I right about that?"

"I think so, yes."

"Who will tend his nets?"

"No nets this year. He might have to sell his boat. That's what Mom says."

"Sell his boat?"

"Mom says there aren't any fish in the lake anymore."

"Sell his boat?" she said again.

"He might. If anybody will buy it."

Signe simply could not take her eyes off her grandmother. They sat there silently for as long as the water took to boil.

Then, while I made the tea, I heard Signe say, her voice almost a whisper, "Miss Grimm?"

Rebekah held her gaze on the window, as if she could see again and the lake was on fire.

"Miss Grimm, why aren't we allowed to know you?"

"Young lady, don't ever doubt that your father knows what's best for you. He learned how to be a father from the best man this town has ever known." She finally turned to her. "He was right, keeping you from me."

I set the tea on the table before the rocking chair and poured a cup for Rebekah. She took a sip and looked toward the staircase. Charlie and Lisbet appeared as if magically summoned.

"You've been telling secrets up here, haven't you?" Lisbet said, glancing at Signe even though her words were meant for Rebekah.

Rebekah leaned toward Signe and whispered, too silently for Lisbet to hear her, "Tell your father I'd like to buy his boat."

I could tell my story didn't impress Gus much. He might even have been getting impatient.

"Let me see if I understand," he said.

"Because Rebekah was once decent to Signe, we should exalt her? Hang up her portrait as the Matriarch of Gunflint?"

"Honestly, you're even a harder case than your father."

"I mean, the simple fact she wanted her portrait done in the first place says it all."

"You're right. She was vain. Because she was beautiful and thought of herself and no one else. I actually think wanting to have her portrait done was an attempt to understand herself differently, though."

"And not because it was my mother doing the painting? Not as a way of getting closer to us?"

"Maybe that was a part of it. But I doubt it."

"Why?"

"How can I say this?" I offered, blushing. "Rebekah, she was the subject of countless photographs."

"Photographs?"

"Yes. One of Hosea Grimm's main enterprises was the distribution of nasty pictures."

"You mean pornography?"

"Old-fashioned pornography, yes. That's why he brought her here."

"Come again?"

"He sold those postcards all over the world."

"Pornographic postcards?"

"Such as pornography was a hundred years ago. Pictures of her in negligees and corsets. Of her bare shoulders."

He turned his attention back down to the painting.

"Yes," I said, "that same woman. Which is to say this wasn't her first portrait. And that wasn't the first she suffered. She was an orphan, as I've told you. She was an orphan who ran away when she was all of twelve years old. The same age as your sister in the story I just bored you with. Think about that. At twelve, Rebekah ran straight into a brothel. From which she was adopted by Hosea and brought here to be his prime subject."

He looked up, his eyes wide and disbelieving.

"She knew nothing in this world except abuse. She didn't understand happiness or even possibility. She was more alone than anyone I've ever known. And she deserves a little dignity." I stood up and spread the sheet back over the painting.

"Gus, you asked me why I'm doing this." I spread my arms as though to suggest the apothecary. "I didn't end up like Rebekah.

Some bluenose in the attic who never had a friend in her life." Just saying those words made me feel as though I'd betrayed her. "All the people who should have loved her. You. Your sister. Your father. All that happiness she might have known. She got none of it. Can you imagine that? All those lives passing right under your window every day and there's nothing you can do about it? You'd go blind, too. Blind and mad." I pointed at the portrait one last time. "I could have been her. I really could've. I got the benefit of your father's love instead. A benefit that might have been hers had things been different.

"But they weren't different, Gus. Things happened just as they did. To all of us." I reached over and took his hands in mine. "I think Signe gave this building away hoping it would erase this part of her life. A part of your family's life. I'm sure that my having a hand in the historical society isn't something she was hoping for. But I want to do it for your father. This seems like something that would please him. And I want to do it for Rebekah. She deserves some kind glances, even if they come from strangers who are only passing through."

He never ventured past the bur oaks again but he went daily to the felled tree, the harvesting of that wood now his sole enterprise.

While he gathered the wood, Harry built a cache and a ladder to reach it, and on those stilts they stored the butchered bear and dozens of gutted fish, packed with snow, that Gus caught in the evenings. Behind the cabin Harry dug a hole, put a box around it, and called it the jakes. He did repairs on the cabin and made a second bunk. His work made Gus feel inadequate, until the last of the oak logs was laid in the snow beside the cabin and Harry said, "That'll get us through." Those simple words buoyed Gus more than he could explain.

Each night they ate bear. One night it was a slumgullion of boiled paws and snout with their last potato and onion. Another featured sweetbreads, which Gus could hardly choke down. Twice it was merely strips of meat fried in the bear's own fat, a meal as rich as chocolate fudge.

After supper Harry labored at tanning the bearskin. With the bear's thighbone he rubbed the skin soft, a practice that Freddy Riverfish had taught him and that had been passed down for a thousand years among his kin. Gus marveled at his father's fluency in skinning and butchering and fleshing and tanning and cooking. It was as if he'd done nothing in his entire life but put a bear carcass to good use. And the work obviously pleased him.

Gus reckoned that the debacle involving the bear had helped his father to regain himself and took comfort in seeing him look and act like the man he had always known. But that same experience cast Gus even deeper into a wilderness of confusion. He responded by abandoning himself to cutting and splitting and stacking the oak. Eight or ten hours a day, for days on end. His hands cramped and callused and grew viselike in their strength. His shoulders and back, which had always been lithe and lean, turned unequivocally muscular after the countless hours spent sawing and swinging a maul.

They were fateful days. The sky was heavy and hard as an anvil at times, then light enough to whisper the whitest snow down on them. It snowed every day, though only twice with purpose. One day it started at dawn and didn't relent until suppertime. When Gus went outside for a night's worth of wood, snow came up over his boot tops. A couple nights later it snowed while they slept, and by morning the lake was solid white. Just like that the bay had frozen and the landscape doubled in whiteness.

When it wasn't snowing, the north wind blew the fallen flakes up in waves, and before long the bay was clear, the ice mirroring the dull sky, and it seemed impossible the world could be so colorless. It took night and the coming of stars to shed any brightness on their lives, and the few nights the clouds parted they stood together on the shore as though it were a Mexican beach and they were tanning their cold faces, staring silently up into the sky, waiting, each of them, for something they could not know.

When he laid the last split log on the woodpile, it seemed nearly as large as the shack. Gus stood back and studied their camp. The shack and the cache and the woodpile. The privy a ten-step walk toward the woods. Their canoes leaning keels-up against a tree on the edge of the clearing. The smoke rising from the chimney and the icicles hanging from the eaves trough. It was the most inexplicable fort in the long and cold history of world. But one he was so glad and grateful of he could not, even now, all these years later, find words to express his relief at its being there.

That night — after the last of the wood was split — they stood together again on the shoreline. The wind still blew from the north. And the ice beneath their feet sent a sudden shiver into the soles of their boots. Then a proper moan issued from the frozen lake. Gus thought it sounded animal and he turned quickly to the woods behind them.

"That's the ice," Harry said. "Must be a spring feeding this bay." He stepped back, and Gus swore he felt the air pulse as his father shook with cold.

The ice moaned again. Now it was musical, like a low note from a clarinet.

"Beautiful, eh?" Harry said. "You've not heard that before?"

"No."

"It's just our bay settling in."

It was such a strange and lovely sound, Gus remembered. After days of hearing nothing but the thwack of splitting wood and the clunk of piling it up, to hear something like music again came as both a relief and a great sadness. Especially because it was native and wild but also because it seemed, inexplicably, destined for just the two of them. As though they deserved that euphonious moment. To prove that life was not just gathering wood and butchering bear. Gus closed his eyes for a moment. When he opened them the clouds in the night sky whistled away and in their wake the stars snapped like embers in a fire. The ice sang on. They listened until it quieted and then turned back for their shack.

Harry seldom spoke of his own father, Odd Eide. Neither to me nor to Gus. Or he seldom spoke of him when he wasn't extolling his command of one of the family trades. Almost everything Gus knew about his grandfather he'd learned from hearsay. From gossip and legend.

So he was surprised when Harry brought him up that night. He'd draped the bearskin over his shoulders and took a cup of coffee to his bunk. "My old man, he never hunted bear. Everything else, but not bear."

Every time Gus looked at the bearskin he bristled and glanced away. "Is it true about him?" Gus said.

"What?"
"That a bear took his eye?"
"Yup."
"That he crawled into a bear den?"
Harry smiled. "It's true. Right on the Burnt Wood. We passed the place coming out here." He took a sip of coffee and smiled. "I guess you and him got something else in common." This was meant to be playful, even sympathetic, but it stung and Gus felt foolish again. "Of course, you got out of your spat with both eyes."
"Some consolation."
"Well, it's better than the alternative."
Harry set the cup on the floor and shifted the bearskin on his shoulders. "I always admired him for doing it. Pretty goddamn tough, if you ask me. He was only about twelve years old."
Over the course of their time on the borderlands Gus would come to learn the whole story. Not only of his grandfather and the bear but of his grandmother and great-grandmother, of the watch salesman and Hosea Grimm. But as of that night of the ice song, he knew only rumors. "It's weird," he said, "how you never talk about your dad. About our family history."
"History," Harry said, as though it were a profanity. "History for us doesn't exist. His-

tory requires proof, of which we have almost none." He looked at his son and then quickly added, "You have plenty of proof. Nothing's ever happened to you that might compromise your history."

"Like getting lost up here?" Gus said. "Or killing the bear? Nothing like that counts?"

"Those are stories, bud, not history. Not yet, leastways. Besides, I talk about my old man all the time."

"Sure, whenever we're cooped up in the fish house working on a boat, you remind me how skilled he was. At fishing, too. But you never talk about anything else. You never told me about when he went into the bear den."

"I've been saving that one," Harry said, a wry smile on his face. "Anyway, I thought you were done listening to my stories."

Gus felt himself blush.

"All right. You want to hear about him?"

"It's just that I've never even seen a picture of him. I wouldn't know him if he walked through the door."

"Well, that ain't happening. But I could tell you about him some." Again he shifted the bearskin, then sat up straight and wiped the hair back from his eyes. "My old man never knew who his father was. Never met him. He also never knew his mother. She died soon after he was born. The story goes, she came from Norway expecting to find the promised land. I guess that didn't work out. But the land on which our house is built? It came down to my father when his mother's people died. You ever hear of Rune Evensen? Our house is on his land. Or what used to be."

"Why didn't Rune Evensen take care of Thea Eide?"

"His own wife strung herself up from the barn roof just to get away from him. He was unglued real good, that one."

"So your dad raised himself?"

"More or less. Learned everything he knew — which was plenty — by trying until he didn't fail. He didn't fail much."

"I guess he passed that along to you."

"Naw, all I got were his good looks."

"Not much of an inheritance," Gus said, and they both smiled. After a moment, he said, "Who would do that? Climb into a bear den?"

"The way he told it, there was no choice in the matter. The hand of God reached down and gave him a shove. He didn't regret it." Harry finally took the bearskin from his shoulders and spread it across the foot of his bunk. "Christ if I know why he did it. Why do we do any of the things we do? Why'd you shoot that bear? Probably you did it for the same reason."

"I shot the bear because we're going to need food. A lot of it."

"You shot the bear because I told you not to. You shot the bear because you wanted to see what it was like."

He picked up his coffee cup and got out of his bunk and went to the pot on the stove. He shook the coffeepot, discovered it was empty, and put it down hard. "Which isn't to say I don't understand. I do. We're men. We need to see ourselves against the world. Against our fathers. I did. No doubt you do, too."

"I bet you never defied your father. I bet you were a perfect son."

"Far from it."

"But a better son than me."

"No chance of that."

"So did you ever defy him?"

"Nope."

"See, you were better."

"I had a better father, that's all."

Gus was old enough to carry his share of the load into that wilderness, old enough to kill the bear and harvest the wood, but he felt like a child when it came to understanding the nature of men. He felt, too, that he would never be old enough to manage to.

"The difference between my father and me," Harry said, "or one of the differences, is that he never would've gotten us in this tangle. He would have squared it all up over a beer at the Traveler's. He had more trouble with those Aas boys than I ever did. That's a certifiable fact."

More confused than ever, Gus wondered how a livelihood mattered more than a marriage. And what the difference was.

"My old man had a saying," Harry told him. "Well, not a saying, exactly, but a question. He asked it of himself and he asked it of me and he asked it of anyone who came to him with trouble: 'Can you get ahead of it?' The answer, for him, was always, always yes." Harry stood in the middle of their small shack, holding his hair back off his forehead. "I should've thought about that before I sicced the goddamn dogs on Charlie."

"Charlie's a killer. He killed his brother."

"And a crook and a thug and a cheat. I know." Harry walked slowly back to his bunk and sat down on the edge. "But the reason I went after him has nothing to do with him killing his brother. It has nothing to do with him stealing from the church coffers. Hell, it doesn't even have to do with his big plans to plunder these wilds." He ran his hands through his hair once more.

"If old Marcus Aas had come after my father's gal, you know what would've happened? He'd have walked right up to Marcus's door and asked him to step outside. He would have told him the jig was up, that if he saw her again there'd be hell to pay. And if Marcus had kept at it, my father would've rolled up his shirtsleeves and gone three rounds with him. If things weren't square after that, he'd have set the bastard's house on fire."

"You said your only chance against Charlie was to get him out here, though. You said that this was a fair place to fight."

Harry looked at him as though at a simpleton. "The reason my father went into the bear den was because Danny Riverfish called him a chickenshit. My father knew, even then, as a boy, that being a chickenshit was about the worst thing you could be in this world." He stared at Gus then for a long time. "I say again, he was twelve. I've got gray hair."

Gus remembered sitting in the shack waiting for his father to say more. Of course, there was nothing more to be said.

Early mornings I went to the apothecary and sorted through the miscellany that Bonnie and Lenora found stashed in every box and drawer and hidden cranny in that old building. There were coded ledgers, correspondence from as far away as France and New Zealand, a passel of letters to and from Chicago and San Francisco, several dozen from Montana. Piled waist-high on the floor, a stack of folios that could best be described as books of spells. Some of the recipes in them called for the blood of wolves in heat or ground stag antlers or the dried wombs of rabbits. There were hundreds of photographs, maybe a thousand, in dozens of warped and yellowed albums. One morning Bonnie brought me eight red-rope legal files, full of documents even young Curtis Mayfair III, Esquire, couldn't decipher. There were boxes and boxes of medical records, including the notes for perhaps two hundred births, among them Odd Eide, Gus's grandfather. All of these the records of Hosea Grimm, who built the apothecary and whose influence lived on long after his death, which came before I arrived here in Gunflint.

Mostly I filed things in bankers' boxes and set them aside, and at the end of a morning Bonnie or Lenora would cart them down to the cellar, where wire shelves had been built and arranged like those in a library. But occasionally something stood out and was set aside as an artifact that might warrant inclusion on the walls or in the glass cases we had ordered to furnish the old sales floor of the apothecary.

One such item was a poster-sized graph of the water level of the Burnt Wood River at the Main Street Bridge for the year 1899, as recorded every day. It charted not only the water level but the phases of the moon, the sunrise and sunset, the direction of the wind at each mealtime, the day's precipitation, and, in winter, the particular quality of the snow, whether heavy or light, dry or wet. As with all of Hosea Grimm's notes and documentation and correspondence, the information was recorded in elaborate and very beautiful calligraphy. The graph itself was hand-drawn and perfect, an accomplishment unto itself. What's most intriguing about it, though, is the note at the bottom of the page, with an asterisk before it: "Aristotle said that venerable and most ancient sage — old Thales of Miletus — decreed all matter and all form were first and last WATER. A fool's metaphysic, as our measure of April One, Eighteen and Ninety-nine, brought with it him who was most decidedly NOT water, but went by the given name of Rune Evensen. Drowned and dead and fished FROM the water."

Everything about the graph speaks to this place. To our need to order that which is chaos and could never be ordered. To our thoroughness in most — if not all — matters. And of course to our feebleness beside this wilderness. When I showed the chart to Gus, he put on his reading glasses and studied it carefully, as though the minute changes in water level nigh a hundred years ago were of great interest and importance.

He took his glasses off. "I've always heard it said Marcus Aas pulled Rune Evensen from the river. That Marcus believed the Evensen property was his by dint of that universal law we now know as finders keepers." He looked up and smirked and sat on the stool opposite the counter. "It's hard to imagine that kind of meticulousness, though, isn't it? Or maybe it's foolishness. To measure a river that way. A sounding a day."

"It's not so strange," I said. "He was a scientist, after all."

"If Hosea Grimm was a scientist, I'm the king of Norway."

"Well, he certainly was meticulous, whatever else he was. A couple days ago we came across the notes he made after your grandfather was born. There were notes for every child he delivered here. Most every letter he ever wrote had a duplicate copy. His record of boats coming and leaving the harbor is more thorough than the lighthouse keeper's."

"Any first-grader can count boats."

"But most don't. I understand you'd deny him any admiration, but he was a man with interesting qualities."

Gus waved this thought away with the back of his hand. He tapped the postscript on the graph and said, "Besides, Thales was right, not Grimm. The human body is mostly water, after all." He glanced at it once more. "Anyway, this" — he ran his fingertip down the column of soundings — "is the simplest sort of inquiry. It rains, the water rises. The snow in the hills melts, the water rises. The last days of a drought summer, the water's lower. You don't need to be a philosopher or a scientist to understand that. People have always mistaken Grimm's fussiness for learning or wisdom. Fact is, he drew pretty pictures with one hand while he strangled people with the other. He was a crook and a bully. Just like Charlie Aas."

Though I mostly shared his view, I said, "That sounds like an opinion your father might have helped you form."

He smiled and put his big, warm hand over the back of mine. "There's more intelligence — more *truth* — in my father's book of maps than there is in the mighty Hosea Grimm's archives." He removed his hand and walked to the end of the counter and removed the lid from one of the three boxes stacked on the floor. "And certainly there's more elegance. Mountains are only mountains if they're mountains."

"About any of that, you'd get no argument from me."

"And still you're busy cataloging his life."

"Gus, honestly. He wasn't the only person who lived here. His story isn't the only one these walls hold. Furthermore, this place" — now it was me spreading my arms to encompass the apothecary altogether — "was, whether you want to see it or not, the centerpiece of this town for most of a century. Some might even say this building made a town out of Gunflint. This place and the Traveler's Hotel. Otherwise, it was a fishing village. A place to load lumber or trade furs, nothing more."

"Of course you're right," he said, but then paused and walked back to me. I was rolling up the graph, tying it with string. "But maybe," Gus said, "if Hosea Grimm had spent a little more time measuring his own conscience instead of the river, my great-grandmother would have lived. Maybe Rebekah Grimm wouldn't have gone daffy. That's all I mean to say. Maybe things in Gunflint would have been different for a lot of people."

"Should I be offended, Gus?"

"Offended?"

"If all of that had happened, you likely wouldn't be standing here with me now, would you?" I smiled, and he did, too.

He put his hand over his heart and said, "How about I take you to lunch before I fill up with my other foot in my mouth?"

Turns out Gus came to town that morning with a relic of his own. We sat in a window booth at the Blue Sky Café and ordered coffee and he pulled from a letter-sized envelope an old composition notebook of the sort schoolchildren once used. The pages were so old and timeworn it seemed a sigh might turn them to dust.

That season on the borderlands began witchy. Snow piled knee-deep in the woods. The sun and moon in their orbits hung lower, just above the tree line, for shorter stretches each day, dawn and dusk fading through all manner of purple horizons, cold getting colder but only yet suggesting what surely would follow. The world seemed restless. And because their firewood was stacked high and the bear meat abundant in the cache, because Harry had built a three-foot-square box and lid to insulate the hole he'd kept open in the ice offshore, because they'd found their routines — for hauling water, cooking their food, stoking their fires — they fell into a kind of early-winter daze. Which in turn made Gus restless. After all, there were only so many games of cribbage they could stand, so many half-conversations, so many quiet hours reading the few books they'd brought along, so many songs he could play on his mandolin. So he went skiing.

Those first couple mornings he made circuits up and down the long lake. He reckoned it was about eight miles from the bay's entrance to the southern end, and another three to the north. The winds that had dogged them for most of their time at the shack had abated, and in their absence a pair of gentle snowfalls had made the skiing conditions idyllic.

On those mornings his solitude was colossal and spectacular. The trees alongshore stood skeletal and shadowed and unalive. Even the green pines appeared black in the flat and sorry light. On certain moments during these tours he felt a kind of exultation he could liken only to the night he made love to Cindy Aas, moments when he felt so emptied and so full and so alone and so ready to push on, when he forgot where he was or who he was. Not in one of them did he care. Just the opposite was true. He thought that if the world ended he could go on here, even without the birds or the deer or the tracks of deer or the tracks of any other living thing. And there were moments when he forgot that he himself was a living thing, when the white plumes of breath that flowered with each push on his ski poles and each kick of his skis seemed more a part of cloudy sky than his own body — and these were the best moments of all, because it was then he could think without feeling foolish that it was all a dream. But he'd lower his eyes and see his own tracks from the days before unfurling and be reminded that he was not dreaming. That he was, in fact and against all odds, a part of that world.

After days of skiing only on the long lake he began venturing beyond. He'd wake in the morning before his father and, with nothing more than the field glasses around his neck, the pistol holstered on his belt, his father's compass in one pocket of his army pants, and a shank of fried bear meat wrapped in cheesecloth in the other, he'd clip into his skis and pole south toward the rising sun, often meeting it before he reached the shoreline, and once there he'd sight a line into the naked winter woods.

Stripped and bare, the woods were easier to traverse than they had been on their route coming in. He could see the game trails and gully washes and vacant creek beds and he followed them, always with thoughts of his lonely night with the bear. But he was careful, and so despite his nagging fear he kept going. He found other lakes and streams and skied across them and still farther into woods. Hours and hours he would go, marking the day against its light, always ready to turn back on his own tracks with enough time to retrace them before dark.

Only when he returned and drank long from the pail of water and told his father about what he'd seen, only after he'd eaten his dinner of rice and bear, only after he sat with his cup of coffee and his mandolin unstrummed on his lap, did he realize how strong he had become, and how much stronger he could still get.

On this point he made sure I knew he wasn't boasting. In fact, he was almost apologetic. But it was not an unimportant part of the story, he assured me, that he was filling into his flesh that season, that, by virtue of his paddling and sawing and carrying and skiing, he was developing a fitness that would have a real consequence for the story he was approaching.

One of those mornings he left earlier yet, the sky raining starlight. He skied the lake and into the by then well-trod break in the woods. He passed through the woods and onto the next lake and then another before the sun was up. He paused on the north shore of that third lake, his tracks from days before heading up the western slope. The land to the east rose sharply, and in the distance he could see a proper cliff jutting into the brilliant morning. The tracks and packed snow beckoned but instead he pushed into the untrod snow, hugging the shoreline still in shadow.

When he went into the woods at the end of that lake he did so without benefit of skis. He took one bearing with the compass and then looked for the earth to rise, which it did, as he did as well. After an hour he stood on the edge of the cliff, looking down on a lake beneath him. The wilderness spread before him in great, gray undulations. He reckoned he could see for thirty miles. Half of the distance home, if he were a bird. Even in the bright sunshine the world was dull and long and hopeless, and for the first time since he'd been in it he saw it for more than it was. For all that it was.

He looked in the opposite direction through the trees, north toward his father and the chanced-upon shack. How far would they have gone if Gus hadn't taken his toilet on the shore that morning? He knew the wilderness never ended in that direction and wondered what that said about his father. Maybe he was crackers. Maybe, Gus thought, he was trying to kill himself. Maybe the whole story of Charlie Aas, of his murdering his brother, of his plans to ruin this wilderness, maybe all that was pure fiction and his father had actually brought him out here to show him how barren the world was, how far away you could get. Maybe his father had already gone too far in his own mind, and so what difference did it make to him how far he went in the wilds? Maybe he was waiting now, not for Charlie, or winter, but for oblivion to come meet him.

Maybe they'd spend the rest of their lives waiting.

He looked back out over the distance. He studied the contours of the hills. He marked the two lakes he could see. Small lakes. He imagined skiing to them. Beyond them. He flexed his arms and shoulders, reached back to feel his hamstrings, bent at the waist and put his nose on his knees and felt the muscles stretch and burn. When he looked up again he saw that wilderness as if for the first time. It was the wilderness of the soul. His soul and all the world's soul. It was untamable and ungovernable and unforgiving and it didn't give a damn about him and his proud thoughts. It was not an idea. It was real and had to be lived in, not just visited. No, not lived in. *Survived.* He had to survive. So he took his compass out again and held it once in each direction and reckoned the world was just that simple if you let it be.

The next morning he left the shack with

one of the Duluth packs strapped to his back. It held the tent and his sleeping sack and a canteen of coffee, a hatchet and saw, and the lantern. And, wrapped in a sweater, his father's book of maps with a composition book and a pencil folded in the moose hide. While he packed it up the night before, his father asked what he was doing.

"I've been skiing south of here. Climbed a cliff yesterday and saw some territory that I want to get to, but I'll need to camp overnight to get there. Just the night. Maybe two."

"What territory?"

"There's a big cut of the woods that burned. I want to see it up close."

Harry smiled. "You remember that night you got our bear?"

"Yeah, and it won't happen again."

"You know that how?"

"I'll be careful."

"You'll be careful."

Gus lifted the Duluth pack, testing its weight. "You can come with," he said.

"I'm partial to our digs here."

"Suit yourself, then."

Harry looked at him for a long moment, reconciling himself to the fact that in dragging Gus up here he'd forfeited the right to tell him what to do or not to do. Still, he was his father. “I’m not sure it’s a good idea, camping overnight. The weather could turn. What if you got lost?”

“I’ve gotten pretty familiar with that stretch of woods.”

Harry studied him again. “What is it you’re really looking for, bud?”

Gus might have answered that he merely wanted the adventure. But that wasn’t true. He might have said he wanted to face his fear, or make discoveries, or simply see as much of the borderlands as he could. But all of that was also untrue. He couldn’t have said any of it and believed himself, much less expected his father to. Decades later, he knew he was simply obeying his instincts by going off into the forest alone. As though he were merely another beast roaming those woods. “I’m not really looking for anything. I just want to go see,” he finally said.

Which was both true and an answer that satisfied his father. Enough that when Gus left with the Duluth pack in the morning Harry only patted him on the shoulder and said, “Be careful, eh? I’ll see you tomorrow.”

By the time he made camp nine hours later — all the daylight spent and a new and bitter cold bearing down — Gus was afraid again. Not of the wilderness or the cold, but because his father had let him go.

He'd stopped twice to sketch the shape of the lakes and mark the entrances into the clearings. He'd climbed the same ridgeline that he had the day before, and blocked out the landscape on a separate sheet of paper. He used the field glasses to scan the distant hills and the compass to assure himself that he was looking either south or east.

Once he got nestled in the tent, the flap pulled back and a fire at its mouth, his belly full and his coffee warm, he had figured out what he was doing out here. He redrew his earlier sketches in the back of the composition book, guessing at distances traveled and seen, detailing any dramatic rises, and any other features of the terrain that warranted attention.

"The next morning I skied what must have been another fifteen miles. Always, always south or east. If I came on some impediment — an impassable stretch of woods, a hill too daunting, whatever — I'd backtrack until I found a route that kept me on course. South or east. No exceptions."

I had flipped through most of the composition book and could well imagine him sitting alone as a boy in the middle of the wilderness, charting his path home. Of all the things I knew about that season and about Gus, this was the most impressive. Even more so than what was to come.

"Anyone who's ever been lost understands the first rule of the cartographer," he said, motioning to the waitress to refill his coffee mug. "I understood it instinctively, and since I gave no credence to my father's maps — which, I might add, I carried with me and consulted often — I was free to follow that first rule without any hesitation. It was a simple undertaking. I had to figure out how to get home when the time came. With no tools at my disposal other than the binoculars and the compass, the task was as simple as could be. Get from here to there, from A to B. From the shack to the Burnt Wood River."

The waitress topped off his coffee and he continued. "I thought often those days of how uninterested I'd been in our route. How trusting I'd been of my father and his plan and his book of maps. I can't say I felt foolish, though maybe I should have, but I was definitely aware that if we were ever going to get out of there, it would be because I'd figured out how to do it.

"Three nights I was gone that first time. Three nights and maybe twenty-five or thirty miles. It occurred to me more than once that we'd only just settled in and here I was looking to get out. At the time I wasn't proud of this. I saw it as a deficiency in my character. But it was merely my nature. I came by it through no choice of my own, just as my father had no choice in his. To get rid of it you'd have to go back a thousand years and across all the miles of the Atlantic Ocean, through all our ancestors and all the qualities of the Northern European people in general." He smiled. "You know something about this particular quality of our people, Berit Lovig. You know it just as well as I do."

"You're talking about more than getting to church on time."

He smiled again, more broadly, and nodded. "I haven't been to church twelve times in my life. What I'm talking about is who I am, and how not even those borderlands could rid me of that."

"Did those borderlands take your father's true nature away from him?"

He thought for a moment. "I suppose my father thought he might feel better up there. Better as in happier, or more capable, or at least more himself." He thought a bit more. "Or maybe he thought he could escape his nature. Just forget who he was. And maybe he did. But any thoughts like this he might've had were afterthoughts. Whatever he thought he'd find there he knew would come with Charlie and all that he'd bring with him."

He gazed for a long spell out the window at the winter waves coming over the breakwater. "The truth is, after everything that happened, he still came back the same man that went up. Even if he spent some time being someone else. But you don't need me to tell you that." He smiled. "You knew him better than I did. Lately, I mean."

"I spent more time with him, but I could never have known him better."

He smiled again. "It was twilight when I got back to the shack after those three nights away. It had been cold. Probably below zero the whole day. And when I walked in and closed the door behind me, I caught my reflection in the window glass. It had been snowing all afternoon, and I was white as a ghost. My whiskers were covered with icicles. My hat was well frosted and covered with snow. My coat, too.

"My father was standing at the stove. There was this delicious smell in the air" — he waved his hand in front of his face as though to summon the remembered smell — "and he had a shit-eating grin on his face. He said he was glad I made it back, as he didn't want to have to eat both grouse himself.

"I peeled off my coat and hat. Emptied out the Duluth pack. Put everything back in its place. Secreted his book of maps and my own new drawings under my sleeping sack after I spread it on the bunk. Finally, I walked over to the stove. 'Grouse?' I said. 'We couldn't have bear for Thanksgiving dinner, now, could we?' he said, turning to me. 'Did you find our old trail out there?' He nodded toward the door. I shrugged and told him, 'I couldn't say. I was just wandering around the woods.' "

Gus finished his coffee there in the Blue Sky Café. He set the empty cup on the table and pointed the handle so it faced south. I noticed that. Then he shifted it east.

"We ate that grouse sprinkled with salt and pepper. Just grouse and coffee. He told me how he'd been passing by a clearing up in the woods when one jumped from under a bush. He shot its head off. Two hours later, he's coming back and another comes out of the same damn bush. He shot its head off, too. And so there we were, eating Thanksgiving dinner at the shack. He didn't ask me about the days I'd been gone except to wonder if I'd seen anything exceptional. That was his word.

" 'Just the cold and snow. I guess it's winter now,' I said."

Gus picked the coffee cup up off the table and looked into its emptiness. "He had an answer for everything, my old man. He might have just agreed. Said, Sure, it's winter now. But instead he reached for his little birch calendar." Gus paused and shook his head. " 'Winter?' he said. 'Not yet, bud. We've got three weeks before winter.' "

Gus made surveying his occupation between Thanksgiving and Christmas, weeks of hush and white and a kind of coldness he'd never known before. Sometimes he was gone for a day, sometimes two or three. Once, he was gone for four nights and crossed the Laurentian Divide. He knew because he came to a river whose south-rushing saults he couldn't cross. His trails in the woods and across the frozen lakes gained permanence. He camped at the same spots and set fires on the heaps of old ashes. The snap of those fires was often the only accompaniment to the silence, and in that faint rasping he heard music unlike any he'd ever known before and to which he composed lyrics he'd never sing. He never once saw another breathing creature that wasn't black-winged and aloft.

Going by an island on a large lake one morning, he saw a dead-looking tangle of blueberry bushes alongshore. The mere thought of a handful of berries caused him such despair that while his mouth watered he nearly wept out of want and felt like a child. If he'd learned anything it was to not want, so he pushed ahead on his skis or snowshoes and found the next vantage.

Sometimes that was a ridgeline, or a bald knoll, or the notch of a remnant white pine he climbed. Thirty or forty feet off the ground, he compared his father's maps with the land and lakes that spread before him. Sometimes there seemed a likeness, but mostly he resorted to his composition book and kept drawing what he saw. On the coldest and brightest days, in the early or late hours, he was blinded by sun dogs that he could only think of as the sort of light he'd likely see at the end of his life. He'd stare into those halos like they had something to tell him, about not only where he was going but also right where he was.

He often thought of the voyageurs his father so admired. And considered how their maps told stories of where they'd been or wanted to go, of who they aspired to be and what they wanted from the world. He thought of their courage and their brute strength — things of legend — and also of their limits, which must have been considerable as well. He wondered if they left wives and children behind, living their lives only looking forward, and he wondered what secrets they kept. He thought their stories were better told on a map than in a song.

One day he discovered pictographs along the umber cliffs above a long lake: a moose chased by three wolves, the sun shining down like God. An hour later he came across a windblown shoreline and in its dark granite he could feel what passed for mid-day warmth. He sat down for a bite to eat, and when he looked at the rock between his knees he saw the vertebrae of some extinct creature, doubtless brought here by a receding glacier. From how far north, and how long did it take that glacier to get here, what force moved it? Instead of feeling less substantial than ever, he felt powered by a force akin to the glacier and knew this somehow was thanks to his own patience. Buoyed by this thought, he looked out before him and drew what he could see of it. The composition book was more than half filled now. Each lake numbered instead of named. Each creek and stream and river noted as frozen or free-flowing, each rise in the land marked as passable or not.

That night he counted the rings on the birch log he stoked his fire with before adjourning to his dreams, which came to him lit by more northern lights. When he woke in the morning he made his coffee and thought of home. He was pleased by his efforts to chart a course to get back, but knew full well that, given the vast number of steps required to get there, it would no longer be the same place he'd left, that the home he'd known was gone forever, and that his next home would be one he'd make himself. Whether that was in this life or the next seemed not so consequential. This thought carried him back toward the shack.

Before he reached their lake he took a detour, changing his skis for his snowshoes and taking an unexplored course along the western shore. For four hours he pushed through the drifted snow, passing islands and rocky shoreline and the headwaters of three streams. At the last of these he took the field glasses from his neck and scanned the wide, frozen world. He spotted the entrance to their bay and the smoke from their chimney rising weakly through the trees, one last mile between him and the shack. Looking north, he could see clear to the end of the lake, some three miles away. He took a last look back at the tracks coming up the shore and meeting him where he stood. With the field glasses back around his neck, he scouted where steps in the same direction would take him, past a gentle shore clear of trees thirty yards up off the water.

And right there he saw the moose antlers, their tips sticking out of the snow only thirty paces from where he'd just surveyed the world. He dug them free of the snow and ice and discovered there were two sets, their skulls locked together eye to eye. On his knees, he peered into the hollow sockets and studied the long teeth and the patterns on the antlers themselves and worried very much about the last breaths of these beasts. He looked around the ground on which he stood — all covered in snow, any trace of the carnage that must have accompanied their death lost to time and water and wind. Still, he could hear the snarling wolves and feel the final desperate kicks of these two bulls writhing on the ground.

And no sooner did he imagine the screaming of the ravens than he heard exactly this — eight or ten or twenty, a whole unkindness, coming over the trees. He watched those living things sharp against the sky, riding gyres up and tucking their wings to veer back down. He might have thought them a warning if he'd had sense to think anything. Instead, he took rope from his pack, laced the heavy antlers to his back, then crossed the lake to the shack.

I'd thought we had finished clearing out the upper floors of the apothecary. We'd stored the last boxes in the cellar, almost finished replacing windows and repairing warped floorboards, and we were to tear out a wall upstairs to make room for a larger office. The plan to open the historical society by April seemed feasible. Put fresh paint on the walls and a coat of lacquer on the floor, then hang a sign out front, and that's all that was left to do on the ground floor. It was a winter's worth of work that I regarded with equal parts satisfaction and doubt and foolishness. Who, after all, would ever visit this old place? No doubt the townsfolk knew enough of their history to want to avoid it. Visitors? They wanted donuts and T-shirts and chance encounters with moose on the trail, not black-and-white photographs and antique housewares and hundred-year-old dresses once worn by the town's mad hatter.

In any case, I hadn't been there in a week when I got a call at home. Thursday last, Bonnie on the other end. "There's something you should see," she said. So I finished my breakfast and drove in.

Up on the second floor, in Hosea Grimm's old office, the contractors found a safe behind that wall they were removing. There had been a heavy shelf on casters in front of it before they'd set to work. Bonnie and I stood where splintered two-by-fours framed a black steel door with the words DIEBOLD SAFE & LOCK CO. arced around the tumbler. "Oh my," I said, my mind wheeling at the possibilities. "What do we do? How can we open it?"

"We've sent for a locksmith from Duluth," Bonnie told me. "I called Buck at the hardware store, but he didn't think he could do it. Someone should be here before lunchtime."

And they were. Two brothers spent the better part of an hour cracking the safe while I wondered if there was anything in the world that might surprise me should it fall out. In all the time they worked I couldn't come up with a single thing. But I *was* surprised when the safecrackers pulled the handle down and swung the door open: a cigar box full of hundred-dollar banknotes from the First National Bank of Butte, the deed to that old cathouse up in the timber, a Norwegian Bible, a fine hairbrush. But what surprised me was a stack of letters bound with a thin leather cord, which I untied. There were twenty-six in all, fourteen addressed to Thea Inger Eide, c/o Rune Evensen, Gunflint, Minnesota. The others were addressed to Odd and Inger Eide, in Hammerfest, Norway.

"I'll get you a chair," Bonnie said, then scurried down the hall. She returned a moment later and set the chair behind me. The brothers from Duluth were packing their bag, and when they finished Bonnie walked them downstairs.

I watched them disappear around the banister and then flipped through the letters one by one, pausing to read the names on each envelope again. *Thea Eide. Odd* and *Inger Eide.* Their names were like some sort of strange proof of their existence, as if Harry and later Gus weren't themselves sufficient. Good Lord, how much had that family endured? Thea came to Gunflint in the autumn of 1895. A sixteen-year-old girl expecting to find her aunt and uncle, she stepped off that boat onto a harsh and bitter shore. Her aunt had hanged herself only weeks before she arrived. Her uncle, Rune Evensen, was crazy before his wife strung a rope from the barn rafters. Perhaps it was a blessing that, instead of meeting him on the Lighthouse Road, she found Hosea Grimm instead. He brought Thea home to Rebekah as though she were a lost kitten.

For a long time Rebekah kept a photograph of Thea on her bureau. Taken by the double-dealing lens of Hosea's Kodak, the same camera that he used to photograph Rebekah. She spoke of Thea as though she was the only permanent thing she ever knew in life. A quiet and pretty and nervous girl, she had an angelic air, and her kindness was the most obvious thing about her. Rebekah once said that the truest testament to her perfection — the word she used — was that Hosea never once tried to take advantage of it.

Two days after she arrived, Thea went to work cooking at a lumbering camp up on the Burnt Wood River. She did not speak English. She was made to live in an earthen grave, serving a hundred rough men three meals a day. Among all those souls she could not count a single friend. She toiled like a slave's dog for a hellish winter, and came back to Gunflint in springtime expecting a child. As Rebekah told it, lots of folks thought, with some conviction, that she was the new Mary, mother of Jesus — so inexplicable was it, her emergence from those woods with a bellyful of child. Later that summer, when the Canadian Mounties brought through an itinerant watch salesman on charges of rape and horse thievery, Thea's virginity was questioned, but never her immaculacy. She went to witness his arraignment with her Norwegian Bible in lieu of a phrasebook, still unable to speak an English sentence.

I used to listen to Rebekah's stories about Thea and wonder that a woman so strange and beautiful herself could hold another in such exalted esteem. Especially one whose whole life in Gunflint seemed built of suffering. But when I later heard the stories as they'd been given to Harry, I began to believe them. He had a triptych of photographs of Thea Eide on his mantel, much like Rebekah had hers on the bureau. In one of them she's holding her infant child, Odd Eide, Harry's father, with a beatific expression on her face that not even the aging, faded paper could diminish. She was dead only a few weeks after the photograph was taken. Died under the care of Hosea Grimm, who had, as Rebekah told me, tried to slice a sadness out of her. A sadness, she was quick to add, that didn't exist. Thea was the most blissful mother the world had ever known. Rebekah was sure of that. Harry spoke of her as divine, as though she had never really existed any more than the heavens must. How he came by this opinion was not hard to imagine, even if his father knew her only for the first three weeks of his life. Maybe Thea Eide did have some communion with the Savior.

And here were these letters. I don't know why, but I wondered most not about lost words between Thea and her parents back in Norway, not about the sadness these letters must have delivered, but, rather, about who had stolen them. Hosea was the likeliest culprit, of course. One thing I'd learned for certain in my months of work on the historical society was that his conniving knew almost no limits.

Good Lord, those letters nearly exhaled their sadness. I thought of the countless ones I'd sorted downstairs, when my job was mostly to slot the daily mail. How many words and wishes had passed through my unsuspecting hands? The I-love-yous and we-regret-to-inform-yous and have-you-heards? All of that *life.* And here were the lives of Thea Eide and her parents. Stolen.

Kept. It brought tears to my eyes.

My own life in Gunflint began with a letter as well, sent by my father to Rebekah Grimm, one that commended me as a chaste, hardworking girl of sixteen from a God-fearing family of store-owners in Duluth, who was interested in the clerk's position advertised in the *Duluth Tribune* and able to leave her studies at Denfeld High School to fill said position at a moment's notice. He included a picture of me as well as a few words about his store, a grocery on the Traphagen Block that his father had founded. What he didn't write about was the larger truth that, like many businesses in Duluth in 1936, ours was failing. The shelves were near empty and we had no credit, despite years of keeping our word and our end of the bargain. Our customers suffered the same hard times as we did. Of course, many suffered worse. But our troubles were plenty and true.

My mother was sickly, my father despairing. We'd already lost our modest home and moved into my spinster aunt's even more modest home. It was a story playing out all over the country, my father assured anyone who would listen. I suppose it was his attempt to console himself for the most difficult decision he had to make, which was to send me off so I might earn a few dollars and ease his burden. I doubt he thought I'd be gone forever.

I did not want to leave my parents, but, even so young and naïve, I understood our situation. It wasn't hard to see how the Depression afflicted nearly everyone. And perhaps because of my youth I saw an opportunity here, and was frankly excited when Rebekah Grimm replied with a letter of her own, addressed not to my father, as might have been expected, but to me.

Miss Berit Lovig:
Find enclosed passage for one aboard the Northland bus service from Duluth to Gunflint for January 13. When you disembark in Gunflint, come without delay to 1 Lighthouse Road. Dress appropriately. No pants. Only dresses, unruffled or otherwise unfancified. If you do not own such dresses, they will be provided for you, and the cost will be deducted from your wages. You will be paid $.35 per hour in accordance with the standard of this town for unskilled lady laborers. Of that wage, you will have $6 deducted for room and board at the end of each week. I expect you to work

daily except Sundays, when you are free to attend church should you go in for that sort of foolishness. I await your arrival.

— Miss Rebekah Grimm.

When I found that old letter in a desk drawer, it took me back to my girlish days with force. There it was after almost sixty years: my passport to the place I've called home for my whole adult life. What if my father hadn't seen that ad? What if he'd felt too weak or too proud to reply? What if I'd seemed unsatisfactory to Rebekah Grimm? These questions troubled me, but I will admit to something: the first thought I had on reading that letter again (for the first time in 708 months, in 21,568 days, I've counted it both ways) was not of my own life, not exactly, but, rather, of what my life would have looked like had Harry been absent from it. It would have been different in a hundred different ways.

Of my bus ride to Gunflint in January of 1937 I remember only the miserable faces, fewer and fewer of them as we passed through each small town, until, finally, only a little old lady and I myself remained. She stepped off the bus before me in Gunflint and I never saw her again. I asked someone for directions to the given address and they directed me the few blocks there. I remember walking up the wide wooden staircase, the cold winter breeze and weak sun on my back. Rebekah stood at the window. She must have been watching me. I carried only one suitcase and a hand-me-down purse my mother suggested would make me seem more ladylike. I set them both down as I entered the store. Rebekah came and stood before me.

"Miss Grimm?" I asked.

She lowered her eyeglasses and looked down her fine nose. She was as beautiful as she was strange, two facts obvious at first glance, and already she scared me.

"You're rather less pretty than I expected," she said. "Less pretty than that picture you sent, certainly." She closed her eyes as though exhausted and said, "Take off your coat and stand up straight. There will be no slouching here."

When I took off my coat and stood up straight, she walked around me as if inspecting a museum piece.

"Another photograph telling lies," she said, somewhat under her breath. "But that's just fine. That's good. Plainness will keep the likes of Charlie Aas from loitering."

She crossed the room to the counter and I followed. When we got there she stopped and looked down her nose yet again. "This is your finest dress?"

"It is my only dress," I admitted.

In my memory, she stared for an hour, but likely it was only a second or two. "We'll have to order you another dress, then. We might fix your hair as well." Seeming satisfied with this assessment, she then began showing me around.

I knew from that first day that in her company I would be lonely. But I knew also that my loneliness — no matter how it came to bloom — would always pale beside hers. In the vacancy of her eyes and the timbre of her voice I could gauge how the years had done their work on her. And in that selfsame moment I vowed I would never become a woman like her.

Gus stood at the glass countertop, where the letters were laid out like a game of cards. I'd called him at the school to ask him to stop by after class, and he came without asking why. After a few minutes he set his satchel down and took off his coat and rubbed his hands through his hair. He picked a letter and looked at it front and back, then rubbed the Norwegian stamp and laid the envelope in its place on the counter. "You found them in a safe?"

I nodded.

"What else was in there?"

"Money. Lots of it. A property deed. A hairbrush with a mother-of-pearl handle. Those letters. And a Norwegian Bible."

"Son of a gun." He picked up another letter, one of Thea Eide's, and inspected it as he had the other. "How much money?"

"I don't honestly know. Scads of it."

"Dirty money?"

"I doubt much clean money passed through his hands."

He set the second letter down. "What actually happened to all his wealth?"

"It went to Rebekah. A kind of justice, really, seeing how much he made off her likeness."

"What did she do with it?"

"Well, she lived to be ninety-four. That alone was expensive. There were those ten years at the rest home to pay for. She took care of me. My pension, she called it. It's how I built my home. How I buy my groceries. She left a huge sum to the Gunflint Historical Society. It's how we're paying for all these renovations." I couldn't tell if he was even listening. "I think she knew that if she tried to give it to your father, or to you, she'd have been rebuffed. She wouldn't have been able to bear any more rejection."

He hefted the Bible.

"That was Thea Eide's, no doubt."

"And the hairbrush?" he said.

I pulled it from my pocket and laid it beside the letters. "I presume this was Rebekah's. Thea's belongings were quite meager."

Gus picked up a third letter, from Norway, and walked over to the front window, held it up to the late afternoon light, and looked back at me. "Can I open it?"

"I figure they belong to you and your sister."

He returned to the counter, took a letter opener from a leather cup filled with pens and scissors and bric-a-brac, and slit the envelope open. He blew gently into it and removed the single sheet of paper and smoothed it carefully on the glass counter. The letter was covered in faint black ink, and Gus looked down on it for as long as it might have taken him to read it.

"Does anyone in town still speak Norwegian?" he asked.

"Signe does."

"And she's in Minneapolis."

I thought about Ingrid Gunnarson, sitting in her shared room up at the rest home, her mind gone much as Harry's had. Her daughter was living somewhere out on the East Coast. It seemed unfathomable that there were no longer any Norwegian speakers here. "I can't think of a single one," I admitted.

"So that's that," he said, motioning at the letters. "They were locked in a safe for a hundred goddamn years and now they're still mute. Jesus."

He cut open another letter, written by his great-grandmother, and stared at it for a long time, shaking his head and gritting his teeth.

"Rebekah used to talk about what a crook Hosea Grimm was. I know a lot of the stories. But this?"

"You think he swiped these letters?" he said.

"Of course."

"What about Rebekah?"

"Oh, I can't see that."

"You said yourself that she was selfish and vain. Maybe stealing the letters was her way of keeping part of something she cared about. Maybe it gave her a feeling of control."

"Let me see if I understand you. On the one hand, you've got Hosea Grimm, the only man as rotten as Charlie Aas who ever lived in this town, a man whose entire life was a fraud, whose every move was calculated for his own gain. On the other hand, Rebekah Grimm, who tried to make a living selling hats in a town of a thousand people. Half of whom were women who knit their husbands and children new hats each Christmas."

"A woman who employed you for twenty-five years, largely for the company. She had no one. You said so yourself. Maybe she wanted to keep something all to herself."

I studied the letters on the counter. This theory of Gus's, it wasn't out of the question. "I suppose it's possible," I admitted.

"And I suppose it doesn't matter whether it was her or him." His face drained of color and he picked yet another letter from the stack and held it at arm's length. "Sometimes there just aren't any words to explain things, are there?"

"Words in any language," I said.

After Gus left I spent a long hour pondering the possibility of Rebekah Grimm's guilt. It had been quite some time since I'd held her up for scrutiny.

Gus hadn't said anything when I explained how she'd dealt out her considerable wealth, but it occurred to me — as it must have to him — that holding on to all of it would have required considerable shrewdness. Lord knows she was at times miserly. I can still see her counting out my weekly wage, her fine fingers dropping those nickels and dimes into my own callused hand. She'd put off a job for a whole summer in order to catch the handyman in his season of need, all so she might save ten bucks on a hundred-dollar job. But she was also prone to great extravagances and cunning business sense. It was one of the few things that surprised me about her. Some people said she was crazy. Others — those who'd known her longest — said crazy like a fox.

I remember, during the winter Gus and Harry spent on the borderlands, when everyone in town was whispering about the fix Charlie Aas was in, Rebekah told me something that she meant to incriminate him beyond doubt. It was a story that went back before my time in Gunflint, to the autumn of 1936, when Hosea Grimm died. His passing hadn't been unexpected. He'd been sick for years, having suffered two brain attacks in quick succession. The first left one side of his face like a melted candle. The second killed him in his sleep.

For years Marcus Aas and his boys had been circling Hosea's holdings, especially the Shivering Timber, a seedy brothel on a lake three miles up County Road Two. It had been around almost as long as Hosea himself had been. Once upon a time a dozen or more molls worked the front porch there, but during the last months of Hosea's life that number had shrunk considerably. Friday nights found only three or four negligeed girls out on the rail. Marcus had it in mind to revive the place. He'd come to Hosea with a middling offer in July of '36, one that a prudent man would have accepted for any number of reasons, not least of which would have been to avoid getting tangled up with the Aas clan. Even as early as then, Marcus and his boys were marking every light post in town. But Hosea said no.

When he passed, Rebekah didn't even have to wait until morning before Marcus rang the bell on her counter. He came in just at closing time, his youngest son, Charlie, at his side like a yearling bear cub. Charlie's eyes darted around, as if he was checking for an assassin. Marcus offered neither pretense nor condolences. He simply told her that he would now be buying the Shivering Timber for one thousand dollars, half of his original offer and less than a quarter of its real value. Charlie, he told her, was going to handle the transaction.

On that day Charlie was just a month past seventeen years old, though even then he had a full, manly beard that he stroked as his father spoke.

Marcus wanted there to be absolutely no confusion about the new order of things. He lectured Rebekah on the diminished nature of Hosea's estate. He told her how it wouldn't be out of the realm of possibility for Curtis Mayfair to poke his head into her affairs and try to arrange for Hosea's chattel to go to Odd Eide. He assured her that would be foolhardy, and beyond the scriptures of law both as the state and the good Lord above saw it. Marcus reckoned Odd was nothing but a prodigal waste. It was Rebekah who had served Hosea dutifully, and in his kindness he would help her manage what Hosea had left behind. Starting with the Shivering Timber. Marcus clapped his son on the back and told him to work out the details.

The details, as the young Charlie Aas made it known, were simple. "Sign over the whorehouse or you'll be back in bed with Hosea before he's underground. We already talked to Lenny Washburn, and it's no trouble at all for him to make a double coffin."

Maybe it was because she was in shock

from Hosea's death. Maybe she simply felt she had nothing to lose. Maybe she was looking for a reason to carry on and a fight with those thugs seemed like a noble idea. Whatever the case, she told Charlie Aas to leave. She told him the resort (as she would reincarnate it) up at the end of County Road Two was not for sale, nor would it be going on the market soon, not until some changes were made. She told him that if he had any concerns she might take them up with her attorney, the aforementioned Curtis Mayfair, who represented everyone in town save the Aas clan.

Charlie, of course irate, left in a tantrum. "You ain't seen the last of me, you lame-brained dyke! I were you, I'd sleep with one eye open! I'll be back and up your ass until we get what we came for! Don't you worry about that!"

She knew very well these were not idle threats. Still, she couldn't help being almost amused by his raving. Even so, that first night she slept with Hosea's Browning pistol on her bedside table. For three or four days she waited him out. She buried Hosea. She had a locksmith add a deadbolt to the front and back doors and a lock to her bedroom door on the third floor. Four or five days after Marcus and Charlie made their offer, as she readied for bed, she heard what sounded like glass breaking downstairs in the apothecary. She went into her room, locked the door, and spent a sleepless night wondering if Charlie was coming to make good on his barking promises.

In the morning she inspected the entire apothecary and found everything as it should have been. That night she heard voices in the back alleyway. She tried to spy out the window but saw nothing, so adjourned again to her locked room. The next morning she studied the *Ax & Beacon* classifieds. The only dogs for sale were a litter of miniature schnauzers offered by a family that she hardly knew who lived down in Misquah. When Claire Veilleux came in for her day's mail, Rebekah asked for a ride down the road.

Rebekah knew that getting a puppy was foolish. Even when full-grown it wouldn't be much bigger than a house cat. But she liked the idea of having another pair of ears in the apothecary, so she brought one home and named her Timmy.

The next morning, while Timmy slept in her basket under the mail counter, Charlie stepped casually into the apothecary. He had shaved part of his face so all that remained were muttonchops. With his hair slicked back, wearing a suit, he came right up to the counter and asked for the Aas family mail. She handed it to him.

"How are things, Miss Grimm? You sleeping all right?"

She didn't know how to explain what was more sinister about Charlie on that morning than there had been less than a week before. It was as if his calmness belied the urgency in him. Like he was dying to make his first mark in the world.

She didn't answer, saying instead, "Is there anything else you need?"

"How about the deed to the Timber? Our offer's fallen a tad but we'll give you forty dollars for it."

"Don't insult me."

"That ain't an insult, it's a life-insurance policy against a slow and painful quarter hour." His voice was steady and calm.

"I've spoken with my attorney, and he advised me that if you made another threat, I could press charges against you for harassment."

"This ain't harassment, you whore. It's your final warning."

"He's keeping an eye on this place," she said. She thought her voice was as steady and calm as his. "He would've seen you come in. He knows the minute he sees you to call the sheriff."

"You think I'm worried about Sheriff Anderson? That pissant? Or old Curtis? You think he's got some jurisdiction up here that trumps mine? It's true what they say, you're goddamn batty."

No sooner did he finish talking than Sheriff Anderson and Curtis Mayfair came hurrying in.

"Miss Grimm," the officer said. "Muttonchops here isn't causing any trouble, is he?"

Charlie swung around. "You're choosing the wrong side, Anderson. Who the hell do you think pays for your wife's fine dinnerware? The good people of Gunflint? Kiss my ass."

"Charlie," Curtis Mayfair said, his voice still booming even at his age, "don't do something you're going to wish you hadn't. As of this minute, there's a way for you to walk out of here without cuffs on your wrists. But that window's closing. Yes, sir."

"You're a goddamn donkey, old man. Keep your nose out of this."

Then it was Rebekah who spoke. "Charlie Aas, I will not sell you any of my property. Your threats or your father's threats, they're pointless. I'm not afraid of you. No one's afraid of you."

This last was a lie, and not a convincing one. Everyone feared the Aases. Clem Anderson, his hand on his service revolver, he was scared of Charlie, and not only because what Charlie had said was true, and he meant to keep his wife happy. No one had been killed yet, but there was a trend and it wasn't veering toward town picnics. But as of that day, Curtis still wielded some moral authority and Clem felt he needed to protect Rebekah, even if he wouldn't feel this way for much longer.

"Hey, Charlie," he said, "let's step on over to the Traveler's and have this out over lunch. What do you say?"

"Daddy's gonna string you up by your balls, Anderson, if you don't step aside," Charlie told him. As soon as the words left his mouth, Clem was on him. He wrenched his arm behind his back and kicked one of his feet out from under him and Charlie's face slammed into the counter. Before he lifted it he was cuffed and knocked to his knees.

"Goddamn you, Charlie. Why don't you listen? Why do you run your mouth like that? Don't you know people don't want to hear that shit?"

Charlie was so red-faced and angry his blond whiskers looked ablaze. He started ranting then, hurling his threats first at Clem and then at Rebekah and Curtis, and then all around three times more. By the time Clem had ushered him to the door, he was shouting loud enough that the lighthouse keeper might have heard him across the harbor.

"You'll next see me through the flames of hell, you crazy whore! I'll burn this place to the fuckin' ground with you in it!"

Clem was telling him to shut up and was smacking him across the back of his head. "Where's your sense, son? You sound like a madman. Folks can hear you raving."

Charlie craned his face into Clem's. "You don't know what a madman is until you see me. You all better keep the bucket brigade ready. This place is gonna burn bright."

Clem took his club from his belt and hammered Charlie's knee. Rebekah didn't hear another peep from Charlie that day.

In fact, it would be a long time before she heard anything at all. His eruption certainly hadn't lacked for attention. She thought maybe that's all he really wanted. Just another Aas pissing on another light post. She'd have to wait a long while to find out how serious he was. For that misdemeanor in the apothecary, Charlie was given a fine and corralled by his father, who couldn't have predicted he would go so far. But even as he checked his son's behavior, Marcus saw something in his actions that he liked. He saw a boy ready to take what needed to be taken. He saw his heir.

Though he never would take a thing from Rebekah. She kept the Shivering Timber from his claws. Within a month of Charlie's arrest, she'd not only shuttered it, but also sent the remaining molls on their way to better days with what she called severance. A thousand dollars per girl, five thousand dollars in all. And passage out of Gunflint.

It was not long after all this happened that I came to town. By the time I arrived Gunflint had changed its collective mind radically about Rebekah. She was still thought touched. Was still eccentric and nearly impossible to know. And people still regarded her as cold. But she was also considered a kind of spellbinder or witch, someone not to be trifled with. Someone who could outstare the pastor or the sheriff or an Aas. Even the moon.

All of which is to say that Rebekah was capable of anything. Maybe Gus was right about her and the letters. About everything.

The first time Gus saw the plane he thought it was the evening star orbiting back into view. Hesperus, his father had called it the evening before, as they stood on the lake fetching water. Before he heard it, Gus saw it bank over the tree line and level out, catching the setting sun on the floats and the silver fuselage. And then he heard it coming in his direction, still a mile down the shore.

He watched, stunned, as the plane seemed to fall right into his ski tracks far off in the distance and ride them toward him. He stood in the shadows offshore, feeling his breath leave him all at once and his pulse throbbing in his neck. He glanced toward the shack, smoke rising from the chimney into the eventide. Then he studied the keener darkness along the shore. *My God,* he thought, and threw his poles behind him and pushed through the unpacked snow for that darkness. He was standing under and behind one of the trees as the plane flew past, so loud he felt it in his eyes.

It was Christmas Eve. There was a hare to butcher.

When he poled up to the shack he found his father standing out by the water hole, staring up at the sky. He wore no coat. No gloves. Only the red hat and his boots and trousers with suspenders over his union suit. Without looking at Gus he said, “That wasn’t Santa Claus.” Then he did look at him. “You got a hare, though.”

Gus planted his poles, bent to unclip his bindings, and stepped out of his skis. “The last supper,” he said.

Harry smiled. “I doubt that. Go on in and grab the lantern. Let’s get that hare ready for the frying pan.”

Harry butchered the rabbit by lantern light outside the shack. The plane wasn’t mentioned. If Harry was nervous or frightened or shaken, he didn’t let on to Gus, who was all of those things and more. Every sound — his father’s blade cutting into the hare, the blood dripping into the snow, his father’s occasional deep breath, the wind rising in the night — put him on edge and sent his eyes darting skyward, even though such gentle sounds bore no resemblance to the roaring plane. He inventoried their camp again. The canoes leaning against the tree on the edge of the clearing. Up in the cache, their ready larder. The saw and maul and their fishing rods up there, too. Everything in its place. His skis and poles planted next to the boats. The stack of firewood still enormous thanks to him. He had a moment of panic at the thought they would not be here long enough to burn it all.

Inside the shack Gus noticed a four-foot spruce leaning in the corner. Harry said, "Merry Christmas, bud." And, sitting on the small table, the twined moose antlers. Gus stood there, unable to move.

Harry took the frying pan from the hook on the wall and went to the stove and started cooking their Christmas dinner. "Get that mandolin out, eh? Play us some carols?" he said over his shoulder. "That tree smells like Christmas, don't it?"

Gus didn't answer. Nor did he get up for his mandolin. Not yet. He just stood there looking at his father and the Christmas spruce in turn, then taking in the rest of the shack. The bearskin on his father's bunk, his daypack at the foot of his own, the pitiful shelves over the stove, his dirty clothes, his father's coat hanging by the door. Seeing it, he took his coat off and hung it over his father's. The tree did smell like Christmas, but never had a day been so at odds with the very concept.

The oleo in the pan was smoking now, so Harry laid the hare in to fry. The smell of the spruce disappeared with the scent issuing from the pan. Gus wanted an orange, a ripe, juicy orange. He'd received one in his stocking every Christmas morning since he could remember. No sooner did he think about that than he felt like a fool. Wishing for an orange. He thought again of the plane flying right at him, straight up the lakeshore. In his mind he could see Charlie Aas's face through the windshield. Of course, that was impossible. Still, he could see Charlie's stupid grin.

"So he's found us," Gus said. He stepped over to his bunk and sat on the edge. "I thought there was no chance of that. I thought we'd just starve to death up here."

Harry turned, holding the frying pan in his hand, and he lowered it so Gus could see fat from the hare spitting out of it. "Starve to death, my ass." He smiled and turned back to the stove, stirring the chunks of rabbit. It did smell fine.

"What's he going to do?" Gus said.

Harry nodded, stirred the meat once

more, and said, "I suppose he'll pay us a visit."

"What does that mean?"

"I suppose he'll land his plane out on the lake. He and whoever's with him will follow your tracks here to the shack. I doubt he'll knock on the door."

"When?"

"Whenever he wants," he said, then salted and peppered the rabbit. "When he's good and ready."

Gus took his mandolin from its case, laid it in his lap, and tried to shake the image of that plane flying toward him. When his father set the plates of food on the small table and called Gus to join him, he just sat on his bunk and stared at the floor.

Harry took three big bites before saying, "You'd better get over here. Don't think I won't eat this whole rabbit."

Still Gus did not get up.

"Come on, bud. Eat a little supper. It's a hell of a sight better than that lutefisk your mother cooks up each Christmas Eve."

Gus started playing then, a sort of medley of Christmas songs. He'd figure out the chords and muddle through the first few bars and then give up and go on to the next. "Silent Night." "What Child Is This?" "God Rest You Merry, Gentlemen." "It Came

Upon a Midnight Clear." Thinking of the words to the songs was a help, but he didn't sing them. Only played round and round. Harry finished eating and sat back in his chair, listening.

After a while Gus started playing something else, a farrago of deep and troubled notes. He played without looking up or stopping. After an hour he got up and ate the plate of hare and wiped his hands on his pants, then played for another hour. The wind now so fierce he could only hear that and his song.

"Snuff out the lantern when you're done," his father said later.

Gus stopped playing. "Go ahead and turn it off now," he said, then kept playing in the dark. By the time he set the mandolin on the floor under his bunk, Harry was snoring soundly. The wind was still rocking the shack, whistling through it, making its own song. Gus couldn't hear the fire ticking in the stove, or his own breathing. So he listened for the words to the song he'd been playing that night. They came to him in those last moments before sleep and were slowly lost in his dreams.

Gus woke up when a candle his father was holding lit the cabin from where he stood at the window. The glass was glowing inside and out, flickering like a strobe light. The wind had quieted but still had some legs. Walking to the window himself, Gus saw his father had the pistol in his free hand.

He looked out the window, pressing his hands around his eyes and against the glass to see better. Out on the bay, a great blazing fire lighted up the thirty yards between it and the shack as well as its own smoke rising into the sky above the flames, now twisting wildly in the wind.

"What is it?" Gus said.

"I'd call it the tip of the iceberg."

They did not light the lantern. In the husky dark of the shack they dressed and drank coffee and Harry reloaded the pistol. The sound of bullets snapping into the clip was paralyzing.

Before the sun rose through the trees they stood out at the remains of the fire, still smoldering and smoking: the scorched skeleton of one of the canoes loaded with all their meat, a can of kerosene smudged black, a dozen unburnt ends of split oak, all of it charred and stinking and ringed and soaking in a slurry of soot and ash and melted snow. Harry knelt and prodded the ashes with a gunwale from the canoe that had broken off outside the fire. Cigarette butts littered the ground around it.

"Add arson to the list of his crimes," he said, slowly circling the ashes, stopping to inspect the boot prints in the snow. Then he walked the trail leading away from the fire for perhaps ten yards and stopped to scan the length of the bay and the woods on either side.

He looked back at Gus standing there. "Well, bud, we'd better find our dancing shoes."

Harry walked back to the ashes and knelt and poked them once more. "Looks like he cooked up all our meat." He pulled a charred-black strip from the steaming heap. "I bet the cache'll be empty." He nodded. "But we should check."

Gus bent at the waist and vomited in the snow, stood upright, then bent and vomited again. He wanted to think it was the dreadful stink coming off the ashes — burnt meat, lacquer from the canoe, the kerosene used to light the fire — but it wasn't this that made him sick. It most certainly was not.

Harry patted his shoulder and led him silently back to shore. He climbed the ladder and peered into the cache for only a second and climbed back down. "Sure enough," he said. "Son of a bitch." He gazed out at the ruins of the canoe. "We should see if we can find the plane. See if they're still around." He looked at Gus.

"One of us should stay here to watch the shack," Gus said.

"I want to stick together. I don't want to leave you alone."

"We're going to starve now," Gus said. "If he doesn't just shoot us first."

"He's not going to shoot us. And we've still got food to eat. He's only testing us. That's good. It's his first mistake."

Gus didn't answer, simply went into the shack to gear up. When he came out he had his pack on, the rifle slung over his shoulder, his snowshoes under his arm. "I'd rather walk than ski."

"Okay," Harry said. He brought his own snowshoes out and they both put theirs on as the sun topped the trees. Side by side they followed the tracks up the bay.

Three men had left them. At the mouth of the bay Harry pointed at an empty fifth of whiskey. The tracks continued north of the bay, though wind had obscured them. Harry stared out across the ice, and Gus did, too.

"That's where I found the antlers," he said, as though they'd just been talking

about this.
"Really?"
"Yeah."
Harry held out his index finger. "I'm thinking we should cross the lake and go north up that shoreline."
Gus had no intuition of his own. "Okay."
"It'll leave us wide open for the time it takes to get across."
Now Gus looked all around. There were hiding places galore in those woods. He felt a moment's panic but subdued it. "I guess we're pretty much out in the open anywhere." He checked around again. "Do you think they're close by?"
"No, I don't. I think they've probably left."
"For now," Gus said, and felt childish about thinking out loud.
"Right. For now."
They began crossing the lake in the tracks of Charlie's gang. Midway, they veered north, and father and son paused. The snow was deep and tough going even in snowshoes and Harry said, "Maybe just keep following the tracks, eh?"
Gus answered by turning into the already trodden snow.
After half an hour they found the grooves of the plane's floats, which spun for the flight out with two parallel sets. There the

men's tracks stepped into packed snow, and Gus noticed how their strides lengthened. He and Harry stepped into the tracks, too, and before long they came to the last of them. More cigarette butts were scattered over the ground here, and Harry muttered that Charlie was a complete pig and then turned and looked back from where they'd come. "I reckon that's a three-mile walk, eh?"

Again Gus didn't answer. He felt somewhat better since they were gone for now and because his father had been correct in predicting they would be; then he tamped the feeling out and told himself to remember exactly what had happened last night. That thought was bad enough, but then he imagined all that was still to come.

Those letters had put a stutter in Gus, and a week passed without my hearing from him. Then it was his wife who called. "Come over for dinner tomorrow," Sarah said. "Gus has been wandering around here like Harry did in the end. I can't stand it. Could you maybe help him get his bearings back? And, Lord knows, I could use the sound of another woman's voice around here. What do you say?"

I should've guessed how much those letters would shake him up. Though I could plainly see Gus's reckoning would require visiting more than his and his father's past, I don't think he did yet. And so those letters pushed him right off course. Got him thinking about older blood. People he'd not thought were involved with the story he was telling.

My initial notion was to decline Sarah's invitation. It was one thing to sip a morning's cup of coffee with Gus at the kitchen table, another altogether to dredge up so many feelings in the evening. But after all the time I'd spent in the shadow of Sarah and Gus's domesticity, sitting vigil by Harry and his sorry thoughts, it would've been rude to say no. So I walked over the next evening.

I should add that Sarah's one of the best ladies this town has. Not only does she keep their woodpile stacked and their home impeccable, not only has she raised two valedictorians of Arrow-head High and kept her husband in starched shirts for twenty-odd years, managed to finish law school at the age of twenty-three, and gotten elected a sixth-district judge right here before her kids were done with grade school, but she did all this without ever crossing another living soul. More than that, she treated folks with a kindness that few of us can even aspire to, let alone reach. She'd certainly been kind to me. More than once she brought me a dinner plate while I sat at Harry's bedside. On the hardest nights — when he was aggrieved and howling like a loon, when his anguish truly found its pitch — she would insist I share a cup of tea with her before I left. She never asked me one question I didn't want her to, either, which might say more about her goodness than anything else.

We were always friendly, but until Harry took to bed we'd never wined and dined each other. Nor even after he did. Sarah and I, we'd say our hellos at the market or the odd social gathering down in town, and wave when our cars passed up and down the Burnt Wood Trail, and we exchanged Christmas cards. But we were not bosom friends. Perhaps this was due to our difference in age or the strangeness attending the fact that I was her father-in-law's ladylove. Certainly it wasn't because I didn't find her charming in every respect. Even so, I admit I wasn't sure what to expect when I went to her home for dinner that night.

Gus was shoveling off their deck when I arrived, their house smelling equally of the fire in the hearth and the soup on the stove. Mushroom, turned out. How she could have known it's my favorite I don't know. But that's another of her gifts.

"It's so nice to have you in our home again," she said. "It's criminal, I know. All winter you've been keeping Gus company and I haven't mustered the courtesy to thank you for it until now."

"Gus and I are just keeping each other company. The pleasure's been as much mine as his."

The table was set as though she were expecting the governor: linens and fine stemware and cloth napkins folded into the shapes of swans, three of each. She knew to mix me a toddy, which she was doing at the counter. She knew to play the music quietly, my hearing not being what it once was.

"Well, there's no excuse in any case." She offered me the toddy. "But you're here now."

I took the glass from her hand.

"Gus told me how much you enjoyed them. I mulled lemon zest rather than simply squeezing a wedge in there." She smiled. "I hope it suits you." She picked up her glass of red wine and raised it. "To righting a wrong. I'm looking forward to this evening."

"Me, too," I said, then took a sip. "Mmmm," I hummed.

She ushered me into the great room and gestured to the chair beside the hearth.

"If I sit there you'll need a crane to get me out," I said, and this was true of the bonded-leather chair as brown as a beaver's pelt and deeper than Lake Superior, sitting under the floor lamp next to the fireplace.

Sarah smiled. "That's Gus's reading chair. He wouldn't admit it, but he very nearly needs his own crane to get out of it these days." She walked to the sofa instead.

I sat down, but before Sarah did, she pulled the screen aside and added two birch logs. The fire flared as she plopped down on the ottoman and took a sip of her wine. She was tapping her toe to the sounds coming from somewhere behind us.

"The music," I said, "it sounds nice."

"That's Gus and Davey Blum. They recorded a CD in Davey's basement some time ago. I guess boys will always be boys, right?" She smiled and had another sip of wine. When I followed suit, she looked straight at me. "I remember what it was like the first few weeks after Greta left for college. Tom, of course, was already gone. I remember how quiet the house was. How strange it was to be here without either of them. Like there was something missing." She smiled again. "Well, something was missing. But we got used to it. Gus started talking more, though it took him a long time to find his voice. The one meant only for me. I think he'd admit that. He started playing more music. That's how he found his bearings. By playing his guitar." She took another deep breath and cocked her head. "I love the sound of a guitar, don't you? And when it's played by a handsome man?"

She fanned herself with her open hand.

It did sound nice, his guitar and Davey Blum's banjo turning melodies together. But it got me to thinking about how Gus would often bring out his guitar while Harry was still here. Usually late at night, while Sarah and I sat on the deck with a cup of tea. Sometimes the guitar was the only thing that could quiet him down enough that he could finally fall asleep. I looked at Sarah, at her beautiful, smiling face, and understood she'd meant the music as a special kindness. "Yes," I said, "I love the sound of a guitar. Thank you for putting it on."

Gus came in through the sliding door. "Hello, hello," he said, stomping his boots on the rug. He unzipped his coat and after he'd hung it on the coatrack he, too, cocked his ear. "Good grief, Sarah, are you playing that CD?"

She looked at me and winked.

Gus walked over to the stereo and hit a button, and the music stopped.

"Party pooper," Sarah said.

"Miss Lovig has heard more than enough of me lately." He stopped at the counter and picked up his toddy before he went over and kissed Sarah on the top of her head. "Berit," he said, and smiled. He admired the fire, which was burning beautifully, then looked again at me. He sat down beside Sarah and put his hand on her knee.

"I'm happy to see you, Gus," I said. "I've missed you this week."

"Thank you for coming. Sarah has cooked us up a right feast, you can be sure of that."

"It smells scrumptious."

She gave his hand a squeeze. "I'd hate to ruin it," she said as she stood up. "Excuse me while I tend to the food. Gus, keep the fire burning."

He stood and watched her straighten her skirt and walk across the great room to the kitchen before he sat back in the brown chair. He put his feet up on the ottoman and raised his mug. "To you, Berit."

I raised my own mug. "And you."

"The new snow'll melt before this time tomorrow," he said. "Why I went out there to shovel I do not know."

"Your father was the same. As soon as it started to fall he started shoveling." I felt the blush rise in my cheeks. "Of course, you know how your father was."

"I never saw him shovel once. At least not that I remember." He smiled. "That was my job." He took another long sip of his drink. "Do I owe you an explanation, Berit?"

"Whatever for?"

"For not being in touch."

"Heavens, no," I said. And I meant it. I admit it had been strange to see him once or twice a week for so many weeks running, then not at all. But certainly he owed me neither explanation nor apology.

He nodded and tried to smile and then glanced at Sarah in the kitchen. "It was those damn letters," he said, speaking into the mug more than to me. He pointed at the counter, where the letters were sitting.

"Should I have kept them from you?"

"No. Of course not. I'm grateful you gave them to me."

"Have you figured out who can make sense of them?"

"Signe will be home next month. For the opening of the historical society. She's offered to have a look at them. I guess there's no hurry." He looked at me. "Right?"

"They've sat there these hundred years."

He smiled.

"For what it's worth, they haunt me, too. I've thought an awful lot about them since they turned up. But I imagine it's a bit harder for you."

He studied them one more time, stood to put a log on the fire, but then saw it didn't need one. "I wish I could say why they're so distracting. I just can't put my finger on it." He sat now on the raised hearth and leaned back against the fieldstones. His eyes caught the fire's flare and shined, and in that instant I saw Harry's eyes and my breath caught. I had to put my fingers to my lips. "Is it strange being here again?" he asked.

"Yes."

He nodded at the far side of the house, into the dark hallway that led to the room where Harry's last days were spent. "I believe it," he said. "I thought maybe you wouldn't want to come. But Sarah —" His voice trailed off and he merely raised his mug in her direction.

"She knows best," I said.

He smiled again.

"I wonder if those letters are bothering you because they make the story even longer, and you might've thought you were nearing the end."

Now his smile faded, even as his face kept a kind aspect. "I guess I figured out some time this winter that the story was never going to end. I didn't want to tell you for fear you'd quit listening."

I didn't have the heart to tell him that I'd known this truth from the first word he uttered. I just hoped he didn't notice I was looking down the dark hallway again.

Sarah called us to the table and ladled three

bowls of soup. She offered wine and water and bread, and butter she'd salted herself. Two candles were guttering above the table. She raised her glass and toasted family and friends and the end of winter, and we ate.

The soup tasted even better than it smelled, and the freshly baked bread was still warm. There wasn't a hair on her head out of place, and if she'd been anyone else I might have resented how effortlessly she managed everything. Instead, I listened to her stories and questions and marveled at how truly good she was.

When we finished the soup she cleared our bowls and plated the main course, baked steelhead trout she'd caught herself. Parsnips mashed with chives. Brussels sprouts sautéed with bacon and garlic. A ramekin of drawn butter on the edge of each plate. More bread. More wine.

The conversation turned to Greta and Tom and the accomplishments of their young lives. I knew them to be outstanding kids. Kind and smart and clever about all the right things. It was no surprise to hear they were doing well, Tom in graduate school in New Hampshire and Greta working as a cub reporter for a weekly newspaper in Minneapolis. It was odd to watch Gus talk about his kids, the expression playing across his face so different from the one I'd grown accustomed to. He was happy, I could see that.

"What was the lucky chance that brought the two of you together?" I asked, surprised, in fact, that I had no idea.

I swear I saw his eyes well up. He took her hand. "Sarah was a ski bunny," he said.

She pushed his hand away but smiled. Almost blushed.

"I swept her off the slopes down in Misquah one winter day."

" 'Swept'? That's the word you'd use?"

He laughed. A hearty and full laugh I don't know that I'd ever heard before. "Okay, okay," he said, lifting his hands in defense. "Maybe it was less of a sweep than a crash."

"He ran right into me," she said, her hand coming up to stifle a laugh. "He had no idea where he was going."

He smiled and said, "Oh, I knew exactly where I was going."

She turned to me. "It was his best move: crashing into a poor girl her first day on skis."

He held his hands up wide to encompass their home, their lives together, that single, splendid evening. "Your Honor," he said, "I rest my case."

She served dessert in front of the fire, a wild-berry cobbler with fresh whipped cream. Gus poured coffee and added a splash of bourbon to his. I declined, though frankly I could have used it. The night was having a cumulative effect on me. All this talk of their lives, their wonderful children, in their warm home. All of it with the dark hallway leading to Harry's last resting place right behind me, and my own past just out the door and up and down the road. I even thought to ask for that whiskey after all.

But Sarah stoked the fire and asked about the historical society, and the whiskey was forgotten.

"It's hard to imagine it being open this time next month," she said.

"Bonnie and Lenora have been working so hard. This town owes them a real debt of gratitude."

Gus said, "Come, now, Berit. This was your idea from the start."

"It was Signe's idea," I said.

"You gave it to her," he told me.

"There's enough thanks to go around," Sarah added.

"Indeed," Gus said.

"I'm glad this came up, actually." I turned to Gus. "Bonnie and I were hoping you'd say a few words at the ribbon cutting."

"A speech?" he said.

"If you'd like to call it that, then, yes, a speech. Anything, really."

"Why?" he said.

"Your family's been here the longest. You teach history at the high school. Everyone respects you." This was Sarah talking, though I could've said the exact same things.

"And," I pointed out, "Signe wants you to. She asked about it a long time ago."

"He'll do it," Sarah said. "He likes to play hard to get but he will."

Gus threw his hands up.

I finished the last of my coffee. "Good," I said. "Everyone will be pleased. Now, Mr. Eide, walk an old lady home?"

He jumped to his feet. "Of course."

Sarah stood as well. "Let's do this again," she said, hugging me and kissing my cheek.

"That dinner was about the best I ever had," I said. "It's a lucky man who gets fed like that."

Gus was already putting on his coat, but he spoke from across the room. "Lucky in every way," he said.

Sarah walked me to the door and helped me into my coat and hugged me again. "You'll be okay to walk home with the snow? Gus could drive you."

"My evening constitutional," I said. "Thank you. Again. A lovely evening."

"It was. Thank you." She turned to Gus. "Be careful in the snow."

We walked home under the vaulted light of the stars. Hardly a word passed between us, which was strange, given our many conversations that winter. Not that either of us minded. I certainly didn't. All around us I could hear the snow melting. Through the trees above I counted my favorite constellations, stars taught to me by Rebekah Grimm of all people, who had learned of them herself from Hosea Grimm. Here the Pleiades were cupped together. There Canis Minor. It's strange to say, but those stars never seemed so close as they did that night. Maybe it was because of the snow melting and dripping from the trees. Maybe, and perhaps more likely, it was simply that there was order in the sky, and order is always comforting.

When we reached my house we stood for a moment on the deck. Gus looked up at the eaves trough and put his hand on the window frame beside the door. He knocked on the rough-sawn cedar siding and nodded. I could see he was thinking of his father. I was, too.

"How was it he came to you, Berit? My father, I mean."

"My goodness," I said.

"We told our story, eh?" He put his hands in his pockets. "I'm curious is all. Don't feel you have to say."

"It wasn't until your parents divorced. Or nearly divorced." I had to think back. "After he built this house."

Gus smiled. "I didn't ask when, Berit. I asked how. I know you're no home wrecker."

I looked up through the trees again, still thinking. The mere act of calling Harry's young face to mind quickened my beating heart. I'd felt so close to him the entire night without ever allowing myself to picture him plainly that to do so standing on the porch was almost more than I could bear. Gus must have sensed it. Or seen it in my face. In any case, he said, "Save that one for another time, eh?"

"No," I said, "it's okay." I looked down from the sky into Gus's eyes, which held stars themselves. "He brought me flowers," I said, "in a manner of speaking. Brought me butterworts he'd picked right outside the old fish house."

There came across Gus's face an expression so expectant and curious that it caused us both to look away. I stepped to the railing and continued. "These weren't the sort of flowers meant to last in a vase. I knew that much, was in fact a sort of expert on butterworts. But that's another story." I closed my eyes against the nighttime, and when I opened them Gus was standing beside me, his hand on mine. I continued without shifting toward him. "I was never so happy in my life. Never. Even without knowing what the flowers meant. Without knowing what his standing there — here, right here, I mean — without knowing what any of it meant."

"He brought you flowers. Beginning and end of story," Gus said, as much to himself as to me. Certainly no question was hidden there.

"It was summertime. Early evening. He was still in his work clothes." I shut my eyes again but what I saw behind them this time was Harry lying in bed all these years later. I opened my eyes quickly and looked up at Gus. "It was the only thing I ever wanted in my life, Gus. The only thing. And there it was. There he was. We were together from that day on."

"That's the best story I've heard in a long time, Berit." He took a step back. "I know it wasn't easy for you, coming to dinner tonight. I said so to Sarah but she insisted.

It's her way, you know."

"I was happy to come."

"We were happy to have you." He took another step. "I'll see you this week."

"Very good. Have a good night."

"Good night." He smiled and started down the deck steps.

"Gus," I said.

He stopped and turned back.

"Will you really say a few words at the opening?"

The starlight caught his smile. "Of course. Anything for you."

Then he walked up the driveway under the same light that lit his smile. His stride was long and easy over the new snow. His hands were deep in the pockets of his corduroy trousers.

After Gus turned down the road, I walked around my deck and stood at the railing listening to the purling river. If I studied the distance hard enough I could make out snow terraces alongshore. Under the light of the night sky everything looked to be keeping secrets.

I wondered, standing there, why I had become so intent on lives of no relation to me. I tried to picture myself standing there in the night but could not. The next morning or the one after, if I passed myself on the Lighthouse Road, would I recognize myself then? Or was I only this now: an old lady alone in the middle of the woods with nothing but starlight and the quiet river? Who would I call if I had to? Who would hold my hand if I needed to be consoled? Those letters stacked on Gus's counter? Had anyone ever written one to me? Had I ever sent one?

I closed my eyes against the night. There was Rebekah sitting in her rocker. Gus's grandmother. My charge. All that time with her and I had what to show for it beyond some modest financial security? Hardly even any memories of my own. And of those I did have, how many were tethered to the Eides? Did any of them belong to me alone? Even this long winter now, all the hours spent with Gus and his reckoning, how much of it had truly been mine? Though it's true I wanted to hear his story — for a thousand different reasons — it was also true I was listening to his stories rather than recalling any of my own.

Motherless. Fatherless. Husbandless. Childless. I was all of these things. If I hadn't chosen my fate, I'd at least — over the years — made peace with it. But to live a life without so much as a story of my own? My God, it seemed nigh impossible. I had my years with Harry, yes, true. And they were good years, to be sure. And happy. Very. But even that epoch of my life closed without a proper ending. Love just vanished into the woods. All the nights I'd stood at this same railing since, shivering against the bitter cold, I'd wept for his absence by myself. *Alone.* I'd never told another living soul of my sadness. I could hardly admit it to myself. Someday — likely someday soon — when I went the way of Harry and before him Rebekah and before her Odd Eide, who would weep at my passing? Who would listen to stories about me? Who would tell one?

I opened my eyes. Clouds had scuttled in and the river was now gone to darkness. Gone but for its murmuring. I wiped the tears from my eyes. Was it warmer even than it had been on the walk home? Was this winter finally breaking?

I turned to face the house. I caught no reflection in the sliding glass door, not in the darkness, not even as I stepped to it and pulled it open. Inside, I sat and took off my boots and wiped my eyes again in hopes of righting myself.

Gus would call in a day or two. We would meet for coffee or lunch and he would tell me how it ended. Once he finished, I would tell him why his father had done all the things he'd done. I would tell Gus things he didn't know because I loved him, I could see that now. I loved him because I loved his father, and because his father never told him where all this started, I would do so myself.

They walked back from the northern end of the lake and entered the bay and passed the smoldering remains. Inside the shack Harry stoked the stove and put water on for breakfast. It was unfathomable to Gus that his father could think of food, or of anything except the men who'd come in the night.

"Who was with him?" Gus asked.

Harry stood over the stove. "Probably Len Dodj. Maybe Len and Matti Haula."

"Matti Haula's an old man."

"An old man without a pension. I reckon Charlie's offered him a fair price for his time and effort."

"What does he have against you?"

"Nothing that I know of."

Gus wanted his father to turn around. He wanted to see his face. "Len Dodj?"

Now Harry did turn. "Len isn't much more than a wood tick what climbed up Charlie's shorts." He poured oatmeal into their bowls, brought them to the table, and sat down. With his foot he nudged the second chair out, but Gus stayed on his bunk. His father's face had given nothing away.

"We're gonna need to hunt," Harry said. "See about getting a deer. This" — he gestured at their meager provender on the shelf behind him — "won't keep us fed for long."

"Hunt?"

"Or fish."

"How about getting the hell out of here?"

"And going where?"

"Home."

"Home." Harry shook his head slowly. "Right."

"We can't stay here."

"Where are we?" Harry said, maybe too sharply.

Gus reached under his sleeping sack and felt the book of maps, both his father's and his own. He thought of the days he'd spent alone in the wilderness, charting what he could of it for the express purpose of escaping this place when the time came. It seemed hardly possible that it now had arrived. But it had.

Gus almost pulled the maps from under his bedding but stopped. He and his father stared at each other for a full minute. Too long. So long they looked away simultaneously and spoke at the very same moment. Harry started to say, "We have to think clearly," as Gus said, "I know where we are." Their eyes met and there lapsed another moment of strained silence.

Harry said, "You know where we are, eh?"

Gus kept staring at him.

"You've been out scouting, is that it? In the middle of all this country, you've put us on the map?"

"I don't think you're one to talk about maps."

"No?"

"Right now I don't think you should talk about anything."

Harry nodded his head as though to admit this truth.

"I don't think you have any idea what you're doing. I think you're crazy." The truth was coming out fast as a spring freshet. Gus felt no control over the things he wanted to say. Or what he said. "You've made a fool out of me."

"Tell me one thing that's happened that I didn't say would."

"Are you kidding?"

"Were you surprised Charlie showed up?"

"Was I —"

"Were you surprised it got cold? That it snowed?"

"You can't be serious."

"Are you snug as a goddamn bug in your bunk over there?"

"It was a miracle we found this place. A miracle *I* found it."

"Don't throw that word around."

" 'Miracle'?" Gus was incredulous. "There're more miracles up here than there are trees. The biggest miracle of all — if that's the word — is that you don't see any of it. The danger you've put us in. How pointless this all is. You're blind. None of this is worth dying for." He thought he might suffocate, his breath was coming so short. "You can give up if you want, but I'm not gonna. I don't want to die. I won't." He went back to his bunk and collapsed, burying his face in his hands to dam the flood.

When he looked up some minutes later his father had his own face in his hands. Gus surveyed the shack, making a quick inventory of their supplies. Charlie and his boys had burned a hundred or more pounds of meat out on the lake. All that remained of their larder sat on the shelf behind Harry. Rice and oats and coffee and half a sack of dried fruit. Some sugar and salt and chocolate bars. Enough to last them a month on starvation rations. Their cookware. Buckets. Tools. Guns. The packs and rope and their clothes, still dirty. Shabby socks and long johns and three shirts, worn hard and missing buttons.

Now Gus looked under his arm at where the maps were bunched up under his sleeping sack. He closed his eyes and traveled in his darkness down the lake and through the woods and for two days beyond. He could picture the clearing in the woods along that creek where he'd twice strung up his canvas and stoked fires. A day and a half south, half a day east, and where was he? Still camped between two spruce trees. Still a long way from home.

Gus looked over at the bearskin on his father's bunk. The moose antlers he'd found across the lake. The Duluth packs hanging from nails on the wall, almost swaying over a draft coming through the shack's pathetic walls. He looked at his father sitting there like a fool. He gritted his teeth against his anger.

And what if Gus had a paved highway between this godforsaken hovel and their house on the river? A full tank of gas and a sack of warm donuts and a thermos of hot coffee in the cab? He could drive home in three hours. But where would he be then?

His anger seemed almost flushed away by a sudden and very heavy weariness. He got up and gathered some of his clothes and laid them on his sleeping sack. He took one of the Duluth packs from the wall and put it there as well. The pot of water on the stove whistled, and Gus took it from the heat and set it on the table. His father still hadn't moved.

He would take the handgun and a pack with the tent and his sleeping sack and enough food for a week. He would strap on the hatchet and saw. He would travel on snowshoes but bring skis, too. A change of clothes. The field glasses. He looked around the shack again. He would leave behind his mandolin and the books and cribbage board. Also the maul. Travel light. Leave right away.

He moved about the shack heavyhearted and slow of foot. Before he packed food he paused to eat the oatmeal Harry had poured earlier. The water just warm. He mixed both bowls and brought the second to his father, who merely set it on the floor between his feet.

What could have been going through his mind? What decisions were left to make? The notion that a fight in the wilderness would be fair no longer had any purchase.

They were marked and immobile. Charlie had the eyes and means of an owl. They were moles.

Gus put his empty bowl aside and took another inventory of his provisions laid across his bunk. He'd need a canteen. And a lantern? Not essential, he thought. He rolled his sleeping sack and tied it off, which reminded him to bring rope. Glimpsing the maps now sitting on his bunk, he remembered once more the days he'd spent making them. It was the only thing he'd done up here. Make the maps and stack the wood and kill the bear. It was hard to believe that the night of the bear was only — what? — six or seven weeks before. Hard to believe how much he'd changed since then. He pictured himself in the woods, lifting the compass to check his direction.

The compass. The goddamn compass.

He spotted it on the shelf behind the stove. *One* compass. Another sitting at the bottom of that stream way back where they started getting lost. One compass and two men, one intent to stay, the other to go.

Maybe he could get home without it. For all the time he'd spent facing south and east, maybe he could tell those directions by sniffing them out and get home by instinct, with help from the sun and the stars. Maybe. But what about those wide-open spaces? The ten-mile lakes and deep rivers and streams winding through the cold and relentless woods? All of those places came back to him as a terrifying memory, and he knew that without the compass he was little better than a blind man.

Gus sat down on the bunk again and looked over at his father. "We only have one compass. I'm going to take it when I leave." Harry still did not look up. "I'm going to finish getting my things together and go this morning. I don't see any reason to wait around here."

Finally, his father's face fixed on him. "Okay," he said, "we can go. But I think we ought to wait till tomorrow. We need to put ourselves right. Make sure we take only what we need."

"I've already figured that out. One light pack. Skis and snowshoes. I'm leaving today."

"Listen, Charlie won't come back so soon. The reason he burned all our meat is because he wants us to suffer. To panic. He's taunting us."

Gus just stared at him for a moment. "I don't really care when Charlie's coming back or what he's doing. I just want to leave. Today."

"We've gone long enough without a plan. That's my fault, I know it. And I'm sorry. But let's put the right packs together and think carefully about what we're doing. About how we're going to get home. We can leave tomorrow morning, the minute the sun comes up."

When Gus didn't respond, Harry stood up, took the pot from the table, and added water for more coffee, then said, "Let's have a look at those maps you've been drawing."

There was little to plan or do. They studied Gus's maps and compared them with the ones Harry had drawn months and years earlier, the books opened like two songs being sung, each over the other. For different reasons both of them worried Gus, but neither as much as the days that surely lay before them.

Harry cleaned and oiled the Remington and the pistol before gathering his own kit. They were both packed and ready before lunch without so much as a word between them. After they ate — rice and dried fruit, a chocolate bar for Gus — Harry brought the maul in from outside. He lined up the moose antlers on the floor, then stood there and looked at them for a long time. What he was pondering was something Gus never even guessed about, but he himself could not imagine those beasts' anguish as their antlers locked. The horrible dance they must have enacted before tripping over each other and falling onto the shore, their eyes just a foot apart. What was one seeing in the other? How hotly did their breath mix in the small space between them? Gus scrutinized the antlers, and what a miracle it was how perfectly they were interwoven, how strong the fibers were that held together the symmetry of their entanglement. More than anything he wondered at their fear when the wolves finally came. For surely they would have come.

Harry swung the maul almost in concert with Gus's final thought. Three swings it took to splinter the antlers apart. Their skulls cracked and rotten teeth scattered across the wood floor. The bone plates at their base split like logs. His father picked the pieces up and laid them into the stove, where the marrow hissed deliciously.

Harry set the maul beside the door and readied a fishing line, then put on his coat and grabbed the wooden bucket and went outside. Gus watched him go to the hole he'd cut in the lake ice, pull off the covering, sit down on the upturned bucket, and drop his line in the water, as if this were just another day of fishing. He stood at the window and watched for an hour, maybe two, until his father came in without anything to show for his effort but two gallons of frigid water.

Gus could not have imagined the depths of his father's thoughts as he sat out there fishing in the cold. Nor the expanse of his memory, nor the horrible things held within it. It was no fault of Gus's that this was true. No fault at all.

Instead, Gus reckoned how impossible it seemed that his father could have spent all these hours and days and weeks up here without giving a single thought to how they would get out. To have left as they did, Gus could see that. Harry had been betrayed and cuckolded, so his anger was explanation enough. But to have had all the time in the world to parse things out and come up with nothing, to have failed to see how he'd endangered them in so many different ways, that seemed — and always would, even with the benefit of thirty-odd years — the most intractable, unforgivable fact of their misbegotten adventure. And then there were all the years afterward, with hardly ever a word between them about their time up on the borderlands. What had those decades of silence actually meant?

They ate an early dinner of rice and Gus filled the stove with wood he'd cut. Before it was dark, they turned in for the last time in the shack. Gus did not dream, at least not that he remembered. But every night after, for years and even sometimes still, he dreamt of fire.

The window shattered and the floor beneath the stove and his father's bunk erupted in flames, the suddenness of all that light and heat meteoric. Gus fell from his bunk as Harry jumped through the fire with the bearskin over his shoulder. "Put your pants on!" he shouted. The flames already governed the shack. "Grab your coat and boots and get the hell out of here!"

Harry had his arm up shielding his face. "My Lord!" He ran over to Gus. "You've got five seconds!" he cried above the pealing flames. "Take the sleeping sack, the pack, and get moving."

Gus didn't need any encouragement. In the time it took his father to bark his orders he'd put his pants and boots on and pulled his sleeping sack free. He had one hand on the door and the other on the Duluth pack, but the door wouldn't budge. He put his shoulder into it three times in rapid succession, then stood back and kicked it with the heel of his right boot, but it didn't give an inch.

Harry was standing beside him, still in his long johns but already wearing his boots and his red hat. "Stand aside," he hollered, his face glimmering with sweat. Even before Gus stepped back his father was swinging the maul at the door. Only because he'd used it on the moose antlers was it in the shack at all.

He swung wildly as the shelf above the stove collapsed in flames. Harry's bunk was engulfed and his sleeping sack blazing. After three or four heavy swings the door flew off its hinges. A piece of split oak had been wedged between the handle outside and the doorframe. The cold air that came rushing in whipped the flames up to the ceiling, and the trusses lit like tinder.

Both Eides fell out the door, Harry pushing his son forward. Under the weight of his pack Gus tripped in the snow, fell on his back, and stared up at the shack. The glare of the fire bright in the doorway. Smoke seething from chinks in the rough-sawn walls. His father started back inside and Gus hurried to his feet and raced to the door himself, lifted his arm over his mouth, and stepped inside.

For all the smoke, he couldn't tell where his father was. The heat was hellacious and he jerked his coat and his mittens from the peg by the door, straddled the threshold, and screamed "Dad!" but couldn't hear his own voice above the howling flames and the pops and cracks of the old wood.

One of the joists crashed down and sprayed fire in every direction, blasting Gus out of the doorway and onto his back in the snow again. When he looked up his father was beside him, the bearskin in one hand, the Remington in the other.

"Is the pistol in your pack?" Harry asked.

Gus nodded yes.

"Loaded?"

Gus nodded again.

"And the maps?" Harry said.

"Yes."

They had to shout in order to be heard over the roar.

"What else you got in there?"

"Tent. Change of clothes." Gus unbuckled the Duluth pack quickly and dug through it. "Rope. Field glasses. Canteen. Compass. Saw and hatchet. Some chow."

"Here." Harry magically produced one handful of dried fruit and another of chocolate bars and stuffed them into the pack. When another ceiling truss crashed to the floor, Harry flinched and looked around blindly, then turned to face the darkness. "Goddamnit," he said. "Goddamnit." He checked the Remington and realized the cartridge was empty. He dropped the gun, stepped toward the burning shack, paused for a heartbeat, then made a second dash inside.

Gus followed, shouting for him to stop. But in the inferno his father either couldn't hear or wouldn't listen and Gus could only stand there, the heat from the fire masking the bitter chill of the air. He could feel the first on his face, the other at his back.

It was only a few short seconds before Harry dove from the doorway and landed on his coat, which he'd covered his head with. Standing up, he tossed Gus the ammo and pulled his coat on. Then he grabbed the snowshoes from the snowbank where they'd been lodged, handed Gus a pair, stepped right next to him, and spoke softly into his ear, as if to keep these instructions secret from the flames.

"Put those on. Make sure everything's in the pack and get over to the oaks as fast as you can." He reached into the pack and pulled out the Ruger, checked that it was loaded, flipped on the safety, and handed it to him. He leaned again to Gus's ear. "Wait for me in that blind you were using. Don't make a sound. Keep alert. Be ready."

Gus did exactly as his father said. He stuffed the bearskin and sleeping sack in the pack, cinched it up and buckled the straps, pulled it on his shoulders. He slipped the tumpline over his forehead and looked around to make sure he had everything while he strapped the holster around his waist.

And then his father was gone. Gus had no idea if he'd disappeared back into the shack or out into the woods or simply turned to smoke himself. Panic welled up but he quelled it as fast as he'd felt it and ran through the weakening glow of the fire until he was halfway across the lake, where there was no light at all. He ran hard, his lungs burning, the snowshoes landing softly and soundlessly on the snow, the Duluth pack clumping against his back. He glanced over his shoulder twice but saw only darkness and the distant fire blooming beyond it.

When he reached the shore he stood behind the nearest tree. Slumped over with his hands on his knees, he finally caught his breath and looked back across the bay. He felt the wind on his face and soon could smell the fire, faint and almost pleasant from a quarter mile away, and growing even as he watched. He heard the boom of the roof collapsing, and in that same exhalation the cache and the closest trees were set ablaze. The glare of the flames was now even brighter and he thought by some miracle he could feel their heat from where he stood. Was such a thing possible? Through all of that cold, could the heat abide?

He peeled the tumpline from his forehead and let the pack slide from his shoulders. He checked the pistol himself, then sat on the pack with his back against the tree. Could he really have been sound asleep in his bunk ten minutes ago?

It might've been an hour later and the fire still burned. The shack was rubble except for the fieldstone chimney. The cache was gone and two trees next to it stood naked of boughs, totems to that unholy night.

Shocked, sitting there against the tree, he felt a strange relief. For the first time since they left home in October, there was only one thing to do. It might be impossible, and they might get killed or die along the way, but there was no uncertainty anymore. Go south and east until they got home or died. Go fast and don't ever look back.

Gus had hardly moved. He sat shivering against the tree, staring as the firelight across the bay faded in gradations until there was none left at all. He looked up at the sky and saw only the black dome of the cloud-covered night. He reached for the holster and gripped the Ruger. There was nothing left to think about. There was only the waiting, so he closed his eyes and did.

What came next was a voice not his father's calling out of the night, from the frozen bay. There was a loud, wolflike howl and then Charlie Aas shouted, "Now for the fun part, you lousy sons of bitches."

Gus pressed his face against the bark of the tree and felt his pulse from his temples to the soles of his feet. He peeked over his shoulder and saw him silhouetted against the firelight perhaps fifty yards offshore. Gus could see him switch a rifle from one shoulder to the other.

"All these years you fool Eides have bird-dogged with the Riverfish clan," he shouted, his voice seeming nearer than his body, "and still you don't know any better than making a trail like a circus leaving town? Old Freddy could track a trout up a stream, that one. But a blind man could follow these tracks. A blind man in the pitch dark." Charlie played a flashlight over Gus's tracks, shining the beam left and right, then lifting it into the woods, where Gus pulled his face behind the tree with the rest of him. The light couldn't reach him but he was glad when Charlie turned it off.

"Of course," Charlie called, then moved forward. "It's only one of you pucker-assed pansies." He switched the light back on and circled the beam all around; then it went out again. "I ain't been shot yet. That must mean it's young Eide on the yonder shore." He cupped his ear and took several more steps toward the shore. "That right? You hiding in those trees, Gus?" Now he straightened up. "You're every bit the candy ass your old man is, ain't you, now? The world hates a gutless man."

He lowered the gun to his waist and pointed it into the woods. "You got the dark on your side. I'll grant that much. But soon the day will break. If you haven't learned a goddamn thing playing woodsmen, I bet you figured that out." He kept moving. "Tell me something, Gussie, you spend much time up here thinking about my daughter with your hand in your pants? You little fuck, you. You poisoned that girl. Yes, you did." He took another step, and now Gus could make out the brim of his hat and the tufted fur of his open coat. "I'm gonna turn you into a damn eunuch. I got a bowie knife here could cut the balls off a dinosaur."

Gus took a gulping breath and thought surely Charlie could hear the drumming of his heart and see the terrified whites of his eyes. Without moving his head, he looked to see the clouds breaking up and the starlight showering down. He slowly lowered his hand onto the pistol grip.

"You've been given every disadvantage," Charlie barked. "I understand that. But the world makes no exceptions and neither do I. You should know it ain't your fault you got found out there. Not one little bit. I want you to die knowing that much. But you should know it was your old man letting you down again. See, it was the smoke from his fire that put us onto you. We been hunting you boys for three weeks now. Might not've found you, either, if you'd saved your fires for the dark, like we did."

Gus snapped the holster, slipped the Ruger out, and held it against his leg. After a long, slow breath he flipped the safety off, then slid down the tree trunk and lay prone on the snow behind the Duluth pack. He elbowed up onto it and raised the pistol. With his left eye closed he sighted Charlie Aas out on the ice.

"Who killed that bear, Gus? I brought a couple chunks home and had your mama cook it up for me. We had a real romantic time of it, she and I. We drank wine and supped and then spent the night tangled in your daddy's sheets. Of course, it wasn't the first time I bent her over that particular bedspring. Won't be the last, neither." He was silent for a moment. "Your sister made us breakfast in the morning. I thought about giving her a go, too."

Gus blinked and took a deep breath before resting his finger on the trigger, thinking of his mother and of Signe and of this man being in their home. He squinted tightly and peered down the pistol barrel.

"That you moving around, youngster? Hiding behind a rock there?"

Gus aimed the pistol a third time and tensed his finger on the trigger. In the starlight he had him dead to rights.

"There's not enough darkness to swallow your ass up. No rock big enough to shield it. Didn't your daddy tell you the only thing you really needed to know?" Now he yelled, "I am the czar and master of these fucking woods! Everybody knows what you don't, Eide! Even your fool dad! And for that you will suffer greatly!" He howled again as he had out on the ice. "But I will wait until morning, so you can see the glint of my blade and the shine of my eyes as I smile down upon you." Charlie shined his flashlight into the trees once more, then turned slowly.

Gus shivered and bristled and took another deep breath as he steadied his gun hand with the other. He sighted Charlie again and closed his eyes, then heard five rapid shots and opened them to see Charlie drop to his knees. Then Gus closed his eyes again, dropped the pistol, and curled up behind the tree.

He thought of those hours often. Too often, he was sure. There remained times, Gus told me, when he felt he was still brooking that darkness, times when a decade of his life seemed a trifle compared with the passing of that single night on the shore of the bay. But it must have ended, that night, because he remembered all the whiteness — the drifting snow, the pressing clouds hiding the rising sun, the frost on the pistol's barrel — and how none of it, not even taken altogether, could bleach the blackness from that daybreak.

And he remembered his father crawling on hands and knees, from the direction of the blind that Gus hadn't even managed to get to. In the hoary first light Harry put a finger to his lips and came up next to him and pulled the bearskin from the Duluth pack and wrapped himself in it, then laid his head back against the tree trunk and took a deep breath. "You all right?"

Gus squeezed his eyes shut.

"Hey!" his father said, the sound of his voice barely audible above the breeze. "Look at me."

Gus opened his eyes. His father's face was only inches from his own.

"Are you all right?"

Gus opened his eyes wider.

Harry grasped the back of Gus's neck. "Did you see Charlie? Did he find you?"

My father let me kill him, Gus thought. He felt dizzy and closed his eyes against the whirl and didn't open them until he was steady again. His father still had him by the neck, so he shook himself free.

"Did he find you?"

Gus lunged on top of him then and tried to punch him but landed only a glancing blow. Harry swept his other arm from under the bearskin to hug him fiercely. "Hey, *hey,* it's okay," he whispered, even as Gus struggled to get free.

"Pull yourself together," his father said. "It's me."

Gus lay back against the tree again.

"Look at me. You've got to tell me, did that asshole find you?"

Gus remembered Charlie's awful voice, his shocking threats, the gunshots. "I shot him."

"You what?"

"I hate you."

"Gus, what are you saying?" He grabbed his son by the front of the coat and pulled him close. "What did you do?"

"I killed him!" Gus shouted.

"Hey," Harry whispered, slipping his hand over Gus's mouth. "Calm down, damnit." He let his hand fall. "Keep quiet."

"How could you let me?"

Harry pulled the Ruger from where he saw it in the snow, flipped the cylinder open, and saw all six bullets. He closed the cylinder, spun it, opened it again. "Did you reload or something?"

Gus looked at the pistol and then out on the bay. The only relief from its grayness was the line of black trees in the distance beyond. He wiped his eyes and tried again, but Charlie Aas wasn't there.

"Gus, look at me. You didn't shoot him. Charlie's still out there."

"But the gunshots? I saw him go to his knees."

"You heard the Remington." Harry grabbed it and showed him the spent ammo. Only one shot remained in the chamber.

"That was me shooting."

"Who'd you shoot?"

"Don't worry about that."

"Did you kill Len Dodj and Matti Haula?"

"You don't know what you're talking about. Just be quiet and listen."

"We have to hide. If Charlie's still out there, we've got to hide." The panic wasn't something he felt as much as he tasted it, bilious and hot. He again imagined Charlie's bowie knife carving the night apart.

Now Harry slapped him. "Look at me, boy!" This wasn't whispered. He took Gus's face in his hands. "Did Charlie find you? Did you really see him? You must have, right?"

"I don't know," Gus said.

"You don't know what?"

"If he saw me. But I sure saw him. He was standing right over there." He pointed. "I shot him."

"You did not. You didn't even fire the gun."

Gus closed his eyes.

"Look at me, Gus. Tell me, what did he say?"

"He said he was going to kill us, so I killed him."

Harry let go of his face, then slumped against the tree. "You didn't kill him, bud.

Charlie's still out there."

"Then we have to hide. He's going to kill us."

"Okay," Harry said, but not to Gus. Once more he checked the pistol and the rifle, wiped the snow from them, and blew through each barrel.

Gus noticed his father had no pants on, only the threadbare bottom half of his union suit and his boots and snowshoes. He was wearing his coat and his red hat, thank God. His mittens he'd thrown down on the snow.

"Okay," Harry said again. "Okay." He took a long look up and down the shore and back into the woods he'd just crawled out of.

"We have to hide," Gus said again. "Now. We can go back to that tree, where you found me that morning after the bear. We can hole up for a day or two and wait."

"Wait for what?" Harry stood and wrapped the bearskin around him like a skirt. "Give me your belt. And the holster."

Gus took them off and watched his father cinch up the bearskin with it.

"We're going to find Charlie's plane before he takes off."

Gus didn't budge from his spot against the tree. "Who did you shoot?"

Harry knelt and buckled the pack shut, then slung it over his back. "We're going to find his plane and we're going to find Charlie. He can't move that fast, not without snowshoes."

Gus still didn't move as his father stood. "Did you kill them?"

"Don't worry about that." Harry handed him the Remington. "Carry this. And remember, there's only one shot left."

Gus wouldn't cry in front of his father. He simply would not. He'd vowed that he wouldn't and he hadn't and he wasn't about to now, much as he felt like it. So he bit down and said, "Why didn't Charlie shoot us when we ran out of the shack? He could've shot us right then."

"Charlie's a pack of rabid goddamn wolves that ain't even hungry. That's why he didn't kill us then. He didn't shoot us for the same reason he burned our meat. For the same reason he sicced his daughter on you last fall." He looked squarely at Gus. "Charlie thinks the world exists for his amusement, and his thoughts are every bit as crooked as the Burnt Wood River. Bear that in mind till all this is done." He took a frantic survey of the woods around them before turning back to his son. "Plus, he's been outed. Everybody in Gunflint knows his game now, so whatever crookedness he didn't know he had in him, well, it'll come to the surface now. He'll play this like a man with nothing to lose, which is what he is. And that's why we have to get after him."

Gus thought of Charlie's first claim out on the bay, that now was when the fun really started. "To kill him?"

"You'd rather he killed us?"

Gus didn't answer.

"Because he will, sure as the day is long. And he'll take insane pleasure in doing it. So I suggest you listen up and clear your head. Get it straight. We're going to find Charlie, and we're going to end this. We'll start with his goddamn plane."

Harry stood up, adjusted the Duluth pack, and rested a hand on the pistol. "I heard his plane come from the north last night. Likely he landed on the south end of the lake, so let's get down there."

"You go."

"Gus?"

"I'm not going anywhere."

"Get up, bud."

"You're a liar." He spoke softly. "You're as crazy as he is."

"Do you have your mittens? Put them on," Harry said. "You get frostbit, your hands'll be worthless. Put your mittens on and get up."

Gus jumped to his feet and sprang again

at his father, punching him in the chest with both fists. Harry stumbled but didn't fall and instead stepped right back in to Gus. He took him in his arms and hugged him so tight it squeezed the breath out of him. "Someday you'll understand all of this. You will. I promise. You have no reason to, but right now you've got to trust me."

Gus pushed him away. "I don't trust you. I hate you. I hate all of this."

"I do, too. I do. But we're in it now, right up to our necks. And I'm not about to leave you here."

Gus sat back down and leaned against the tree.

Harry knelt again. "Do you remember, way back when, that I said you were my advantage?"

Gus didn't so much as look up.

"This is what I was talking about. You are my advantage now."

"What're you talking about?" He put his hands up over his ears. "I can't listen to you anymore. Go. Jesus Christ, get away from me!"

"He wants us split up, Gus. That's the only chance he's got left."

"Why don't you ever listen? I couldn't care less about your fight with Charlie. I don't even care what happens next. Just leave me alone."

"You can't stay here, Gus. We have to get the hell moving. Listen to me, bud!"

"You listen." Gus finally looked up at him. "Go to hell. Just go to hell."

"You have to come, Gus. You can't stay here. This is no place to be."

"Well, it's where you brought me."

Harry took the pack from his shoulders, pulled the sleeping sack out, and tossed it to him. Then he handed him the belt and holster. "Don't move. Don't start a fire." He buckled the pack again, put it on his shoulders, shook his head, and slipped it off again. "If you have to run, take the pack. Better still, stay here and don't move. I'll be back."

I visited Rebekah Grimm the day before she died. She had a private room at the rest home, a single bed pushed up against one wall. A small black-and-white television on a shelf under a window that overlooked a grassy, man-made knoll where Norway pines had died not long after they were planted. There was a painting of a schnauzer dog hanging on the wall above her bed, a mirror hanging over a small chest of drawers. Hairbrushes and bottles of lotions and perfumes sat atop the chest, giving off a lovely fragrance. Getting to her room was always a relief, as other rooms reeked of soiled bed linens and heaping ashtrays, the stench leaching into the hallway.

The day before she passed, she was sitting in her bed and staring out the window. A sorry view, compared with the one she'd had for so many years from the third floor of the apothecary. Even though she was fully blind by then, this irrelevant fact saddened me more than any other about her condition and situation.

She always kept herself neat. Whereas most of the folks waiting out the last years of their lives here were happy to spend all day in their pajamas, or even less, Rebekah dressed every day, bathed twice a week, and, when Bonnie Hanrahan's daughter came for just this purpose, had her hair done each Saturday. But the day before she died she was especially done up, in a pink cotton dress and a white cardigan sweater and the pink cloche hat she saved for only the best occasions. Her fingernails had been painted to match the hat. She held a black patent-leather purse in her hands.

"Well, aren't you a picture of pretty?" I said.

"I wonder if you'll take me to lunch, Miss Lovig." All those years after we met, that's what she still called me.

"Are you sure?" I said. "Did you run this past Janice?" This was the head nurse at the home.

"Am I a prisoner here?"

"Of course you aren't."

"Then I'd like you to take me to lunch at the Traveler's Hotel." She lifted herself from the bed and into her wheelchair, which was required in the halls of the home. "If you would."

Once we were seated, she ordered tea and rabbit stew and spread her napkin across her lap.

"This is the first time you've been out in a long while," I said.

"I don't feel the need all that often."

"Until today." And this was a question.

She fingered the napkin on her lap and turned her eyes up to the window. They were as milky as the pitcher of cream waiting beside her tea. "When I die," she said, "I would like to be buried in the cemetery, under a marble pillar with the words 'I Have Loved' inscribed beneath my name. Lenny's boy, Mace Washburn, has been paid for this. He understands my wishes."

I didn't — couldn't — respond.

"Is that too much to ask?"

"Why are you talking about this now?"

She wiped the corners of her mouth with her napkin. "Miss Lovig, I'm as old as the town itself. If I don't die tomorrow, I will soon enough. I'd like to have this settled before then."

"Of course."

She sipped her tea and wiped her lips again. "And please make sure my grave is as far from Hosea's as possible. Would you do that?"

"I will."

"When I'm buried, make sure I'm well dressed. I'd prefer to be wearing a hat — this hat, my pink cloche." She reached for her purse on the edge of the table, opened it, felt inside, and pulled out a photograph. "Make sure this goes down with me." She handed me a snapshot of her and Odd Eide standing outside a brick building, dressed to the nines. The resemblance between generations — Odd, Harry, Gus, and his son, Tom — was uncanny. They were all the same men, just wearing different shirts and trousers. "It will be in this purse, which will be in my closet. That is my final wish."

The waiter brought Rebekah's stew and set it before her, then laid my salad in front of me and offered to refill our teacups. Once he left, Rebekah felt for her spoon with one hand and the rim of the bowl with the other. Before taking a bite, she lifted her blank eyes to me and said, "Thank you," then chewed slowly, her eyes closed. When she opened them, she said, "Miss Lovig — Berit — you've been very good to me. I couldn't have lived as well as I did without you."

She didn't eat another bite of her stew, and when I finished my salad we left. She asked me to walk her down the Lighthouse Road. It was warm and breezy and she covered her hat with her hands. Once we got to the lake, she just stood there. No easy thing for her. I asked if I could help but she shushed me. She waited there for a minute, feeling the wind on her face.

"Will you take me back, please?" she said.

And I did.

The next morning I woke to the telephone ringing. It was Janice from the home. Could I come quickly? When I hurried there, Janice was at the front door. She squeezed my hands and walked me down the hallway to the room where Rebekah lay in her bed, the sheet pulled up to her neck. Her eyes were closed. She was still as a stone.

"She passed away about an hour ago," Janice said.

I dropped to my knees at the bedside, and reached under the sheet for her hand, which was still warm.

"She asked that we call you when this happened," Janice explained. "You were the only person who ever visited her, Berit." She put her hand on my shoulder. "You're a saint. She would've died five years ago if not for you."

I looked out that sad window, at the dead trees and the emerald-green grass on the knoll. "Isn't it strange," I said, "how different our men and women die?"

"Most of the folks here, men and women alike, they sit around all day begging to die. They've had enough. They don't want to eat or sleep or go to the bathroom. They certainly don't want to be sick anymore. They don't even care to be visited." She moved her hand from my shoulder and pushed a lock of hair from Rebekah's forehead. "This one, she did want to live. Fiercely, in fact. And we all loved her for it. She was never sick. Never had headaches or colds or indigestion. The doctor came once every year, but there was never anything wrong. She had the constitution of a hunk of granite."

"Then how did she die?"

"Without complaint."

I called Harry from the front desk. "Rebekah Grimm has passed away."

There was a long silence on the other end of the line before he said, "Today?"

"Yes. Around seven o'clock this morning."

Another pause. "I guess she couldn't stand the thought of another bowl of the oatmeal they serve up there."

"I guess not."

"You're there?"

"I am."

More silence. A deep breath.

"I was with her yesterday. We had lunch at the Traveler's."

"Gus mentioned seeing you."

Now we were both quiet for a moment. "Yesterday, she gave me all her instructions. It's like she knew she was about to go."

"She knew everything, didn't she?"

"Harry, stop. There's no need for that today."

"No need. You're right." He took a slow, deep breath. "Is there anything you'd like me to do?" It was as if he was at the market, offering to pick up a pound of butter.

"Do you want to come up here?"

"Why would I do that?"

"Harry, love, your mother just died. It's just you and me talking now."

"Let me know if there's anything I need to do," he said. "I'll be happy to pay for any arrangements. Just say the word, eh? In the meantime, I'll be down at the fish house."

"Harry. She's your mother."

"I never had one of those," he said, and hung up the phone.

My first instinct was to scold him. To march right down to the fish house and give him a good talking-to. But as that morning moved along — first the doctor, then Mace Washburn from the mortuary — I became less and less judgmental. I remembered when my own mother passed away. This was some five years before Rebekah's death. Harry came with me, stood at my side, offered his handkerchief when I cried. He said he was sorry and put his strong arm around me.

The strange thing was, standing beside my mother's open coffin, I couldn't really see her. All those years I lived only a hundred miles up the lakeshore, even as often as we saw each other, which was pretty frequently, she had become someone else. She became a person I only used to know, and not very well at that. My father was an even more distant memory.

And so I became as much Rebekah's daughter as theirs. Two days after I got that call from Janice, we buried Rebekah in the hillside cemetery. Her coffin was silk-lined. We put her pink cloche on her gray head. We dressed her in a beautiful gown. Down in the cellar at Mace Washburn's mortuary, I slid the picture of her and Odd Eide into her hand before he closed the coffin lid.

Merely a handful of reliable citizens gathered in the cemetery. I stood among them, huddled against a faint summer rain. I remember looking up the hill and seeing

Harry and Gus and Signe. She'd come home for the occasion. They all stood beside Odd's grave marker, looking down as Rebekah was lowered into the earth. It was nearly gallant, Harry's being there at all.

I watched Harry and his children as the pastor spoke of dust and life eternal. I thought solemner words had never been whispered on that hillside. But of course more solemn words were just waiting. They always were. They always will be.

Every person, I have come to believe, has a moment or a place in life when all four points of the compass converge, from when or where their life finally takes — for better or for worse — its fated course. For some, like myself, whose moment came when Harry Eide knocked on my door with a handful of butterworts, it's a quiet moment. I knew, or anyway hoped, that the very scene that did come to pass eventually would. I had imagined it a thousand times. I had believed in it. And, most luckily, I knew it when I saw it and lived the rest of my life accordingly.

But for others, perhaps most, the moment is blindsiding. Not only do they fail to see it coming but also might never even catch its trail or notice at all that it has passed. I cannot say if one way of recognizing that moment is preferable to another, or if there are cases when the profit is in never knowing.

But I count Gus among those whose moment was missed. A pity, too, considering how fateful it was.

That morning when Harry went after Charlie, Gus stepped into the sleeping sack and arranged the Duluth pack under him and sat back against the tree again. To wait for something he couldn't truly imagine. He hated his father. He'd established that much. But as soon as Harry was gone he wanted him back. Gus was exhausted after no sleep. He was cold. The snow still fell.

And Charlie was near to hand.

Something like half an hour went by. During his months on the borderlands, Gus had become an expert keeper of time. He knew the hour by the sun and by feel and even in his distress of that morning he marked the minutes as they marched by. He was an Eide, after all. In fact, he was more intent on the movement of time than he was on movements in the woods, and at first he mistook the shifting trees for the snow playing devil with him. Three times the forest blurred and then refocused, and the fourth blurring was accompanied by Charlie's voice. This wasn't Charlie shouting from thirty yards away on the bay, but behind one of those tripping trees not thirty feet from where Gus sat in the sleeping bag.

"What kind of a father would leave his son out here?"

Gus could see Charlie's long gray fur coat, half of it anyway, the hem of which met his leather galligaskins. Gus could see one of his eyes and the brim of his black hat. He could see one hand and the fingerless gloves and the blueing of the .38 Special held in it. He saw all of that and also the cigar hanging half chewed from Charlie's red face.

"Don't shoot your dick off with that little popgun sitting on your lap. You move one muscle and I'll put a bullet right between your eyes."

"I could have shot you last night," Gus said, his voice cracking.

"You should've. You missed your chance. Seems to be a common refrain among you Eide assholes. Always missing the fucking chance."

Gus looked down for only a second, and when he looked up again Charlie had moved to another, closer tree. Now he had his .38 Special raised in his right hand and with his left he lit his cigar.

"Smells good, don't it?" He blew a long stream of smoke toward him. "I'd offer you one, but you won't live long enough to enjoy it."

For the second time in five hours there

was a gun between the two of them, a thought that was, to Gus, as incredible now as it was then. And no less horrifying in either decade. He was sure of that.

"I was thinking," Charlie said, "sitting here listening to you and your old man jabbering, that I actually admire your moxie, Gus. Getting your hate out like that? I approve. I get a brotherly feeling with you. Yes, I do."

"You're nobody's brother."

"Sadly." He took a puff on his cigar. "I suppose your old man's been filling your head on that subject. Don't believe everything you hear, son."

"Don't call me son."

"I'll call you whatever I goddamn please." He had a couple more puffs. "You don't even know where you are, do you? That fucking bungler took you all this way and you don't have a goddamn clue."

"I know right where I am."

"You don't know your ass from a tea kettle. Shut your goddamn mouth."

Charlie walked a few steps closer, and now Gus could see the gray in his whiskers. The shine in his eyes and the rifle barrel poking over his shoulder.

"I'm gonna tell you what your problem is. What your old man's problem is, anyway, and since it's his I presume it's yours. It ain't that you're up here playing voyageur. Hell, we've all got our heroes. The problem is, you've picked the wrong goddamn heroes. Who wants to be the asshole trapping the beaver? The right man wants to be the guy wearing the beaver-skin hat. That would be me, wearing that fucking hat. Do you understand?"

"You're crazy."

"I'm the sanest man you ever laid eyes on. Know why? I got everything I ever wanted. You should judge a man by what he wants — and what I want, I got. Including you in my crosshairs." He puffed the cigar. "It's a sad sack of shit I see over there, too." Charlie cocked his head and stared at him for a long time. "How does it feel, all of this nonsense coming to an end like this? Think of the effort it took you to get here. All those portages lugging your gear through the woods. All those times you wanted to spit in your daddy's face. All the fear you felt. All the times you just wanted to curl up on your mama's lap." He smiled ghoulishly. "And who was there with her? Not you. Not your daddy. Me, in this beaver-skin hat. I was in her lap and up her ass and everything else."

He pointed his cigar at Gus. "Now you got that want-my-mama look. All you Eide boys, loving your mommies. But where is she? Where's your daddy's mama?" Charlie cleared his nose and throat and spit yellow sputum onto the snow. "You could go back to the first Eide mama that ever lived and she still wouldn't be there. Probably because she was out in the barn with the guy in the fucking beaver-skin hat."

"You don't know anything."

"I know everything, boy. I know what's mine and what will be. I already told you, I'm the czar of this world and what I say goes. I could tell this snow to stop and it would obey before the next goddamn flake." He stepped out from behind the tree and started walking sideways toward Gus. "I know Daddy-Boy left you sitting here because he was scared shitless of the czar. I know you've got a sleeping bag full of piss over there." He stopped twenty paces in front of Gus, nothing between them but a bare stretch of frozen, snow-covered ground. "And I know you're dead. It doesn't even give me a minute's pause to say it. You're as dead as goddamn Kennedy. And your head's about to look the same as his, too."

"Gus was right. You don't know anything."

Then they both looked toward the oaks, where Harry was no more than ten yards away, crouched on one knee, with the Remington rock-solid in his hands.

Charlie took a last puff from his cigar and dropped it into the snow, eyes jumping between the Eides — quickly, but not in a panic — before he settled them on Harry. He kept the .38 Special aimed at Gus.

"Gus, listen to me," Harry said. "I want you to close your eyes. Close your eyes and don't open them until I tell you to."

"You say one more word and I'll shoot your worthless fucking son."

"You be quiet," Harry said. Then, to Gus, "Close your eyes. None of this is happening, bud. None of it ever happened."

"Lying right up to the end, huh?"

Gus closed his eyes.

"You've upset your boy, Harry."

"Don't mention him again."

"This is a hell of a knot here," Charlie said. "I can't say I saw this coming."

"I did," Harry said. "Now put the gun down, Charlie."

"I don't think so. I was just telling Gus what I was about to do with this here gun. How his head's about to look like our former president's. And you, asshole, are next in line."

"Why the hell do you keep talking about the president?" Harry said.

"See?" Charlie said. "You come up here and live like hermits while the world passes you by. President Kennedy was assassinated, you dipshits. The world ain't what it was before. It never was. And you just never saw it, did you, Harry?"

"I saw plenty, Charlie. What I didn't see, I know that, too. I know you killed your brother. I know there's only one way of stopping you, sad as I am to say it."

Charlie laughed uproariously. "You think you're up for this? With your little boy crouched in the snow over there? My money's on no. I don't think you got the sand to see this through." He held the Colt on Gus and swept his gaze to Harry.

Gus closed his eyes so tight it hurt.

"I won't ask you to put that gun down again," Harry said.

"Tell me one thing," Charlie said. "How do you think your wife'll feel about all this? You think you've got troubles now? Just wait on that."

"Gus, are your eyes closed? We're not here, buddy. We never were."

"You can keep your fucking eyes closed, boy, but that don't mean you ain't here. You sure as shit are."

"Do not open your eyes, Gus. Sing to yourself."

"There's only one song for this rat fuck," Charlie said. "And it can't be sung without a church choir and an organ playing alongside."

"Shut your goddamn mouth, Charlie Aas. Shut your mouth and put that gun on the ground. This is the last time —" But there were no more words, just two shots, fired practically the same moment, two claps of thunder in the woods — *Boom! Boom!* — and then a silence as profound as a corpse.

"One of the last things my father ever said to me, or one of the last things before he started to lose it, was about those gunshots. Christ, Berit, I can hear them still, honest to God. And not just figuratively. That sound's in me yet, like a scar from some childhood pox."

Gus's voice was barely louder than the snowfall coming down outside the apothecary.

"He said he was an ugly man, and that ugliness first found him when he shot Charlie Aas. He said it wasn't the only ugly thing he'd ever done, that there was plenty of ugly to go around. But he also said that all of his ugliness and failures, all of the things he'd done wrong and regretted, they were all worth it because of how beautiful Signe and

I were. He said that the beauty of our lives made the ugliness of his worth it. Even our time up on the borderlands, horrible and wrong as it was, turned out to have its own benefit — in his life and mine, he thought — because it proved to him how deep his love truly was. Despite those gunshots.

"You knew him, Berit. Probably you knew him better than I did myself in his later years. So you know I never could've doubted his love. It was as unequivocal as Lake Superior, and I took it just as much for granted. But to have heard him say that? About our time up there, after all these years? I don't really know, Berit."

He looked out at the snow and studied it.

"There've been many days in my life when I might've sworn it never happened. The whole adventure, but especially that morning. I actually swore once — with my hand on a Bible in the Arrowhead County Courthouse — that it never did happen. And that's how it often felt. Except for those two gunshots and their echoes through me all these years."

I watched him there at the window and thought maybe I'd been wrong about him. Maybe *that* was his moment of reckoning, not that morning against the tree on the bay of that remote lake. Maybe it had taken him that long for the four directions of his compass to come together. Maybe he might now have some peace.

"Those echoes, they're like part of my own heartbeat, Berit."

He turned to look at me, but then closed his eyes and lowered his head.

"I kept my eyes closed, just like he told me to. Ever the obedient son." He closed his eyes tighter still. "And then those gunshots were alive. So loud and close I felt them not only in my body but through the tree I was leaning against. They'd become part of me the second I heard them. Two shots, and for the third time on the borderlands I was dead. The third, but not the last time."

The first letter was about trees. "I had begun to think that trees were not real," she wrote her parents. "When the boat to Tromsø came through the fog and the shore was there, I saw them. I was very happy." The rest of that first letter, dated 11 October 1895, and the next several were like a strange trip through time. They recounted in childlike detail Thea Eide's passage to America (pregnant cabinmate, stillborn child), her landing in Gunflint (no one to meet her, wild fear), meeting Rebekah ("The saddest person you ever saw"), and her opinion of Hosea Grimm ("A nice man, even if he's strange sometimes"). She told her mother that her sister — Thea's aunt — had passed away tragically, and that this had rendered her uncle unfit to help upon her arrival or since. She wrote in detail about the conditions of the logging camp where she found work as a cook and spoke highly of the kind, rough men who felled the trees. On the subject of the dogs guarding the camp, she wrote a whole letter. "One I have named Freya. The top of her head comes up to my belly. Each morning and each night I bring them scraps. They are beautiful, like bears. We all feel more safe for having them."

But the most revealing letters were the last two she wrote. The first was dated 23 April 1896.

> Kjære mutter og pappa,
> I am happy to tell you that I have married a man named Joshua Smith and we will be having a child. We were wed in Immanuel Lutheran Church here in Gunflint, Amerika, by Pastor Erolson. Mr. Smith is a watch seller and is eight years my senior. He is a kind man and God fearing and I am happy and lucky to have found him. We will live in town. I will send a photograph of the child and his father when he is born. I am not afraid of bearing the child. Mr. Hosea has always been kind and he will see that all is fine with me. My love to you both.
>
> Kyss og klem —
> Dine Thea Inger

I looked up. "My goodness."

"You can say that again," Gus said.

"What about the last letter?"

He handed it to me, translated in his sister's elegant scrawl, and the photograph that had waited in the envelope for a century. I looked at a black-and-white snapshot worn almost to the point of invisibility, though the outline of a cherubic babe was plain to see. I stared at it long enough that there passed from one minute to the next a likeness to each of the Eide men: first Odd, then Harry, then Gus. Even Tom, Gus's grown son. I felt a chill go up my back.

"Read the letter," Gus said softly. "It's the last one she sent. The last she *meant* to send."

There was no date on that letter, though on the back of the photograph Odd's birthday was written: 26 November 1896. The letter began as they all did.

Kjære mutter og pappa,

This is my son. My dear sweet son. Odd Einar, I call him. He is all mine. Pappa, I have named him for you. Maybe he will grow to be as good. He will. I am certain he will. He is so gentle. You sent me to Amerika for happiness and I have found it. He will have his own happiness someday. I only wish you could hold him, Mutter. Since you cannot, I will hold him for us both. I am well. I was brave. I remember how brave you were, Mutter. I was you. I am so happy! If I die tomorrow my only unhappiness will be that I can't see my Odd Einar grow. I love the sound of his cry. He cries now. I must feed him. But I will write again soon. Thank you for sending me to Amerika.

Dine Thea Inger

"I didn't think Thea Eide was ever married," he said.

"She wasn't." I set the letter down among the others.

"But —" Gus picked it up and held it limply, as though offering a piece of suspect evidence in a trial whose verdict had already been decided.

"I guess she had her own stories."

"I expect she did." He scanned the letter again before putting it atop the others. "It was often said that my grandfather was misbegotten. Like my father after him."

"That's what I always heard, too."

"From Rebekah?"

"Yes. Though she wasn't a proper storyteller, as I'm sure you know. But she occasionally muttered something, and of course there has always been the gossip and scuttlebutt. In any case, I think what we've heard about your great-grandmother is true more or less."

Gus looked at her. "But she put this differently. Why do you suppose?"

"She could hardly tell her parents the truth, could she? I imagine she needed to say something, to let them know they were grandparents, even if only from half a world away. That's what people do when they have children, isn't it? Spread the good news? Who else did she have to tell? Her folks were the only people she had in this world. Which means she had no one. Imagine that. How very sad."

"What a shame those letters never reached them."

I shook my head. "To say the least."

"Tell me, what's the story as you know it?"

"You could walk over to the courthouse to find half of it signed and sealed. As far as I know, Joshua Smith was the itinerant watch salesman he's said to have been. A strange vocation, that, but of course the lumberjacks needed timepieces, each and every one of them. Smith came through the first winter she worked up at the Burnt

Wood camp. A famous winter it was, for both the cold it wrought and everything that happened up in the woods."

"The winter of 1896?"

"That's right."

"You know," he said, "the *Ax & Beacon* compared this winter to the one we're talking about. This is the second coldest on record — 1896's number one."

"Exactly a hundred years apart. Did that occur to you?"

"Yes, it did."

"Puts a nice shape on things, doesn't it?"

"I'm not sure I thought of it that way."

"So what did you think?" I asked.

"Not much, actually. Maybe that a hundred years isn't such a long time. Not when it's measured out against a place like this."

"It's practically the whole history of this town, though. That's something. Even you can admit that."

"Maybe I should've said measured out against a family like mine." He looked at me. "I consider you part of the family, Berit. I would've said that for years, but I say it with even more conviction now."

"That's very kind of you."

"And not just because of what you meant to my father."

I saw the blush rising in his face as I felt it

in my own. "Well, now," I said, "be careful not to sweep an old lady right off her feet."

He tucked the letters in a neat pile. "I thought they'd say more. To be honest, I thought they'd make me cry."

"I can't say I had any expectations, not particularly. But they certainly do break my heart a little."

For three days and three nights Gus hadn't checked his maps. On the fourth morning, soon after they'd broken camp, the wilderness — though it hadn't, in fact, changed at all — became a foreign land. So he took the compass from his pocket and confirmed his direction. All that day they continued south or east. He kept one eye on the woods ahead and the other on the needle of the compass in his outstretched hand, always south or east. When they crossed a river flowing down that same course, he knew they'd bridged the divide.

Gus wore his snowshoes and his coat and hat. The Duluth pack had been fashioned into a harness and from it a length of rope was tethered to the canoe, where his father sat cocooned in the bearskin and wool and down of the sleeping sack, his red hat pulled down over his ears. His union suit was soaked through with a fevered sweat. One foot was in his stinking boot and the other wrapped in Gus's T-shirt and stiff with frozen blood.

Pulling that load was, on the lakes and frozen rivers, with the north wind at his back, surprisingly easy. But up in the woods, through the underbrush and beneath countless soaring pines, around rocks and deadfall, into and out of the steep gullies of ancient streambeds, it could take an hour to cover a hundred yards. He consoled himself with the thought that hauling his father through the wilderness — bringing him home — was an act of deliverance, and then he felt he was sailing among the clouds. Until the straps of the pack pulled against his galled shoulders and returned him to earth.

And so when the going became most difficult he would hum those old chansons he'd learned the season before and press on, even as he sometimes plunged through snow up to his waist.

That fourth day, he labored through the gloaming and pitched camp between two trees alongshore. He packed the snow with his boots, hardly able to lift his legs after his day in the harness. At the mouth of the tent he built a fire, then gathered wood to last the night and melted snow in the pot he'd salvaged from the fire and forced his father to eat a ration of dried fruit and a chocolate bar. He had the same himself, blocked the wind with the upturned canoe, curled into the sleeping sack and the bearskin beside his father — now fallen into some fantasia between sleep and death from which he didn't stir, except to eat and sleep and, later, rant and moan like a lunatic — and fell himself into a dreamless slumber. He woke on the hour to stoke the fire but knew this only because when he rose for good, ten hours later, the fire was still ablaze.

In that predawn darkness he melted enough snow to fill the canteen and ate the last of the chocolate and a handful of the fruit. He took down and rolled up the tent, and lifted his father into the canoe, pulled on the Duluth pack as later in life he would slip his blazer on for a day in the classroom, oriented them southward, and finally struck out across the lake for home, their campfire still burning behind them, the only thing warm or light in the entire world.

By daybreak snow was falling, and by noon even harder, but it did not start blowing until that night, when Gus raised the tent in a blizzard. Somewhere that day he'd lost one of his mittens.

■ ■ ■ ■

Five days earlier — the morning Harry shot Charlie — Gus had kept his eyes closed for a long time indeed. So long it might have seemed he was sleeping. But when he finally opened them he saw an inch of powdery snow had covered his sleeves and the Duluth pack. The silence was deathly until he heard his father dragging himself back through the trees farther inshore, a trailing blood came along and his face was already ashen, his eyes nearly uninhabited. Gus would not allow himself to look around the woods for Charlie.

"Now it's up to you," Harry said as he tossed the Remington in the snow and collapsed beside him.

"What happened?" Gus said, pointing at the spattering in the snow. "Whose blood is that?"

Answering, Harry pulled his foot around. His grimace only made the colorlessness of his face more profound. The boot was shot half off and blood bubbled from the wound like a stew simmering on the stove. His hands were smeared with blood. Gus looked at his father's bloodstained coat and union suit and asked him if he'd been shot more than once.

Harry shook his head, his eyes fluttering.

"Where's Charlie? What happened to him?"

Harry tried to focus on Gus but was too far gone. He did manage to say, before he passed out, "Charlie who?"

Gus wrapped his father in the sleeping sack and the bearskin and ran back across the bay to where the shack used to be. All that remained was the chimney and foundation and the still-burning cord of oak that hissed and smoked in the snowfall. The warmth of the fire was splendid after the everlasting night beforehand. He was hoping the remaining canoe hadn't burned, and indeed it had not, set off as it was on the edge of the clearing. He cleared off the snow and dragged it out to the icy shore. He went back for one more look at the fire, and that's when he saw the pot sitting atop the ruins of the stove. He kicked a charred two-by-four that must have fallen from the joists and picked it up to reach for the pot, which was still warm to the touch.

Harry had pulled himself up against the tree by the time he got back. The bearskin and sleeping sack had slid off, and Gus pulled them back over him, then set about making a fire to melt water. The richness of this was not lost on him: setting another fire.

After he'd melted water he examined his father's boot. This roused Harry, of course, and he came from his blackout like a man who'd been underwater — gasping for air, eyes wide in terror. But as soon as he understood who and where he was he asked Gus for something to bite down on.

The blood came steadily as Gus removed the boot. Its cap had been shot off, and so it was his father's toes that were bleeding — three injured, two blown off altogether. He used his pocketknife to cut the sock away, and by the time he'd washed the foot with warm water and wrapped it in a T-shirt, Harry was unconscious again.

It was still midmorning when Gus fashioned the Duluth-pack harness and tied it to the forward thwart of the canoe. He had already arranged his father in the boat, resting his back against the yoke with the tent underneath him. The rest of their outfit Gus stored in the stern. The food supply was so sorry there wasn't enough to feed a small child for the time it would take them to get home, never mind two men, one with the hardest job of his life before him. With no lantern. No fuel. His father didn't even have any pants, and only one boot. Nor was there a first-aid kit.

And, for all they lacked, the load would still be too heavy, and Gus could not see how he would be able to pull his father home. Not even on a highway of ice did it seem possible. But that first morning he took one step and then another, and in fifteen minutes they had reached the fishing hole his father had cut from the ice. He filled the canteen, drank it down, filled it again, brought it to Harry, roused him, and made him drink. He filled the canteen a third time and stowed it in the canoe's stern. The Remington sat among their provisions, and he lifted it out and started for the hole in the ice.

"Where are you going with that?" Harry said.

"We're out of ammo."

"So what." His voice was already growing weak. "That's my gun."

"I'm sick of this shit." He opened the lid. "Fuck it all." And he dropped the rifle in the water. Then he pulled the harness back on and took a step. And another. And then he was at the beaver lodge out on the lake he did not have a name for, his father trailing silently behind. Gus turned south.

■ ■ ■ ■

On the sixth day Harry began babbling and hallucinating. The sound of his ranting served only to make Gus feel more alone. All those solitary days he'd spent charting the land away from the shack had trained him to live in silence and the peace of his thoughts, which now was broken, profoundly, by his father's whimpers.

"The ice is breaking. Papa! The fish. Papa! The ice. Look out!"

Gus would pause and take deep breaths with his elbows on his knees, his face down so he wouldn't inhale any snowflakes.

"Why didn't she ever come down? What's wrong with her?"

Then Gus would straighten up and take another twenty steps before he'd rest again. One hand always freezing, because he had to switch the mitten back and forth, a great annoyance.

"Nous étions trois capitaines, / de la guerre revenant / brave, brave / de la guerre revenant bravement," he sang, his voice half croaking and half wheezing.

Snow fell in streamers throughout the windless day. Gus could hardly tell when he'd come out of the woods onto a lake.

He'd walk and rest and walk and rest and for most of that day he was on a lake bearing east. As night gathered, he thought he saw lights in the distance.

"There are tracks, my son! There are *tracks*! Gus, *mon fils*! Please, stop. My boot. I've lost my boot!"

Perhaps it was merely a trick of the darkness, but the snow seemed to fall even harder as night came on. Gus — hoarding the last handfuls of dried fruit for a more desperate stretch of miles — had eaten only snow for twenty-four hours. He'd been walking for the last sixteen. His body no longer ached. It was no longer even a part of him. But it kept moving. It kept moving, and then they were in a tangle of frozen reeds alongshore.

"There were snakes, Gus. *Mon fils!* You missed their tracks. All across that lake. I believe they are following us. The ice is cracking, Papa! It's coming apart."

Now the snow was relenting, and sometime that night the sky unfolded its light and Gus could see they were on a frozen river. He turned to look at his father in the moonlight. He had removed the sleeping sack and bearskin. His jacket was unbuttoned and he'd even taken off his red hat. Gus stepped out of the harness and went back to the canoe. His father's lips had split and bled and now were frozen. He looked like a corpse. Gus found the canteen but the water, too, had frozen. He would have wept if he'd been alive. But for the fourth time he had died on the borderlands. And he had killed his father. They were both dead.

He then looked at his hand in the moonlight. It was the same color as the moon itself and hurt like hell. He opened his coat and put his hand in his armpit, and he was not dead, because he was bleeding. His shoulders were bleeding and his shirt was soaked with icy blood. He covered his father again with the sleeping sack and the bearskin and then stepped back into the Duluth pack and walked on, the river purling beneath his feet, giving the melody to the song he now sang: *"Par ici t'il y passe trois cavaliers barons, Dondaine, don, dondaine, don, / Que donneriez-vous, belle, Qui vous tir'rait du fond? Dondaine, don, dondaine, don . . ."* At some point he imagined — or maybe heard — his father singing along with him.

There were last days on the borderlands, of course, and for Gus and Harry the end was also the beginning. Of the river, that is.

Its headwaters were frozen. The canopy of trees spanning its shorelines arched above in a snow-covered tangle, a high tent. He came to it in the late afternoon and thought of setting camp — he'd slept only a few hours for two nights and had little to eat beyond a moose's fare of twigs and grass and bark, the fruit still in the canoe — but the mere thought of pitching the tent and building a fire sent him walking forward in a different sort of suffering.

As evening fell the river spread before him and the snow gave way to coursing water. He stood at the shore and considered the dark current flowing into the twilight. Was this the Burnt Wood River? Was such a thing even possible? He took out his father's book of maps and opened it to chart 8, the facsimile of Thompson's map of the lake and the river's headwaters. Gus studied it longingly, as though by sheer force of wishing he could place himself on that page and in doing so save them both.

Since he had no paddle, he found a log as big around as his arm and as tall as he was, settled into the canoe, and used it to push off the shore.

The water under the keel ferrying him along was the sweetest sensation he'd ever felt, and it revived him before lulling him to something like sleep. He ought to have feared the saults and rocks and icy shores stretching before him as inevitably as the next hour, but he had no thoughts left to use. Or anyway no worries. What would come would come. It had been coming and it came and it would keep coming.

His father was sleeping. At least Gus hoped he was. Surely the sound of the water, warbling and piping and gently lapping against the canoe, was a song to set a man asleep. And the pull of that same water beneath the canoe? It was as if Morpheus was pouring it to seduce his dreamers.

Gus rode the canoe through the night, in and out of sleep as the boat bumped against rocks or the soft snow banked alongshore. At times the river was wider and slower or narrower and faster, but in either case it was doing his work for him, and for this he was more grateful than he'd ever had occasion to be. And the day broke to a bright sunrise through the trees as they sailed toward it.

Gus filled the canteen and guzzled the water and he filled it again and scooted up to his father, who was unconscious. The water merely leaked through his beard onto the frozen bearskin. So Gus settled back in the stern and covered his eyes with his arm. He slept, and then woke when the canoe was caught in a slurry of snow and ice above a frozen lake. Gus pushed for the bottom with the log pole, and after an hour's hard work and the very last of his strength he had the canoe on solid ice and moving across that small lake. He could have sworn, looking onto its shores, that he'd slept there once upon a time. When he reached the far end of the lake the river opened again and he sat himself down and the canoe floated on.

The rest of that day the river flowed up through the keel of the canoe and into his spine and then through his mind, and his mind was flooded and would remain afloat for many, many years to come. He slept and dreamt of the water now and felt flooded.

Not drowning, just coursing through him. Near dark, he woke as the canoe came to a slow and sliding stop, and he heard in the absence of its movement a waterfall, thunderous or perhaps not. Conceivably, it was instead all the water that was washing through him.

But what was unmistakable and certain — and proved by the story as it was later told to him — was the whining of snowmobiles. He tried to open his eyes but could not. He could not even open them when he heard voices familiar and gentle and strong coming through the gloaming. It was the last time Gustav Eide would be that far up the Burnt Wood River until his father went walking early this winter.

You're not dead until you're warm and dead. That's what they say about hypothermia. When I saw Harry the night he was brought out of the woods, he looked more than warm — he looked like a burn victim. And I couldn't believe he was not dead. Not even for all of the medical equipment and the doctor and nurses that surrounded him at the Gunflint hospital.

I had sneaked up there after dark to see for myself what was being whispered in town: that he and Gus had been delivered by the Riverfish brothers, and that Harry would not survive the night.

The tip of his nose and his cheeks above his beard were frostbitten, blistered, and red. He was covered from ankles to chin by an electric blanket. One foot was covered, the other elevated and being treated by a nurse. His faintly orange ankle deepened through peach, umber, rust, and brown until it finally turned black near where his toes used to be. When the nurse saw me — it was Ana Olsson — she smiled and covered his foot and stepped out from behind the curtain.

"What are you doing here, Berit?" She put one hand behind her back and touched my arm with the other. "I didn't know you were friendly with Harry Eide."

How could I explain? Even to myself? I had gone up to the hospital because I could not wait a minute longer to see him. When I'd first heard about Harry and Gus paddling up the river, I thought, with some certainty, that I had seen the last of them, a feeling that filled me with regret and shame. So when word filtered through town that they were back, and in such shape as they were, I would not be stopped.

"Of course, you spent so much time with his mother," Ana said.

I smiled weakly. "What happened to his foot?"

"Hunting accident."

Harry? A hunting accident? I thought. *In January?*

She still had one hand behind her back. "His foot is the least of his problems. His body temperature was well below ninety degrees when we admitted him a couple hours ago. We're warming him slowly, hoping to avoid cardiac arrest. He needs to make it a couple more hours. That's what's important now." She spoke in a whisper and nodded behind the next curtain, where Gus slept like he was on fire. His right hand was wrapped in gauze, his hair a bird's nest of matted curls, his young man's beard only an inch long where it had grown in full, and I couldn't help thinking he resembled a child because of it.

"Has his mother been here?" I asked.

"She left twenty minutes ago."

"Will the boy be all right?"

"He's skinny as a newborn fawn. Has a little frostbite of his own, on his hand and up on his cheeks. But mostly he's just tired."

"Is it true Freddy and Marcel Riverfish brought them in?"

"Honestly, Berit, it was the damnedest thing you ever saw. Those two and these two, right out of the woods."

"Where did they find them?"

"I heard they were about to die up on the Burnt Wood River. Not twenty paces from the Devil's Maw. Their canoe had caught in a snowbank alongshore. A few more feet to the right and they would've been swallowed whole." The nurse looked at Gus for a long time and then back at me. "He looks just like his pops, doesn't he?"

"Yes, he does."

She patted my arm again and told me to have a seat. When she pulled the curtain to step back to work, she did so with the hand she'd been keeping behind her back. On it was a plastic glove covered in blood.

News of Harry and Gus coming out of the woods that January day in 1964 spread through town even faster than reports of JFK's assassination had two months earlier. Some folks were already calling it a miracle. Others said that fate had smiled kindly on them. Surely it was a bit of both. A few even said that between Thea Eide, Harry's grandmother, and Odd Eide, his father, the family had endured a generous portion of misfortune, and this was God's way of evening the score.

But I could have told you, sitting in the corner of that hospital and watching that man's suffering, that this was a godless business. The only credit I was willing to give providence was for making our winters what they were, and for making Harry the man who he was and his situation as devilish a thing as anyone could ever imagine.

It seems so recently that I sat through that night. So little time since the great happiness of my life came to bloom. It's true I hardly knew Harry then. And it's true I didn't know exactly why I'd gone to the hospital or what I expected to find once I got there. Certainly I had no idea what he'd been through in the months he'd been gone, or any sense of what it was that drove him into the wilderness in the first place, but I did know — sitting there that night — that the care he was receiving in that hospital room would have less to do with his survival than my love of him would. I knew this because of how powerfully my feelings were welling up in me. And I was right.

First I sat there and thought about all the lost time. Not his stint on the borderlands but all the time before that. The years since I'd first laid eyes on him in the winter of 1937 and the day we'd stood there with the butterworts six months later. It pained me to think of what had been squandered to those years. It pained me also to think of what Lisbet had gained instead: Gus and Signe, their beautiful home on the river, all of that time with Harry, all the dusky nights and bright mornings, all the happiness of a full life. I even wished for the spats and sadness and hard and hateful moments that I knew they had and that we, too, would inevitably have shared. All of it should have been mine.

Now, before you judge me I should say that I knew even then what an ugly thing it was to covet. But I had waited. I had been patient. I had lived my life and had done so without objection. Indeed, I had lived it as well as I could. All the friends I had. All the books I'd read. All the quiet and soulful evenings when I'd felt near to bursting because of how beautiful this place was. All the snowfalls and sunrises. All this added up to a life of plenty, that's for sure. And as I sat there, watching Harry not die, all those things, and everything else, was suddenly larger and more stunning because I saw what I'd always really known — that I would love this man.

It's an amazing thing — the most amazing, in fact — to sit through a night and know in the morning that you are in love. That it's not a dream or a fantasy or something to covet, only something to fill you up. There are those people who say it's a folly or that only fools rush in, but I have lived all three ways — without it, with wanting it, and with it in my hands — and I say the latter's by far the best.

Before it was even light outside, I opened my eyes to old Willem Lundby standing above Gus, holding his notebook mid-inquiry, his badge on his chest. Gus was picking pieces of dried fruit from a plastic bowl. Before Willem noticed I was awake, I closed my eyes again and listened.

"So you never saw Charlie Aas?"

"No, sir."

"You never saw his plane?"

"No, sir."

"Because no one has seen Charlie or his plane for coming up on ten days now. The last time someone did see him, he was heading over the hills above town."

"I don't understand what you're saying. My dad and me, we were just wintering."

"And where did you say you were wintering?"

"I don't know exactly."

"You don't? Really?"

"No, sir. I don't know exactly. Somewhere up on the borderlands. We got lost."

"Huh. So you got lost?"

"Yes, sir."

"And not even Charlie in his plane could find you?"

"Not even God could have found us."

"What about your old man's foot over there? He step in a wolf trap?"

Gus looked over at his father. "We had a hunting accident."

"A hunting accident?"

Gus nodded.

"Your old man never poached a day in his life, so why start now?"

"We had to eat. We were trying not to starve."

"Had to eat." Willem shook his head. "Good God almighty," he said, and shook his head, flipped back through his notebook, tapped his pencil on his mustache. "Most folks figure Charlie went up to find you and your dad. On account of the hot water your old man put him in."

"How could he find us, though?"

Willem looked up from his notebook. "That's what I want to know, son. Or, rather, I'm wanting to know what happened when he did."

"But he didn't. Nobody could find us. I told you that. We couldn't even find ourselves."

On it went like this for some time, Willem sure there was a connection to be made, and Gus, still nibbling on his dried fruit, insisting there was not. In the end, Willem smiled and shook his head and said, "I'll be damned. You Eides can really tell a story after all." He pocketed his notebook and pencil and took his brown felt campaign hat off the chair beside the bed and put it on his bald head. "I just hope your old man tells the same story when he wakes up."

Maybe Harry had been awake during Willem's questioning of Gus. Maybe they'd talked it through before, on those days they spent escaping from the wilderness. Maybe he simply knew through their consanguinity what Gus would have told Willem or anyone else like him. Maybe — and least likely, I think — he actually was amnesiac and simply couldn't remember the details of their last days. Maybe their story was merely telling itself. Whatever the case, when Harry woke the next morning and Willem came back to put his campaign hat on the chair beside his bed, the story did stay the same, what parts of it he could remember, anyway.

Ana assured Willem that it was natural Harry could have lost some of his memory. Hypothermia did that, stripping things from your mind. And even if the hypothermia hadn't, the shock and trauma of their experience might well have. Indeed, that was likely, too. So Willem left again, the story still the same.

A week after Freddy and Marcel Riverfish delivered them to the emergency room, they came back to drive them home. Or to what was left of it. Lisbet had moved into the same attic apartment where I'd spent so much of my life, an irony that's still not lost on me. (It wouldn't be long before she left Gunflint altogether, a divorcee headed back to Chicago and whatever might have been there.)

The whereabouts of Charlie Aas was the only thing Gunflinters talked about the rest of that winter. Many folks were ready to believe that he'd merely skipped the country and had flown his plane into Canada to avoid his local legal troubles, which were by then considerable. The authorities would find it impossible to prove he'd killed George, but all the rooting around they'd done investigating that charge had unearthed dozens of other crimes on top of the good work the *Tribune* reporter had done. By the time Charlie left Gunflint for the last time he'd already had his real-estate license revoked, he'd been placed on unpaid leave as mayor, and his wife — long-suffering — had filed for divorce. His daughter, Cindy, hadn't spoken to him in months, not since she'd been brought down to Duluth to get better in the psych ward at St. Luke's.

There were others who believed his last flight was a suicide mission. These were predominantly the same people who blamed the Cubans for JFK's assassination. Folks like Len Dodj, who, instead of being with Charlie on the borderlands, was mopping the floors at the hospital where Harry and Gus ended up. Matti Haula was seen plenty around town, usually plunked down at the Traveler's Hotel, and he had his own theories about where his pal had disappeared to.

But no one knew, not even Lisbet. She told Willem first and then the federal authorities who came later that when Charlie left on that January morning she knew neither where he was going nor who was with him. I never doubted the veracity of this. No one else did, either.

It wasn't until early April that the speculation came to an end. A Canadian trapper on a lake called Hagne — deep in the Quetico — found Charlie's Cessna, undamaged and empty but for a pack of American cigarettes, a box of rags, and three empty Mason jars. A twenty-gallon jug of airplane fuel sat on the ice outside the plane.

The trapper reported his find to the ranger at the Cross Lake Station two days later, and in turn he dispatched a party to retrieve the plane. Because by then air-traffic restrictions were already in place for the entire borderlands wilderness, Charlie's plane being where it was at all made this a criminal investigation from the outset. But the search lasted only one day and included only the three men whom the ranger had sent out there. By the time the plane was linked to Charlie, and Willem and the federal investigators were alerted, he'd been given up for dead.

Charlie Aas, and the two men who'd been with him, left no trace.

"This is your first time back here?"

"Yep."

"What about when you were searching for your father?"

"I stopped below the lower falls that night." He threw his thumb over his shoulder as though to say, *Down there.*

"Is it strange?"

"No. I don't think so." He stepped up to the railing on the lookout and peered over the edge. "In a way it's like I never left. Lately, it sometimes feels like that."

There was still snow in the woods, and ice knurling from the fissures above and below the falls, but the birch trees upriver were greening.

"Do you think it's true that people have thrown pianos and cars down there?" Gus said, pointing at the Devil's Maw.

"I've heard those stories, too."

He looked around. "How could you even get a piano up here?"

I shrugged. "I don't know whether to hate you or thank you, Gus."

He looked at me like I'd slapped him.

"I know you meant no harm. I'm just certain of that. But you have to understand something about all that you've told me."

He stepped away from the railing, toward me. "What is it, Berit?"

It was only as I stood there looking at the falls that the notion had come to me at all. Rather, it was only by standing there that I was able to start making sense of it myself. "We almost never talked about that year, your father and I. When we first started seeing each other I asked him what happened up there. He told me only what he'd always told the authorities. He said the story was out there for anyone who wanted to hear it. As though the whole thing had been written in some book."

Gus now wore the expression of a scolded child.

"I believe there was only one other time," I continued. "This was maybe five years ago. I asked him about it after Charlie's wife, Maddy, passed away. In fact, I didn't even ask him about that winter, simply what he thought had happened to Charlie." I looked at Gus, who was standing so near I could've reached up and touched his cheek. "Your father said that Charlie probably got lost in the woods and froze to death up on the Îles des Chasseurs. He said he hoped he'd died slowly."

He had such an expectant look on his face, Gus did. Like I held the secret answer to the whole riddle. He seemed almost to be tipping over. So much that I put my hands up as though to catch him. "I don't understand," he finally managed to say.

I took a step back. "We were together for more than thirty years, Gus. Think of that. He knew me better than anyone. A hundred times better."

He still looked at me like he couldn't understand.

"And all that time," I explained to him, the falls rushing, the falling water rising again in cold mist, "I did not know him. Actually," I said quickly when he raised his hand to object, "I meant to say I didn't know one of the most important things about him. His secret, if you will. All you've told me, it's got me wondering if it changed who he was — if it changed who we were together?"

There's a little wooden bench up there on

the lookout, and I sat down on it. I felt dizzy. I put my hand to my head and tried to press the whirling sensation out of it with my fingertips.

Gus sat down beside me. "I'm sorry," he said.

It seemed wrong for him to apologize, and I told him as much.

"I didn't give enough consideration to how this story would affect you," he said. "I really didn't. I'm sorry."

I looked at him and saw that boy in the hospital bed all those years ago. For a long time I kept looking. Also seeing someone else.

When he started talking, I could barely hear his voice above the river. "When we got back, after Dad got home from the hospital, I used to sit around the house with him. Just waiting and hoping he'd say something. Anything. An apology, sure. That's what I wanted most. But eventually I would've happily taken a simple glance."

He scooted even closer to me now. "I had no idea what was happening, since my mom and Signe were staying down at the apothecary — it was only me and Dad. Not so different, really, than it had been in that shack.

"In my memory he never spoke at all, but he must have. Just not about what had happened. So it was mine to live with, that winter, as it turned into spring. Mine alone. It began to seem — and I'm sure this sounds crazy — like he wasn't even there. That I was alone again up on the borderlands." Now he paused and took my hands, exactly like he had the morning after Harry disappeared, back in November. "I should've been more thoughtful, Berit. Should have considered how hard it would be for you to hear all this. I didn't, and I am truly sorry."

"I was never anxious to know much about the things your father kept to himself. He never told me about the war. I know very little about his marriage to your mother. At least not as told by him. He was intent to remember the good times, the happy times, of his life."

"My God. I'm such a fool."

"That's not true."

He let go of my hands and gazed down between his feet for a long time. I thought of so many things in those moments. I thought of Harry, of course. Of how much I missed him and how much I loved him and how much I would've given to have him sitting there next to us. I would've gladly traded whatever time I have left on this earth for one more hour with him. But I also thought about Gus and his adventures up there — I glanced above the falls — and how it still wasn't finished. It never would be. And anyway, weren't my memories as much a part of Harry as he was of them? Especially now? I could let it all be. Could leave it all just as it had been. That was my prerogative, right?

I turned to Gus. "Don't fret about it, please. Nothing could change how I felt about your father. Nothing in this world, much less something that happened so long ago."

When it was time to go Gus stood and offered me his hand, helped me up, and said, "Are you ready for the long walk back?"

"I guess I'd better be."

We took one more long look down at the Devil's Maw and turned to go.

What I didn't tell Gus as we walked through the woods back home — what I might have told him, and maybe should've — was that I'd been up here myself only a week before. The walk had been even harder than I knew it would be, especially for an old girl like me, but I'd wanted to make it alone. To be the first to visit.

I didn't bring flowers, as I perhaps should have, but only that pompom from Harry's red hat. I brought it along with the last bits of my anger and threw it all into the river above the maw. I watched them funnel into the chute that dropped into the hole and saw them disappear. And I was content that my final gifts would find the bottom and be gone forever. And that maybe Harry's spirit or his soul or some such might see the pompom and know that I'd not stopped thinking of him. And that I never would.

The day before the ribbon cutting, I walked down to the outfitters on the end of the Lighthouse Road. In the back of the shop, behind the Duluth packs and cook kits, they keep a supply of maps. One of the kids who work there came back to help me.

"Miss Lovig," she said. I think she was one of the Veilleux girls. "Are you planning a canoe trip?"

"I've never set foot in a canoe," I said, hoping I sounded playful, as I'd meant to.

"Most folks looking at the maps back here are planning a trip. That's all."

"Once upon a time I might've tried it. But these days I prefer my feet on solid ground." Now I smiled, trying to assure her I wasn't the old crank people so often mistake me for. "But I am looking for a map. Maybe you can help me."

"Of course."

"There's a lake up in the Quetico called

Hagne. I'd like to see it on a map."

If this girl knew that lake had any significance, she didn't let on. "I'm not sure where that is, but we can figure it out." She pulled a map from one of the slots below, one of the yellow Fisher Maps. *E-15,* it read in the upper right-hand corner. "This is the whole boundary waters–Quetico wilderness." She smoothed it atop the rack. "Almost all of it, anyway. You said it's in the Quetico? What's its name again?"

"Lake Hagne. Or Hagne Lake. It's a big one."

She ran her finger across the map. It was painted red, her fingernail, and it went right to a spot in the middle of the map. "Hagne Lake." Now she reached below for another map, *F-18.* "This is the map of that area." She laid it beside the other. "Here's Hagne Lake." Again with her red fingernail.

"Thank you," I said. She didn't leave, so I said "Thank you" again.

Then she did step away, saying that if I needed anything else I should give her a shout. Before I'd even looked back down she stopped and added, "I can't wait to see the history place. Our whole family's coming."

I looked over at her and smiled. "That makes me glad. Pray for some sunshine."

She went off toward the front of the store.

First I studied the map of the whole wilderness and noted, in the key, that each inch equaled two miles. Therefore, the full map from west to east covered eighty miles, fifty miles from north to south. Four thousand square miles. Was that right? There must have been a thousand lakes. A hundred streams and rivers. In the middle of it all was Hagne Lake, my eyes drawn back to it from everything else like it had a magnetic pull.

I cannot say, exactly, what had led me to the map. Some need of proof? Did I expect the Fisher Map would be marked with a skull and crossbones? Or a note in the key reading: *Here rests Charles Aas?* Or did I just want to put my unpainted nail down on a map and announce: *Presto!* Even if Gus didn't know or want to, would my own knowledge make the endgame permanent and put it finally and fully to rest? If I was expecting any of that I had clearly been mistaken, but there was a sense of calm that came upon me. So I rolled up the map and brought it to the girl at the cash register. Maybe I'd make it a gift for Gus. More likely I would put it on the desk in my den, along with every other memento and bit of evidence I'd compiled in the months since

Gus came knocking on my door.

The next morning Gus and Sarah picked me up at ten o'clock. Signe was with them, sitting in the backseat of his Subaru, and he opened the other rear door for me.

"Hello, Berit," Signe said.

"It's so wonderful to see you." I squeezed her arm.

"And you," she said back.

"Today's the big day," Sarah said from the front seat.

Gus climbed back behind the wheel. "Ladies, shall we?" There was a lightness to his voice I'd not heard in a great many years.

"I'm so excited for you," Signe told me.

"Oh, it has nothing to do with the old postwoman."

"Nonsense," Gus protested, peering into the rearview mirror. "It has everything to do you. Well, with the two of you back there." I could see his eyes turn up in a smile.

We drove down the Burnt Wood Trail, the winding road crossing over the river in three spots before dropping us in town. I could still see ice drifting along the Lake Superior shore, and there were piles of snow in the ditches along the road, though a restless energy was everywhere in the woods, and the first songbirds of spring could now be heard in the mornings.

"It surprises me every year," Sarah said.

"What's that?" Gus asked.

"That winter does actually end. That the snow melts away and the trees' leaves grow back." She smiled at him and then turned around to us. "But it happens, every April, almost like clockwork."

"Last year it snowed on Tom's birthday in May," Gus said.

"I watched it snow in June one year. The lilacs took a real dusting."

"Well, there'll be no snow today," he said.

"Certainly not," said his wife.

We veered right at the stoplight and drove toward the Light-house Road. When the apothecary came into view three blocks away, Gus craned his neck and said, "What's that?"

Sarah was looking at Gus. So was Signe. But I was watching the expression on Sarah's face as Gus drove. Something about her eyes reminded me of the fresh green of the grass on the roadside. We parked in back and Gus jumped out of his Subaru and started around to the front. By the time we caught up with him he was standing by the boat, one hand under his arm, the other on his chin. Sarah stepped beside him and put her arm around his waist. Signe moved to one side of them, as I did to the other. He glanced quickly in both directions, pausing once on each of us.

"Well?" Sarah said.

The boat had been my idea. For some thirty years it sat in the carriage house behind the apothecary, forgotten for so long. A more dilapidated thing you've never seen, but there was plenty still true about it. The keel, for instance. And the lapstrake planking. When Signe donated the apothecary and we took our first inventory — Bonnie and Lenora and I — we were surprised to discover it in the carriage house, covered with canvas on a trailer with four flat tires, a home for mice and chipmunks. But it also had an air of latent perfection, of incorruptibility, and we all agreed it would make a perfect showpiece. I asked Chuck Veilleux if he would restore it. He couldn't, but knew who could. So, one day last November, he pulled it out of the carriage house and hauled it down to a place in Duluth. Sargent's Boatwright and Chandlery, it was called. They spent the winter rehabbing the boat, not to make it seaworthy again but so it could sit out front of the Gunflint Historical Society with dignity.

Gus stepped over the hawser that had

been strung around it and walked up its starboard side, his hand on the newly lacquered hull, the three of us behind him like schoolchildren trailing their pied piper. But at the stern he stopped and covered his eyes. The boat had once been named *Rebekah,* but I'd asked the men in Duluth to give her a new name, specifically the name of the man who'd built it: *Odd Einar* was now painted on the escutcheon.

"I thought it was gone," Gus said. In the sunlight we could see his eyes get glassy.

"Nope," Sarah said. "Berit kept it safe all these years."

"No, Rebekah did," I said.

Signe stepped over the rope and stood beside her brother. "Rebekah bought the boat the year you and Dad went wintering. He thought it was sold to some fisherman in Sault Ste. Marie. It's been stored here in the carriage house all these years. It seems everyone forgot about it."

"I never did," Gus said. "I dreamed about it a million times."

"Well, now you have it again," Sarah said. "We all do."

Four sets of bleachers had been erected on the Lighthouse Road in the shape of a horseshoe surrounding the *Odd Einar.* A podium and microphone had been set up in the bow. Bunting was hanging from the apothecary's windows. The high school marching band stood off to the side, ready to play. At one o'clock folks started turning out, pretty much the whole town. The bleachers started filling up, and so did the lawn all around.

At one-thirty Mayor Bear Anderson stepped aboard the *Odd Einar,* welcomed the townsfolk, thanked the members of the historical society — singling out Lenora and Bonnie and me — and then reminded everyone that after the ribbon cutting there would be a pemmican feast sponsored by Sons of Norway and Immanuel Lutheran. It didn't take him more than thirty seconds to get to introducing Gus. "We're lucky up here, having such outstanding citizens. I bet if I asked any one of you about this next gentleman, the first thing you'd say is 'I know Gus. He's a friend of mine.' That's what I think of him, that's for sure. This boat I'm standing on now was his granddad's. And his great-grandma came walking down the Lighthouse Road about a hundred years ago. That's how long the Eides have been here. I can't think of anybody better to say a few words about this here historical society, the renewed heart of our beautiful town. So, without further ado, here's Gus Eide." He laid out a welcoming hand. "Gus, come on up here."

He climbed the makeshift steps and shook Bear's hand and pulled his speech from his coat pocket, laid it on the podium, then buttoned his coat and pushed his windblown hair out of his eyes. Smiling weakly, he looked at Sarah and Signe and then at me. When he put his mouth up to the microphone, it screeched, and he stepped back and smiled and then adjusted it and began.

"Thanks, Bear." He nodded at the mayor, still right behind him. "You've done a lot for this town, a lot for all of us, and I think I speak for everyone when I say we appreciate it." Everyone clapped. "See?" he said, and turned again to look at Bear, who waved like a grand marshal.

"And you're right about us being friends. Friends and family. We're lucky indeed." He took his reading glasses from his chest pocket and squinted down his nose at his sheet of paper. He took one deep breath and then another and then took off his glasses and slipped them back in his pocket.

"Maybe I'd do better to wing this." He swept his hair back again and began in earnest. "Without these three women down here, none of us would be standing here to celebrate the opening of a society dedicated to who we are. Bonnie Hanrahan, Lenora Lemay, and Berit Lovig, you've accomplished something really wonderful." He gestured back at the apothecary. "Almost from the time folks started settling here, this building has been the center of Gunflint's life. Your hard work ensures that it will continue to be. Every one of us thanks you deeply."

He paused to collect his thoughts. "Miss Lovig tells me the walls of this place went up in the summer of 1893. Ever since then we've all called it the apothecary, even though not a single aspirin's been sold here in about seventy-five years. I suggest that from this day forward we say it's what that shingle up there says it is: the Gunflint Historical Society. Can we agree on that?" Again the crowd clapped.

"I've seen the exhibits inside and can tell you there's something for everyone. We've got a rich and colorful past. And a complicated one. But I think it's important we hold our past near to us. That we learn from it and keep living by it. In fact, I think we're nothing without it." He stared up at the pinnacle. "This building will help us keep our past to heart. It will help us keep it alive." He nodded his head, satisfied.

"So, Miss Lovig, and Bear, why don't you join me at the front door so we can cut this damn ribbon."

At four o'clock we locked the doors. Bonnie and Lenora were behind the counter counting up the donations — a fair number had been made — and Sarah stood at the window. Gus, who'd been quiet, almost taciturn, all afternoon, was beside her, staring across the room at the portrait of Rebekah Grimm.

All the townsfolk had come through the exhibit, and by any measure the grand opening had been a success. I was relieved, as Signe was. It seemed an odd time for Gus to seem so melancholy, so I walked over to him.

"You look glum, Gus."

"I'm not," he said. "I was just looking at my grandmother over there. She's still keeping an eye on us, eh?"

"I suppose she is."

"Do you remember the first morning I came to visit you? After my father disappeared?"

"Of course I do."

"I said maybe you'd be able to help me understand why he'd set off again."

"I remember, Gus."

"I thought if I told the story of that winter, if I told you all those secrets, I'd feel better. I thought life would make more sense."

"Do you feel better?"

"I believe I do."

"And does life make any more sense?"

"Does it ever?" He nodded at Rebekah's portrait. "You know, there's more than a glancing resemblance between her and Signe. I'd never really noticed before."

"I often thought the same thing. Not about the painting, but about the two of them."

"No, life doesn't make any more sense." He turned to me and smiled. "Let's go upstairs. For one more look from on high?"

Up we went, those steps I'd walked more than any others in my life.

On the third floor he said, "What a rousing success, eh, Berit?"

"It was quite a day."

Out the window, down below, a crew was disassembling the bleachers.

"You've really done something amazing here. I wish I could have articulated that better in my speech."

"It was a beautiful speech."

"I'd written something, but, standing on that boat, with all the kids from town there with their parents, it suddenly felt entirely too academic. So I winged it."

"Even so, it was lovely."

"I'm not fishing for compliments." He smiled almost to the point of blushing and then turned to gaze out the window.

After a while he said, "I was thinking about my dad an awful lot today. Especially standing on that boat."

"I thought of him, too."

Another moment passed.

"I was also thinking today about our walk up to the Devil's Maw, Berit. About what you said."

Now I turned to look at him.

"About my father keeping some secret from you. And how that made you feel."

I kept my eyes on him until he faced me. "What about it?" I asked.

"You're not the only one he kept secrets from. That's all."

"I guess we all have some."

"You sure do," he said, then gave me another weak smile.

"Not so many as you might think," I said.

Now it was Gus keeping his eyes on me.

"What?" I said.

"Downstairs just now, I said life didn't make any more sense now than it did on that day Dad disappeared. But, still, I think I understand it better. Can those things both be true at the same time?"

"I'm a small-town girl, Gus. I never went to college. Never traveled the world. I wouldn't have an answer to that question."

"You've never fooled me, though."

I smiled.

"Tell me that story, Berit. The one that started all of this. Tell me that, and then I promise we can move back to the here and now."

"I knew this was coming. It had to. I'm glad you see that, too."

"So you'll tell me?"

"No, I won't. I can't." I took my purse from my shoulder, opened it, and removed the envelope I'd been carrying around in there for weeks. "Maybe I should've told you all this back in November, when Harry vanished."

He took the envelope and flipped the unsealed flap open. "What's this?"

"It's something I wrote down for you. Things I didn't think I could tell you. Maybe this will help you understand."

Your father and I didn't speak often of what happened to his own father, though I recall those conversations very well, and one in particular. We were sitting on his deck on a late-spring afternoon. This was some ten years after the Riverfish brothers rescued the two of you. The Burnt Wood was surging with snowmelt and two days and nights of wild rain. We could feel it thundering through our bodies even a hundred feet away. Your father cradled his coffee in his hands, his eyes fixed on the river. He was quiet. As always, he was quiet.

I watched him staring at the river, then watched it myself. I remember thinking what a raucous and beautiful thing it was. And how patient it was, too. It had flowed for thousands of years to make itself as it was just then. I'd seen it freeze and thaw and freeze and thaw over and over, year after year, and this was only the merest fraction of its existence over those millennia. What a beautiful notion this was.

As he did so often, your father read my mind. "I was reading a book by Louis Agassiz last night," he said.

"Was he a scientist?"

"That's right. He thought there was once an enormous sea here. It was called Lake Agassiz."

"Back in the Ice Age?"

He nodded.

"I believe I've read about that myself," I said. "What of it?"

"You think it's true?"

"That this land was once a sea?"

He nodded again.

"I do, yes."

"Think it will be again someday?"

"Someday?" I said, and caught him with my smile. "The way that river's running, it might be as soon as this weekend."

Precisely then we heard a terrific boom. We flinched simultaneously and looked hard through the mist and saw a lump of ice the size of a misshapen truck that had rolled out and flattened several trees on the other shore.

"My goodness," I said.

"Let's have a look."

We walked across the clearing and stood

on the river's edge, which was some thirty feet higher than it would be come August. The water was one long manic sault, churning and lapping furiously back on itself. Countless chunks of ice were coursing down the current, but this massive piece that must've calved from the falls upriver was now dragging the felled trees along with it, completely at odds with its essence, but in fact no different from the livid river itself. It was the same stuff, after all.

I could see from the look on your father's face that this ice troubled him, too. As if he'd seen a ghost. He stared at it for a long time before saying, "I never thanked you."

This perplexed me. "Thank me?"

"For those fried potatoes."

I must have looked stunned.

"On the day we first met."

"I know what you're talking about," I told him.

Now, understand, my memory is a cursed thing. It grabs hold of everything without my say. It always has. And it stays with me. I sometimes have trouble remembering where I put my teacup, but I can tell you exactly what I wore to Rebekah Grimm's funeral. Exactly who was there and what the pastor said. I can recall whole conversations with my mother from sixty years ago.

In many ways it has been unfair, going through life not being able to forget. But what is sometimes a curse also allows me to conjure up the story of what happened to your own father when he was still just a boy. It was, I am sure, the prologue to all his life after.

It happened on a morning in February, an easterly wind blowing cold across the lake. The sun rose over low clouds. Snow was in the offing from the east, as it had come overnight and would again that morning, blowing up off the lake and over the breakwater. But just then the sky above was blue and unbitter, and your father and his father, Odd, hauled their toboggan out from the cove. I cocked my ear to the ceiling above and listened for the sound of Rebekah's arthritic feet crossing the floor.

I sorted the mail, keeping one eye on your father as he augured holes a quarter mile offshore. I watched them sit on the upturned buckets and drop their lines in the water as I slid letters into boxes and wondered why, after nearly a month here in Gunflint, I'd never seen that boy — your father — anywhere but out on the ice.

At nine o'clock I went upstairs and made tea for Rebekah, as I did each morning. She d, as she nearly always did, at the indow, her fingertips touching the glass, her head down, and her eyes fixed on the lake. She turned when she heard me. "Oh," she said. It was the first thing I'd heard from her in weeks. Maybe it was meant as thanks.

At ten o'clock — I know this surely, because I can still hear the soft ten gongs of the grandfather clock — it started happening. And though I saw it with my own eyes, I've always remembered it through your father's.

First, the *crack.* From nowhere and like gunshot, which it might as well have been. Folks in town heard it carried in by the wind. I heard it even inside the apothecary. Your father was hurled onto the landfast ice, his father in the opposite direction. Odd landed on his gut, looked up, and saw the ice breaking before him as though exploded from beneath. He clambered to his knees just in time to duck a swell. After wiping the water from his face, he turned back to Harry. Already the ice stood jagged between them. Like a stone fence or a range of mountains in miniature.

Odd surveyed the lake as it was opening up all around him, ice floes colliding and cleaving with an urgency he could not believe. In all his years he'd never seen anything remotely like it. Neither had your father, of course. At that age, he hadn't seen much that Odd had not seen right alongside him.

On one great swell and then another, the block of ice that Odd was on floated out toward open water that thirty seconds before had been frozen solid. When a third wave broke, his ice block was halved and he had to scramble to stay out of the water. He held his balance and glanced down at his feet, one of his boots now missing. On a still-intact sheet of ice, water spewed through the fishing hole he had augured just a couple hours earlier.

Your father gazed up at the sky above his father and saw clouds dashing across the dull blue as fast as the lake ice was coming apart. He watched his father fall to his knees and then stand again to look back at him. Harry had a rope in his hand and was throwing it hopelessly into the wind. He was bawling, but his father never could've heard him.

Odd was floored once more and once more stood. He watched your father hurrying toward shore.

The floe yawed again and Odd was dropped a final time. He removed his mittens and clawed at the ice until his fingers bled, but there was nothing to seize hold of. The water was growing even bigger, and some cruel, ungodly force was pushing him farther out even as all the powers of nature ought to have been bringing him in.

The townsfolk were quick to act. Nils Bargaard and two of his sons pushed their skiff across the harbor ice and met Harry before he made the breakwater. By the time they were in open water, Mr. Veilleux was lowering the town tender from its launch. Two other boats were searching before I took an accounting of all that was happening. Once tallied, I went upstairs to give Rebekah the news.

But she hadn't budged from the window except to raise her chin. I went to stand beside her. If she noticed me, there was no sign of it. I watched as the boats plied the water, searching. I saw your father brace himself in the bow of the Bargaard boat. Even from so far away I could see his frantic eyes. Or perhaps I was only imagining them. He searched and hollered and cursed God.

There was much desperate searching that day. Only the old men stayed ashore. As did the Aas clan, who leaned against the cable on the breakwater to watch as the boats crisscrossed open water and the snow began in earnest. They kept cruising for hours, until, one at a time, they came in. By noon — the lake mellowing, the snow falling harder by the quarter hour — the only vessel left on the water was the one that had gone out first. Nils steered the outboard, his sons praying and searching from either side of the boat. And your father? Harry stood on the forward thwart whispering, "Papa, Papa, Papa."

It was dark when those four pushed the Bargaard skiff back across the harbor ice. I was locking the front door when I saw them coming. They put the boat ashore and walked up the Lighthouse Road and came straight to me. Mr. Bargaard in front, then your father flanked by the two Bargaard boys. The younger boy carried a single boot.

I unlocked and opened the door and stepped aside as they walked in. Mr. Bargaard said not a word, only brushed some snow from your father's coat and held his shoulders for a long moment, stunned silent by his downturned eyes. Then the Bargaards turned to go. The younger boy left the boot on the floor next to your father.

This is when I first met him. Your father was sixteen years old. So was I.

He looked up at me after I'd returned

m closing the door. "Would it be too nuch," he said, "to ask for a cup of coffee?"

I nodded and went up to the kitchen on the third floor. Rebekah was no longer at the window. I don't know where she was just then. I put the water on. I diced a potato and put it in a frying pan with a spoonful of bacon fat from a jar I kept in the icebox. I made a roast-beef sandwich and cut a pickle in half and waited for the water to boil. When it did, I poured it over the grounds and stirred the potato until it was done frying. I sprinkled salt and pepper over the skillet, then poured a coffee cup full and set it on a tray with the sandwich and pickle and scooped the potato onto the plate and carried it downstairs. All that time, I'd been crying for the boy I now thought of as an orphan waiting for his coffee downstairs.

When I got to the bottom of the stairs I saw Rebekah standing off to the side. I couldn't tell if your father had noticed her. She followed me as I crossed the floor and placed the tray on the window seat.

"I made you something to eat," I said, wiping my tears with a handkerchief I kept tucked in my dress sleeve.

Your father looked up at the tray of food and picked up the mug and took a sip of it and then unfolded the napkin and tucked it into his shirt collar. "Thank you."

I turned to watch as Rebekah stepped forward, her chin upheld. Now your father looked at her. She nudged me aside and bent down to lift the wet boot. She stared at it for a long time and then said to him, "Who are you?"

The snow had melted off your father's coat and pooled on the bench and floor beneath him.

"Who are you?" Rebekah asked again.

This time, when your father didn't answer, she turned to me and said, "See to it this mess is cleaned up before you retire for the evening." Then she walked back to the staircase and went up.

This town has always been good at having secrets, and terrible at keeping them. As I sat behind the counter watching your father finish the last potatoes, I realized I'd been wrong while I stood over the stove just half an hour before. He was no orphan. He was eating supper in his mother's parlor. How easily lies pass as truth. How easily we overlook what is obvious and plain to see.

What I didn't fail to see that evening, what has been the one sure thing in my long life, was that your father's grief in that hour —

gh I felt it as surely as if it were my wn — would not be the saddest part of this day. Not for me.

I watched him wipe his mouth with the napkin, lay it on the tray, and lower his head. I crossed the room again and gathered the tray and brought it up to the kitchen. Rebekah was back at the window, looking out into the starless, moonless night. What did she see in that darkness? Odd, no doubt. But what else?

Did she see her son crossing under the streetlights? Did she see him ducking into the alleyway past the Traveler's Hotel? That's surely what he did, your father. For when I went back downstairs he was gone. Only the puddle of melted snow remained.

Here's what I knew right then: As long as your father was alive and still living here, I would be, too. And however long it might be, I would wait. I would wait for him as Rebekah had. The only difference was that I would not go crazy while doing it.

And I didn't. I was also right about that. These stories that we live and die by, I've learned this much about them: They never do begin and they certainly never end. They live on in the minds of old ladies and locked in antique safes, in portraits on a wall and in renovated boats sitting on a lawn. Somewhere, deep in the Quetico, there's one pile of ash and another of bones. They, too, are just stories.

Why have we told them? You to me and now me to you? We've told them because we need proof of love, and that's what they are. More than anything, they are exactly that.

ACKNOWLEDGMENTS

My father first took me to the country described in this book when I was a boy. For this and so many other reasons, my love and thanks.

The lyrics to the chansons that appear sporadically throughout were found in Grace Lee Nute's splendid *The Voyageur.* Her book was indispensable, as was John Jeremiah Bigsby's *The Shoe and Canoe.* Thanks to Amy Greene, Laura Jean Baker, Tom Maltman, Emily Mandel, Jarret Middleton, Chris Cander, and Lance Weller, who all read earlier drafts of this book. And to Bill Souder, ballistics expert. Matt Batt, brother, you're such a fair reader and bosom pal, thank you over and over again.

Thanks also to Steven Wallace, Jason Gobble, and Joseph Boyden. Heartfelt thanks to Greg Michalson. And to Pamela Klinger-

Horn, patron saint of mine. And to Ben Percy, counsel and confidant. Laura Langlie, flowers for you. Thanks to Ruthie Reisner, for walking this dunderhead through the woods.

Gary Fisketjon, the next one's on me. Thanks for making this novel better, word by word. Thanks also for bringing to the world so many of my favorite books over the years.

Finn, Cormac, and Eisa, thanks for making every day matter.

Dana, thank you for all you've given me, and for your unfailing support over the years.

ABOUT THE AUTHOR

Peter Geye was born and raised in Minneapolis, where he continues to live. His previous novels are *Safe from the Sea* and *The Lighthouse Road.*